Donor

Donor

Elena Hearty

SAMHAIN
PUBLISHING

Samhain Publishing, Ltd.
11821 Mason Montgomery Rd., 4B
Cincinnati, OH 45249
www.samhainpublishing.com

Donor
Copyright © 2011 by Elena Hearty
Print ISBN: 978-1-60928-671-2
Digital ISBN: 978-1-60928-658-3

Editing by Don D'Auria
Cover by Scott Carpenter

First Samhain Publishing, Ltd. electronic publication: December 2011
First Samhain Publishing, Ltd. print publication: March 2012

Dedication

This book is dedicated primarily to my husband, who manages to see me in the way I wish I could see myself.

Chris, Mom, Dad, Cara, Randy, Malbert, Steven & Alex,

You are the main characters in my life. Thank you for being a part of my story.

Chapter One:
The Basement

Lenore stood at the entrance to apartment B14 as her host fumbled with the keys. All other doors along the basement hall appeared to have been boarded up or hastily filled with cement. A single lighting fixture flickered above, causing Lenore's shadow to dance against the wall. It looked like it was running.

"Don't get many trick-or-treaters, huh?" she asked, eying three deadbolts on the door.

Richard smiled as he wrestled another key from countless others on the ring. "Never had a trick-or-treater. B14 is a sort of misnomer, by the way. This place was built in 1907 and originally had 14 apartments to a floor. When my great-grandfather bought the building in 1920, he moved into this unit and started expanding as vacancies emerged. Now just about half the floor is this apartment, and the rest is filled with utilities. You'll see—my place is about 4500 square feet, when it's all said and done."

"So it's just you down here?" Lenore would later remember this moment with longing, as it was her last possible opportunity to escape.

"Yep. Just me." Richard turned the final deadbolt and opened the door. "Ladies first."

Eager to lay her eyes on the urban mansion, Lenore stepped into a sprawling foyer and was not disappointed. She marveled at marble floors and ornate ceilings as the door closed behind her, thinking that for someone who did not appear to be out of his late twenties, Richard had quite sophisticated taste. The interior design was distinctly art-deco, punctuated by eccentric touches, such as the bright orange coat rack on which she hung her jacket.

"I'm impressed. This isn't what I was expecting. Not after the outside." She stopped herself, not sure if she was being rude.

Richard seemed too distracted to care. He cocked his head to the side as if straining to hear something and then brushed past Lenore on his way down the hall. Not knowing how else to respond, she followed his lead, and the sound of a woman crying emerged as she walked. Hadn't Richard claimed to live alone? Her pulse quickened.

Lenore turned the corner into a large parlor and jerked to a stop. Something was wrong. Richard leaned against a pool table, joking around with another man who appeared to be covered in blood. A disheveled girl cried loudly over a sopping mound of flesh in the center of the room. It still wore the clothes of a man.

Ripped apart and badly mutilated, the corpse resembled something a tabby might leave at its master's doorstep. Taking a step back, Lenore could make out a trail of blood all over the floor and assumed that the victim must have struggled before expiring next to the coffee table. The girl wailing beside him would periodically lift the head in a hopeless attempt at revival.

The lamentation of the mourner on the floor struck Richard and his blood covered friend as high comedy, every sob evoking a new string of ridicule. Richard facetiously suggested she try mouth to mouth resuscitation, which threw his companion into a peal of laughter. Neither man appeared to acknowledge Lenore's slim figure in the entryway. They were entirely too delighted with the harassment of the other woman to pay her any notice.

Lenore took a few slow steps back into the hallway and sat on the ground. She needed to think. Whatever had happened to the man on the floor had not been an accident, and the reaction of the men in the parlor suggested indifference at best. No one was making any motion to call the police. She needed to get out of there as soon as possible.

With stealthy deliberation, Lenore made her way back to the front door and tried the handle. It rotated, but the door did not open. The deadbolts had been turned with a key from the inside. Richard must have sealed her in the moment she walked through the door.

A hand touched her shoulder. She jumped.

"You weren't thinking about ditching us, were you? You just got here." Richard stood grinning behind her.

Lenore's mouth trembled. "Listen, I—I don't know what's going on, but it looks like you've got a lot to take care of right now. I can take a look at your record collection another time, ok? I'll—I'll email you tomorrow—is that cool?" Richard kept smiling, but made no motion for the keys. "Please...I really don't know what's going on. I don't belong here."

He grabbed her by the hand. "But Lenore, I think you *do* belong here. Let's head into my living room and we'll figure this whole messy situation out. What do you say?"

She tried to wrestle free of his grasp, but found this to be impossible. Eyes dashing wildly between Richard the door, Lenore realized that even if she were to break free, there was nowhere to go. Silently, she walked with him back to the living room, where Richard released her hand and turned his attention to the woman on the carpet.

"Hey, Angela, why don't you come with me?"

Angela's face distorted into a terrified grimace. "*No!* I want to stay with Lance."

"Lance isn't lookin' so hot, kiddo. C'mon and don't make a show of this. Let's go."

Angela sprang to her feet and ran to the other man in the room. "Please," she said, clinging to him. "*Please.* I'm sorry. I'm so, so sorry. Please don't let him take me. Call Charles. *Where's Charles?*" She screamed as Richard started moving toward her. "You can't let him take me. Don't do this. *Please.*"

Richard's friend held Angela in his arms for a long moment and kissed her gently on the forehead. "So long, kiddo," he whispered. Then he handed her to Richard, who carried the pleading woman out of the room and into the hallway. A door shut in the distance, and Lenore could hear muffled screaming on the other side.

The blood covered man grinned at Lenore. "Rich asked me to entertain you while he talks to Angela."

She froze as he approached, clutching her purse to her chest like a shield.

"I know what you need," he said. "You need coffee. It's late. I'll bet I can figure out how to work the coffee machine if you give me a chance. I need to get a paper towel anyway."

He led Lenore to a sparsely stocked wet bar beside the pool table. When she got there, she planted herself on a stool and wrestled her oversized hobo bag onto the counter. She dug through its contents, swiftly producing a large bottle of pills, a pack of Marlboro Lights, and a disposable lighter. Lenore pulled a cigarette from the pack and attempted to light it several times before throwing her lighter down in exasperation.

"Here, let me." A blood stained hand lit her cigarette. "I'm Paul, by the way."

Paul dampened a paper towel in the sink and began to wipe his face. The features revealed were average, with the exception of Paul's eyes. The deep creases around his lids suggested a playfulness and wisdom that made their wearer look kind, even when slathered in blood. Once cleaned off, it was evident that none of the blood on Paul had been his own. Aside from his crimson stained polo and khakis, the only evidence of altercation was what appeared to be a deep burn on the back of his left hand.

He discarded the towel and pondered the coffee machine in front of him as if it were an ancient Chinese puzzle box. "I feel like Angela pours the coffee in the top or something, right?" He removed the lid and winced as the scent of rancid coffee filled the room. "Hang on I'm going to wash this thing out...that's fucking filthy." Paul looked up at Lenore as he rinsed the pot. "You know, Rich is going to kill me for letting you smoke in here. He hates it when people stink up his apartment." As an afterthought, he reached behind the bar and set an empty glass on the counter to serve as ash tray.

"I—I can put it out if you like. I don't want to make him mad..." No, she certainly did not want to make Richard mad.

He smiled, taking an exaggerated breath. "Nah. Smells great in here to me." Then, looking thoughtfully at the man on the floor, he grabbed another glass from underneath the bar. Leaving the water still running in the sink, he ran over to the body and filled the container to the top with blood, then walked back carefully so as not to spill the contents. He took a large sip and went back to scrubbing. "I know that's really rude of me and I shouldn't do that type of thing in front of you."

Lenore frowned at his drink. "Are you supposed to be some sort of vampire or something?"

Paul turned off the water and began to dry the pot with a towel. "Something like that." He grinned up at her. "You don't believe me, do you?"

"Nope."

He motioned to the pills on the counter top. "What're those for?"

"Anxiety. It's Xanax." Lenore lifted the bottle to show him the label before pulling six pills from the container.

"Jesus! Do you usually take that many?"

"Nope." She swallowed the pills dry.

Paul opened several cabinets until he found one filled with coffee grounds. "Okay we've got French vanilla, regular, bold...Jesus...how much of this shit did Angela own, anyway? What do you drink?"

"Bold works for me."

He started the pot, which comfortably churned in the background. "You know, I knew you were on something," he said, leaning over the counter and pointing to the bottle of pills. "You're way too calm to be totally sober. Most people with a dead body in the room would have thrown up by now, or would be freaking out pretty bad like Angela."

"I took four before I came here," Lenore said. She thought it was the best decision she'd ever made.

"So do you take them all the time, or just when there's a dead guy on the floor?"

"All the time. I'm agoraphobic."

"You hate gay people?" Paul chuckled quietly at his own joke, but got no response from Lenore. "I'm kidding. I know what agoraphobia is. You can't go outside, right? Like, you're scared of being out of your house?"

"Yeah that's pretty much it. I have to take Xanax every day to function, basically."

"Jesus. I can't imagine. So what are you afraid of? Are you like afraid of diseases or something?"

Lenore shook head. "It's not disease, but if I tried to explain it to you it wouldn't make any sense."

Paul nodded understandingly. "Well at least you've got medicine. Like, it hasn't stopped you from getting out of the house."

"I'm pretty sure I'm going to regret leaving my house this evening." She took a long drag on her cigarette.

"You've got to open yourself up to new experiences," he said, displaying his glass in front of her as an example. "I just realized you never told me your name."

"It's Lenore."

"Huh. You know you don't hear that one a lot anymore."

"My mother had this idea that you should give your children old fashioned names. That way, they can't go out of style, something like that."

"Any brothers or sisters? Any more interesting names?"

"Just me," she replied, expelling a large cloud of smoke.

Paul nodded and polished off his glass. He held up one finger, motioning for her to wait while he ran back to the body for a refill. Lenore watched as he put one foot on the corpse's chest in an effort to pump it for blood.

"You know you're going to make yourself sick doing that," she said when he returned. "I think human beings can only drink so much blood before they throw up. That's why you put your head down when you have a nose bleed—you need to make sure you don't swallow anything."

"Wow I love the fact that you're on Xanax. This isn't freaking you out at all. I don't even feel bad about drinking in front of you anymore." He grabbed her pack of Marlboro Lights and pulled out a cigarette. "I'm going to steal a smoke from you. I haven't had one of these in a while."

Paul practiced blowing smoke rings while Lenore's mind raced toward a plan of escape. She looked around the room and noted there were no windows in sight. Cell phone. If she could reach the phone in her purse without attracting Paul's attention, perhaps she could call for help. Would he become suspicious if she asked to use the bathroom and carried her purse inside? It was worth a try, and sooner rather than later.

"Hey is there a bathroom around here that I can use?"

"Yeah. There's a bathroom down the hall to the left."

"Thanks." Lenore grabbed her purse and headed out the door.

"Hey! Leave that here!" She looked at her purse and thought for a moment that Paul was on to her scheme, but he was pointing to her lit cigarette instead. She extinguished it before leaving the room.

Following Paul's directions, Lenore entered a small powder room and locked the door. She used the toilet and then ran the sink while fishing through her purse for her phone. Her heart sank when she pulled it out and saw there was no reception. Was there no reception in just the bathroom, or everywhere in the apartment? Lenore turned off the sink and walked back to the parlor, checking the phone in her purse every few feet for signs of service.

The only evidence that Paul had moved at all while she was gone was a refilled glass on the countertop. He looked somewhat relieved upon her return, stating, "I thought for sure you were going to lock yourself in there and I'd have to come and get you."

She looked inside her purse again. Still no service.

"Are you thinking about making a call?" His lips curled knowingly. "You can't get a signal in this basement. Sucks if you're expecting a ring. Hey, the coffee finished while you were away." He grabbed a cup from underneath the counter and filled it with light brown liquid. "You know what? I should have offered you something stronger." He turned around to ponder the modest assortment of liquor behind the bar. "You want me to make this Irish?"

She nodded. Paul poured a generous amount of whiskey into her drink. He started nursing his own again.

"Hey is there cream or sugar around here anywhere?"

Paul hunted around the back shelves. "Oh, yeah—yeah I think it's...somewhere...right over... Aha! Found it." He produced a box filled with Splenda and a canister of non-dairy creamer. "Sorry, this is all I got. Angela was lactose intolerant and constantly on one of those sugar free diets or whatever." He waved his hand dismissively.

Stirring the powders into her cup like an expert alchemist, Lenore noted with some measure of disconcert that Paul had referred to Angela in the past tense. But none of that mattered now. The six Xanax were kicking in. Waves of calm spread throughout Lenore's body, and she celebrated the tranquility with large sups of spiked coffee. Closing her eyes, she imagined herself falling back into a large leather sofa, and the name of that sofa was Xanax.

She drowsily looked over at Paul. "So did you kill that guy?" It was an awkward question.

Paul looked down at his blood stained clothes and grinned. He was always grinning. "Yeah I messed up," he said, "but I'm not beating myself up about it. I didn't even know him. He was Angie's friend."

"So what happened?"

"Well, in a nutshell, he shouldn't have been here and now he's dinner."

By Lenore's account, Paul had thrown back two glasses of blood and was working on a third. The vampire act was pretty convincing, she thought, and not just because Paul drank blood. There was something catlike in his movements, and when standing still he appeared not to breathe at all.

Loud screams emanated from down the hall. "What's going on in there?" she asked.

Paul looked in the direction of the screams with evident disinterest. "Richard's chatting with Angela, that's all."

Lenore could now hear banging noises in addition to the screaming. "So how do you think that conversation is going?"

Paul giggled. "Doesn't sound like it's going so well for Angela, does it?"

Lenore finished her coffee, which had almost a full shot of liquor waiting for her at the bottom of the cup. There had to be a way to turn this situation around. She had to convince Paul to let her go, but needed to present the idea to him in a way that did not sound desperate.

"Any chance you've got the keys to the front door?"

"There's an excellent chance I have the keys to the front door," he said slyly. "You thinking it's time to boogie?"

"Yeah it's late and this has all been a bit much for me."

Paul shook his head. "I don't know why you're bothering asking me to let you out of here. I'm obviously not going to, and I think you already knew that." There was a weary irritation in his voice.

"Oh God, are you guys going to kill me?" Lenore immediately wished she could retract the question. So much for sounding calm.

Paul bit his lower lip to stifle a grin. "That's the elephant in the room, isn't it? What do you think?"

"I think if you weren't going to kill me you would have let me go by now," she said, and as the words come out of her mouth, she knew they were true.

Lenore's Xanax patina was starting to crack. She opened her purse and started sifting around for more pills. Only two remained.

"Jesus. You're going to take *more* pills? You just took *six* ten minutes ago! I don't think two more are going to make any difference at this point."

"What's it to you? If you really wanted to help me out you wouldn't be monitoring my dosage, you'd open the fucking door."

Two pills went down the hatch. Lenore's hand trembled as she pulled another cigarette from her pack.

Paul looked at her sympathetically and gave her a light. "You're right," he said. "How did Rich talk you down here in the first place?" He grabbed her empty cup from the counter and started fixing Lenore another Irish coffee.

"I was looking for old records and he posted an ad online. I met him at a coffee shop a few blocks down and he told me he was bringing me here to show me his collection. We exchanged emails—I'm sure they'll trace that. Someone will come looking for me."

"I'm sure they will," he said distantly. "You know what's funny? Rich actually owns a ton of old records." Paul leaned over the counter and spoke to Lenore with confidential flair. "No offense, but most of the time if he brings someone in here, it's to kill them." His brow furrowed. "But I'll bet he was going to show it to you. I don't think he was planning on killing you at all."

"What do you mean he kills them? Oh God, does Richard think he's a vampire too? Are you kidding me? You're grown men. You can't go around killing people. There's no such thing as vampires. Drinking blood isn't going to make you live forever. All you're going to accomplish is catching AIDS, not to mention throwing up." Paul's perpetual grin faded a little as she said this. Now she'd gone and done it, she thought; she'd pissed off the serial killer. Lenore stopped talking and put her hands over her mouth like a self imposed muzzle.

Paul took a deep breath, running his fingers over the edge of his glass. "Okay let's get something straight. I don't kill people. I slipped up, but I almost never kill anyone. Rich, on the other hand—"

The muzzle broke. "Wait wait wait wait wait. There's no 'I almost never kill anyone'. You either kill people or you don't. That's not one of those subjects where there's a ton of gray area." She stared deeply into her cup of coffee as if it were the only sane thing left in the room.

"Just out of curiosity, are you supposed to mix Xanax and alcohol? You slurred half of that last sentence."

"No of course I'm not supposed to mix them." Lenore chugged down the rest of her drink. Paul motioned to give her a refill, but she stopped him. "You know what? Just give me the bottle of whiskey." She took a hefty swig, making a bitter face as she tried to swallow it down. "Dammit I never could develop a taste for this shit. I hate shots. I hate liquor, period."

"There are other drinks in the cabinet." Paul started bustling around for alternatives.

"Don't bother. God I'm hoping to pass out soon. I don't know why it hasn't happened yet." Lenore did not want to be awake when the two serial killers decided exactly what it was they were going to do with her. If their intention was to kill/rape/eat her, then she wanted to miss the show entirely.

"Yeah, yeah, I know what you're trying to do. Rich is going to be pissed that I'm letting you. He probably wants you awake if I don't kill you first."

"What? Why?" Her face began to crumble.

"We all like a little cat and mouse from time to time." And with that, his grin widened, and Lenore winced as she saw two fangs descend. Nothing about Paul looked human anymore. Even his stance had adopted a predatory hue.

She covered her eyes with both hands like a child avoiding a horror movie. "Please," she whispered. "I'm so scared already. Please stop making that face."

"Oh Jesus...okay. I'm sorry...one sec...okay, they're gone. You can open your eyes."

Peering through squinted eyes, Lenore dropped her hands to see Paul apologetically staring back at her, his carnivorous grin gone completely.

"You've been such a good sport so far," he said. "I don't know why I went and did that." He rubbed his teeth with his finger. "See? All normal again."

Lenore heard footsteps in the hallway and realized that the earlier screaming had abated some time ago. The footsteps grew closer and then faded away. A door shut, and she could hear water running in the distance.

The thought of Richard-who-kills-people's return was starting to gnaw at Lenore's sense of drunken complacency. Was passing out really such a good idea? What was her alternative? She looked down at the mangled body on the floor and had her answer; she didn't stand a chance.

"I guess Richard finished talking to Angela," she whispered, mostly to herself. Lenore was through talking to Paul. The cat and mouse comment had rubbed her the wrong way.

"I guess so."

They sat in silence. Lenore wished someone were there to comfort her. Thank God for Xanax.

The footsteps grew louder again, and Lenore forced herself to take another gulp of whiskey as Richard entered the room. With damp hair and a fresh change of clothes, he stepped carefully around the body on the floor and leaned against the pool table with a disgusted expression on his face.

"This whole place smells like an ash tray now," he said, glaring at Paul. "Not only did you completely fuck up my living room with that stupid body dripping all over the *four thousand dollar rug*, but you're letting her smoke in here as well?"

Paul chuckled. "I didn't mean to overpower the smell of death in here with cigarettes."

18

Richard ignored him. "You are cleaning all of this shit up. I hope you understand that." He glanced at Lenore, who, to his obvious consternation, kept right on smoking. "Well, look who's still breathing." He wrinkled his nose, examining the bottle of whiskey. "How much has she had to drink at this point?"

"I don't think she's had that much, actually. But get this—she took *eight* Xanax." Paul held out eight fingers for effect. "Wait, it's more like twelve because I just remembered she said she took four before she came by."

"What, is that a lot or something?" Richard spotted the empty Xanax bottle on the counter and read the label aloud in monotone. "Take one half to one as needed for anxiety every four to six hours."

"I think she's pretty fucked up about now. She's like on a mission to pass out or something. How did it go with Angie, by the way?"

Richard chuckled. "Well, your stories didn't match up, that's for sure. What freaks me out is how she got the knife in here in the first place. We're going to have to ransack her room later. Clear it out."

"You're overreacting. We're talking about a *knife* here. You act like it's fucking plutonium. Could've come from Lancie over there. Wasn't necessarily Angie's in the first place."

Richard shook his head. "Well, you'd know better than I would—you were her babysitter and all." Richard shot the body an appraising view from where he stood. "I'd never even *heard* of this guy until he wound up on my carpet. Where'd you guys find him, anyway?" Then he smiled. "Oh no, wait. Let me guess. Your friend Charles found him on the Internet! Am I right? Do I win something if I'm right?"

Paul rolled his eyes. "You know, you knock him, but Charles has scouted out a *lot* of meals for you—"

"That guy is a freak and he attracts other freaks—"

"—*and* he goes to the store for you when you claim to be too busy—"

"Because he's a freak! Who *does* that?"

"—*and* I'll bet you use him to find your next donor," Paul said

19

triumphantly.

"Oh, another Angela? Thanks, but no thanks. I think I can handle it on my own. God she was strange. I probably did her a favor by putting her out of her misery."

"She's dead, Rich. Cut her a break."

"Oh, I'm sorry. Was I being insensitive? Because you look really broken up. I didn't realize how upset you were. Can I get you a handkerchief?"

Paul chuckled. "I'm crying on the inside. Seriously, I liked her okay. I don't know why you always had such a big problem with her."

"What kind of person signs up for this shit? You'd have to be sick in the head."

"Did you see what she did to me, by the way?" Paul drew up his sleeve and turned Richard's attention to the back of his hand. The entire forearm was swollen and appeared to be inflamed.

"Man, that looks like shit."

Paul winked at Lenore, who wanted no part of their conversation. "Yeah, but you should see the other guy."

Richard snickered.

Lenore focused intently on passing out, which was proving to be an elusive goal. She held the bottle of whiskey to her mouth again, but could not bring herself to take another sip. The pungent odor of the past two gulps was starting to rise in the back of her throat with the full force of yesterday's dinner and, to her horror, twelve pills of Xanax. She put out her cigarette and rested her head on the counter, willing herself not to throw up.

"Hey, why don't you go lie down on the sofa?" Paul suggested, tapping Lenore on the shoulder.

She shakily descended from the bar stool and stumbled toward the sofa, nearly tripping on Lance's remains on the way. Holding back the rising swell in her esophagus, she attempted to make herself comfortable on stiff cushions and closed her eyes. Twelve feet away, she could hear Paul and Richard discussing her as if they were now out of earshot.

"Hey, was she part of the plan here? She said she was going to buy some records from you or something. Are you still trying to get rid of those things?"

"The *plan*? What *plan*? I didn't know this evening was going to go all triple homicide on me. I'm trying to clear the records out of storage. They're just collecting dust these days, and they sound like shit. You know, I don't get why people are into collecting vinyl anyways. It's fucking retarded. CDs are much better."

"Okay so she's just in the wrong place at the wrong time? That sort of thing? I mean, she's not your usual fare."

"And by that you mean she's not homeless, right? I shouldn't have brought her back here. I just didn't feel like lugging a bunch of shit down the street. I go out for a few hours and all hell breaks loose."

"Yeah tell me about it. I didn't realize we were going to get back so early. I should have texted you or something."

"It's okay. This shit happens."

There was a pause in their conversation, and Lenore could hear someone walk by her, and then walk away.

"Hey, Rich," Paul said. "I think she's going to pass out soon. Her breathing has gotten really slooow. Once that happens, take care of her quickly and we'll clean up the mess. I have shit I want to do tonight."

"Take care of her? Oh, now that you're finished playing with her? I just drank. Why bleed her until I'm hungry again? Besides, we haven't disposed of Angela yet, or Lance for that matter. She needs to take a fucking number."

"Rich, don't be a dick, man. She didn't exactly ask to be here. She's all but euthanized herself over there."

"Umm, *none* of this shit would have happened if you hadn't splattered that guy all over the floor. She'd be listening to those shitty vinyls in the comfort of her own home right now if it weren't for you."

"Whatever."

"Look, if it's really that important to you, then you can have her when she passes out. I'm sure it won't be long now, but take her down the hall so I don't have two messes in here to clean up...make that *you* don't have two messes in here to clean up."

"But I just fed."

"Exactly. That's what I thought. Leave her to me, then. I'll be totally humane."

Paul snorted. "Oh yeah? Just like with Angela? Could you have dragged that out any longer?"

"I don't know. Let's ask the guy you ripped apart on the floor over there."

"Ooooh," Paul said in mock offense. "Touché."

Lenore lifted her head and opened her eyes to see the room spinning, only half aware of the conversation going on around her. Not quite a cogent thought, there was a nagging sensation that she should be running for her life right now, but her system was entirely too sluggish to comply. She could hear a soft moaning sound and wondered if it was coming from her lips.

Paul eyed Lenore. "Do you think I should get her a blanket or something? She looks pretty uncomfortable."

"Knock yourself out. Get a bucket, too, while you're at it. I don't want her throwing up on the couch. That's just about the only thing in this room that isn't going to have to be replaced."

Barely conscious, Lenore was dimly aware of a blanket being placed over her legs and a pillow being slipped underneath her head. She opened her eyes for the last time to see both Paul and Richard standing over her, talking to one another in hushed tones and glancing in her direction. Then the room spun into oblivion, and Lenore slid gratefully into the awaiting darkness.

Chapter Two:
Angie's Room

Lenore awoke to a wet splashing sound and took a moment to realize that she was throwing up into a large blue bucket on the floor. There was vomit in her hair and all over the collar of her shirt. It lined the creases of her neck with a cold, sticky residue. Wiping her mouth with her forearm, she looked around and noted that both the body and rug underneath had been cleared out of the room while she slept. The exposed marble tile was bespeckled with what fluids had leaked through to the floor. She rolled onto her side, opting to go back to sleep for a while rather than face what was in front of her.

Several hours later, the blue bucket received another deposit, and this time Lenore had a pounding headache to boot. She closed her eyes and tried again to sleep, but could no longer manage to do so. Several painkillers lay inside her purse, which to her relief was still atop the wet bar on the far side of the room, exactly as she had left it. In her current condition, however, anything outside of arm's length might as well be on Pluto. Summoning all of her will, Lenore shifted her body into a sitting position, taking great care not to topple the bucket beneath her. She discarded the blanket in her lap and walked toward the bar, head throbbing.

The side pockets of Lenore's oversized hobo bag were a veritable pharmacy. The left pocket contained all of her painkillers—these included Tylenol, aspirin, ibuprofen and Percoset from a previous surgery. The right pocket contained antihistamines, Benadryl, cough drops, eye drops, sleeping pills, nasal spray and until the night before,

Xanax. Curiously, her pack of cigarettes was nowhere to be found.

Wincing at the pain behind her eyes, Lenore hunched over the sink and ran the water, halfheartedly glancing around for her cup from the night before. Cupping her hands, she washed down three Advil and three Tylenol, figuring that if those did not kick in within the next twenty minutes or so, aspirin could be added to the equation.

The chemically induced serenity from hours ago had disappeared, leaving Lenore nervously in tune with the present danger. She looked around. No Paul. No Richard. Would the front door still be locked? Probably, but it was worth a try.

Apprehensively on the lookout for her captors, Lenore ventured down the hall and toward the foyer. When she got there, the front door would not budge despite furious, yet knowingly futile, pulling at the handle. She took a step back and thought for a moment. The next best course of action would be to try to locate a land line somewhere within the apartment, given that her cell phone was unable to pick up a signal in any of the locations tried so far. But where to begin? Sensing another wave of nausea, she decided to make that decision after visiting the bathroom.

Lenore heaved over the toilet for a five minute span that felt like hours. When she could heave no more, she sat with her eyes closed in the middle of the floor, willing her headache to go away. Massaging her temples, Lenore pondered the awful knowledge that three Advil and three Tylenol floated in the porcelain bowl. And now came the classic hangover dilemma: risk throwing up again to take more pills, or forego the pills and endure the headache? Whenever there was a fork in the road, Lenore veered toward the path that involved popping pills.

She slithered over to the sink and took three aspirins, accidentally catching a glimpse of her reflection in the mirror. The woman staring back at her looked dreadful. Lenore's angular face was gaunt from restless sleep. Deep bags had formed under her dark brown eyes, accentuating half-mast lids. Specks of vomit littered her mousey brown hair like green and yellow confetti. Although she knew that she had better things to do, Lenore took the time to wash her face and attempted to pick her hair clean of sickness before leaving to explore the rest of her surroundings.

Down the hall and past the parlor, she entered a large library. Wall to wall bookshelves housed an eclectic collection of nonfiction, home repair manuals, National Geographic magazines, comic books, and stashes and stashes of old newspapers. A glass display in the center of the room showcased several antique baseball cards, some of them dating back as far as the 1920s. Next to the display were two leather sofas sitting across from one another, with a work desk in between.

And on that work desk sat a laptop computer. Perhaps she could communicate with someone through email.

Impatiently, she sat down with the opened computer in her lap and waited for it to boot up, growing nervous that Richard would return to find her sifting through his possessions. The boot screen on the computer gave way to a Windows password prompt for user "Rich." She pressed Enter in hopes that the password was empty, but was denied access. The prospect of guessing Richard's password seemed a hopeless endeavor, not to mention a dangerous waste of time. She had to keep moving. Before stepping back into the hall, Lenore switched off the machine and placed it, she hoped, back on the table exactly as she had found it.

Where should she go next? The apartment appeared to be laid out in a "T" shape, with an entrance at the foyer that opened to separate left and right wings. So far she had only explored the left wing, which included the parlor, the library and three closed doors at the end of the hall. Opening those doors seemed like a foolish idea; Richard might be on the other side. The prospect of traversing the right wing was equally discouraging. This was the direction that Richard had taken Angela the night before, and Lenore was afraid of what she might find.

Without Xanax to mollify her, Lenore began to panic. She had to find a phone. She needed to get back to her apartment where 90 more pills waited in the medicine cabinet. A threat, possibly one more frightening than Richard himself, had begun to emerge.

Withdrawal.

25

Lenore gritted her teeth and walked toward where Angela was last heard screaming. There was a large modern kitchen to her left. She glimpsed along its walls for a mounted phone but did not find one. A formal dining room adjoined the kitchen, complete with banquet table and chandelier. But again, no land line.

There was a shut door to the right of the kitchen, which at first glance appeared to be covered in dirt. Taking a closer look, Lenore saw dried blood caked in the hinges and smeared on the knob. This must have been where Richard had taken Angela. She thought about how Angela had screamed on her way down the hall. Lenore's mouth ran dry. Beads of sweat formed on her forehead. The items in her purse were shaking, the arm that held the purse was shaking, and so was the body to which it was attached.

"Making yourself at home, I see." Lenore recoiled to see Richard standing quietly beside her. How long had he been there? She was too frightened to reply.

"Would you like me to show you what's behind this door?" He smiled wickedly. There was something about his smile that jogged an uneasy memory form the night before. Paul had grown teeth when he smiled like that, hadn't he? Surely that was some sort of a dream, but it made her skin crawl nonetheless.

Lenore shook her head and could feel frustrated tears popping out of her eyes. Richard stared at her for a moment with his arms crossed and nodded thoughtfully.

He had changed clothes since their last encounter. Muscularly built, his designer apparel complimented a tall figure and cruelly handsome face. Lenore remembered being quite intimidated by Richard when she first met him at the coffee shop; people like her and people like him did not get along. She felt momentarily embarrassed as his eyes studied her vomit stained shirt and hair. Attempting to gather back some of her composure, Lenore stood up straight and wiped away her tears.

Richard lifted his eyebrows and opened his mouth to speak, but then closed it again. Instead, he turned around, signaling Lenore to

26

follow. He led her to the kitchen sat down at the table. "Have a seat," he said.

She followed his instructions and sat across from him, nervously looking down at her hands.

"Are you hungry?" he asked. "You slept for nearly sixteen hours."

Lenore shook her head and mouthed the word, "no." Sixteen hours? She wondered what time it was.

"Excellent." He smiled. "Neither am I." And, looking at her to establish eye contact, he added, "But I will be in about a day or so, and when that happens you're in a heap of trouble."

Lenore was confused. "Why? What happens then?" She could feel tears welling back up behind her eyes.

"That's when I'm going to kill you."

A new wave of tears descended, and Lenore turned away from the man in front of her. She wanted to say something, anything, that would convince Richard to let her go, but knew whatever escaped her lips would come out as a sob.

Richard's lips curled in a half-smile. Was he enjoying this?

Leaning back in his chair, he continued, "I'm not telling you this to upset you. Do you understand that?" Lenore did not understand that. "There's a point to all this—I wouldn't bother having this conversation with you if there weren't."

Richard looked around the room impatiently as Lenore attempted to stop the ebb of tears. If he was going to kill her, why couldn't he have done it while she slept? Why wait until she was wide awake and terrified?

When there was a sufficient break in Lenore's sobbing, Richard continued. "So I don't think I had an opportunity to introduce you to Angela. She was the dark haired girl in here last night. Do you remember her?"

Lenore nodded. She was not sure where this was going.

"And you remember my buddy, Paul, from last night, too, right?"

Lenore nodded.

"I had a chat with Paul after you went to sleep and he admitted to me that he did something very rude in front of you."

Now Lenore could see where this was going. "He drank blood," she whispered.

Richard smiled at this. "That's right. Paul and I suffer from a similar..." He lifted his head, struggling to find the right word, "...condition." He looked at Lenore to make sure they had an understanding on that point before moving on. "So I'm sure you can imagine, it's very difficult for me to find people willing to let me drink their blood on a voluntary basis. Angela was one of those people. Now, as Angela is regretfully not with us anymore, I'm in a bit of a tight spot trying to replace her." He paused for a moment. "Do you—do you understand what I'm telling you so far?"

Lenore had stopped crying and stared back at him. "I think so," she said.

"Wonderful. So one of two things can happen when I get hungry again." Richard held up two fingers and cleared this throat. "The first option is that I'll take you inside that room over there." He pointed to the blood stained doorway, the very mention of which made Lenore gasp. Richard raised his hands and added, "I swear on my mother I'll be as quick as I can possibly be, so relax. That's the worst case scenario." He smirked. "So let's call that option 'Door Number One.'"

Lenore did not know what the second option was, but she was pretty sure she was going to go with Door Number Two.

"The second option—and this one is tricky, but I've gotten pretty good at it over the years—is that I can feed without killing you, if you do *exactly* what I tell you to do."

Lenore raised her eyebrows. "And then would you let me go?"

Richard smiled and shook his head. "Obviously no. I can't do that. See—see that's why you might want to think about this before making a decision right away. There aren't any windows in this place. No phone. No friends or family. For all intents and purposes, you're dead, you're just dying slow is all. It works out better for *me* because I don't have to worry about where my next meal is coming from, but I'll be the first person to admit that I'd probably be doing you a favor finishing you off quickly. It really isn't any kind of life I'd want."

"So why did Angela do it?" she asked. "Did you tell her all this?"

"Nooooo... That was a totally different situation altogether. See, Angela was into this lifestyle that was all dark and alternative and she sought this type of thing out. She wanted to be like Paul and me and thought that by offering herself up we'd eventually turn her. I can't even tell you how much that was never going to happen. Anyway, the reason that I'm telling *you* all of this is because you don't seem to be one of those wannabe freaks that I'm fucking sick of, which is good on one hand because it means that you aren't crazy, but it's also bad because it means that you don't exactly want to be here."

"So Angela wasn't the only one who's done this?"

"No, there have been several other donors...and I'll even level with you...they all wind up dead. Eventually everyone sees the back room over there." He grinned. "How's *that* for a sales pitch?"

"How long do I have to think it over?" she asked. But she had already made up her mind. Door Number Two sounded almost as bad as Door Number One, but at least it would buy her time to formulate an escape.

"Take as long as you want, but really think it over. I'm not going to bother you until I'm hungry again, and until then you're my guest here, okay? Angela kept a ton of food in the pantry. You're welcome to it. I'm not going to sit around and make you coffee like Paul did, but feel free to help yourself to whatever you want. Just clean up any messes you make. That's all I ask." Richard eyed Lenore's shirt. "Actually, come with me first."

As they walked out of the kitchen, Lenore became suspicious that Richard was leading her straight to the slaughter room a few feet away. She relaxed as they walked past it to the other end of the hall. Richard stopped in front of the set of closed doors that Lenore had been too frightened to open earlier.

"Angela packed her entire life away when she came here," Richard explained, opening the door farthest down. "I know you guys aren't exactly the same size, but maybe you can find a fresh change of clothes in here. Angie had her own bathroom—you can take a shower too if you like."

Lenore walked inside the hole-in-the-wall bedroom and found it to be a mess. Drawers were thrown open, the bed was turned upside down, and items were littered all over the floor like something out of a drug raid. From where she stood, even the bathroom appeared to have been ransacked.

Richard looked sheepishly at Lenore and said, "Yeah, I know it looks pretty bad in here. Paul and I went through her things yesterday. It didn't always look like this."

"What were you looking for?" she asked, more out of reflex than curiosity.

"It's not important," he said dismissively. "Listen, I'm heading out for a while, but you should be all set as far as clothes and food and such. Is there anything else you need?"

There was one thing. "Do you know what happened to my pack of cigarettes? I usually keep them in my purse but I can't seem to find them."

"You mean these?" Richard fished her pack of Marlboro lights from his back pocket. "I'm saving these. If you decide to go out the quick way, I'll let you smoke one beforehand because I'm not a complete asshole, but if you're going to stick around here for a while then you better figure on quitting smoking. Deal?"

"Deal." What choice did she have? Besides, cigarettes were soon to be the least of her problems. An unpleasant metallic taste was forming in the back of Lenore's throat, and this was regularly the first symptom she experienced when going into withdrawal. Another day or two without Xanax and things would deteriorate exponentially.

"Okay, if that's all, I'm going to get out of here."

When Lenore turned around he was gone, and she was left standing alone in all that remained of Angela's short legacy. Although it was difficult to picture what the room had looked like before being been torn apart, it was plain to see that Angela had lived a very lonely life. The walls were barren of any decoration, and Lenore noted that not a single picture of a friend or loved one existed on the threadbare furniture. A small wooden bookshelf was filled to the brim with romance novels and brain teasers. On the floor lay a thirteen inch television, having been knocked off its entertainment center. It was connected to an Atari and eight bit Nintendo.

The vanity along the wall revealed Angela's other pastime, which was evidently taking care of her nails. The surface was littered with hundreds of polishes, decals, extensions, trimmers and countless files. Lenore frowned as she pictured Angela sitting on the bed, day after day, painting her nails in the blue light of the television. She thought back to the image of the girl sobbing on the carpet and wished she could have done something to help her.

Willing herself to change focus, Lenore walked to the dresser and started hunting for a change of clothes. She was not optimistic about her prospects. At five pounds underweight, Lenore did not imagine she would fit into items tailored to Angela's midsized frame.

She was pleasantly surprised. The top drawer contained a pair of jeans that might stay up if she could find a belt. The drawer beneath contained an oversized t-shirt that proudly displayed the words: YOU CALL ME BITCH LIKE IT'S A BAD THING, but it was clean and that was all that mattered. Now came a more difficult decision—did she use the dead woman's underwear? Lenore located the underwear drawer and was delighted to find several banal choices forged from 100% cotton.

Gathering up her finds, she stepped into the bathroom, careful to avoid the scattered remnants of the medicine cabinet strewn about the floor. She drew the shower and discarded her vomit stained clothing. Stepping into the stall, she closed her eyes and sighed as a stream of hot water ran over her body. Angela had several scented soaps, and the aromas threw Lenore into relaxed contemplation.

She wondered if anyone had missed her yet. It seemed unlikely. Lenore had no immediate family to speak of and worked from home with remote clients and far away deadlines. Eventually, she mused, her landlord would wonder why she was behind with her rent, but it was not due for another three weeks. By the time anyone had noticed her absence, the trail would be completely cold.

Surely her host was not *really* a vampire, but a mounting uncertainty had started to fester in the back of her mind. In the end, did it really make a difference one way or the other? If Richard was going to kill her, it did not matter if he was the Easter Bunny or the Angel of Death himself; the threat was still the same and the need to escape just as real. Thinking about this fact shot Lenore into another round of hysterics and she could feel tears merge with the steady stream from the showerhead. This was weakness. She needed to pull herself together.

Taking a deep breath, Lenore stepped out of the stall and donned her new attire. Angela's pants sagged loosely about her waist. She looked around for something to tie them with, and her eyes hit upon a lace scarf lying amid the clutter on the floor. As she attempted to thread it through the belt loops, Lenore realized that her hands were shaking. Muscle tremors—another sign that her body was starving for the next dose of Xanax. It took three attempts to tie the final knot.

She stepped back into Angela's room, noticing for the first time that a round clock hung on the wall beside the entertainment center. Its hands read 2:43—was that a.m. or p.m.? Did it matter?

She turned the mattresses over on the bed and lay down, uncertain of what she should do next. She might as well check her cell phone one more time. Reaching into her purse, she pulled out the phone and was devastated to discover that the battery had died while she was in the shower. There was no hope of calling for help anymore. No one knew of her plight, Richard was going to return, and—more importantly—she was out of Xanax.

Lenore restlessly contemplated her withdrawal symptoms and

wondered how long they would last. She remembered the humiliating lecture she received from her general practitioner the last time she found herself in this predicament. "You'd better have kicked this for good or the next time you might not be so lucky—benzodiazepine addiction is serious and if you go off too quickly you could have a seizure."

And she *had* been lucky, hadn't she? Foul taste, insomnia, muscle tremors, not to mention exquisite mood swings, but no seizures, and after three weeks she felt right as rain. That was only from 12 pills a day, however, and this time she was coming down from over 20. Lenore had four separate doctors prescribing the drug. What she did not spend on rent or food went to four separate pharmacies, only one of which billed her insurance provider.

A full blown panic was beginning to take hold. Lenore needed to distract herself, but how? Food. Food would mask the terrible taste in her mouth. Food would take her mind off the trembling in her hands.

She slid out of bed and walked down the hall to the kitchen. Richard's pantry contained several unhealthy choices, including Lenore's favorite: rippled potato chips. It also contained dozens of bottles of Gatorade. Angela must have loved that stuff.

Angela loved Gatorade. She also died across the hall. Right behind that door over there. Remember how she screamed? Lenore turned her head toward the blood stained door and shuddered. It seemed to be moving closer to where she stood. She pictured Angela crouching behind it, getting ready to leap out and drag her inside.

Lenore's pulse was racing. She grabbed the bag of chips and hastily shut the pantry. She then sprinted back to Angela's room, feeling as though the dead woman's ghost were chasing her the entire way.

Panting, Lenore threw herself on the bed and thought about her next move, which was likely to involve the sleeping pills in her purse. They offered a temporary escape, even if it wasn't the physical kind. It might be best to wait on that plan, however, and only use the pills in an emergency. If she had not been so hasty with the Xanax the night before, she might still be enjoying them now. Scared and in desperate need of distraction, Lenore busied herself with one of the novels left by the room's former occupant, only succumbing to the call of Ambien ten hours later, when the clock on the wall read 12:04.

Lenore woke again at 8:57 (a.m. or p.m.?), her system feeling entirely out of whack. She wanted to take more pills and sleep off the withdrawal, but knew she needed to stay awake for a few more hours in order to harness their effect. Fitfully, she picked up the romance novel she had been reading earlier before placing it back down in distaste.

There had to be more palatable alternatives in Richard's library. The walk down the hall ended in a hasty U-turn, however, as she glimpsed a male figure sitting on one of the sofas. Lenore's heart raced. Richard must have returned while she was sleeping.

"Hello, Lenore," Richard sang out as she scurried back to Angela's hole in the wall. She slammed the door and sat down on the bed. Silent as a mouse, she listened to the sound of footsteps approach and stop at the entryway.

"It's okay—you can come out of the room if you want," he called through the door. "I'm not going to hurt you. I'm still not hungry. You sound like shit, by the way. Your heartbeat's all irregular."

How would he *know* that?

"Hiding in here isn't going to do you any good, by the way. When the time comes I'm just going to come and get you, so you might as well come out. Were you coming to get a book? You can, you know. I'm sure you're bored in there." There was silence for a moment, and then the footsteps faded back into the hallway.

After giving it some thought, Lenore decided nothing was worse than sitting perfectly still and waiting for Richard to come and get her "when the time comes." She rose and opened the door, this time walking cautiously back to the library to find Richard sitting exactly as he was before.

She browsed the collection of items on his shelves, taking care to avoid all eye contact with her would-be murderer. Richard, for his part, appeared entirely too engrossed in a task at the computer to pay her any notice. After hasty deliberation, Lenore selected a collection of short stories entitled "The Lady or The Tiger" and took it back with her to Angela's room. She read until the clock struck 1:15, at which time she took another round of pills.

Lenore awoke to a rapping at the door. She peered through half-shut eyes at the clock on the wall. 6:47 (a.m. or p.m.?). She rolled over as the cogs in her mind sluggishly turned. Richard. Richard had come to get her. Startled, she shot into a sitting position with her back pressed firmly against the headboard. Then she watched, unable to breathe, as Richard came in and sat on the opposite edge of the bed.

Looking at him now, Lenore was unable to rekindle her feelings of fear and desperation from the last time they met, although she certainly was afraid. She concluded that her recent preoccupation with Xanax must have achieved a somewhat desensitizing effect. Either that, or the sleeping pills were not quite out of her system.

"How was your nap?" he asked.

Lenore did not respond. Upon waking, the taste in the back of Lenore's mouth was almost unbearable. What had started out as something vaguely metallic had morphed into what she imagined might be the gustatory equivalent of Athlete's foot. She swallowed fitfully.

"I think it's time I ate," he said congenially. "So what's it going to be? You want to do this the quick way or the slow way?"

She hated the way he phrased her options. "The slow way," she whispered.

Damn that taste.

"Yeah I was pretty sure that's what you'd say," he smirked. "You didn't seem too keen on the back room earlier."

It was subtle, but Richard's appearance had changed over the past two days. Pale to begin with, he seemed positively white at this point, an unflattering contrast to the bags that had formed beneath his eyes.

35

He *looked* hungry.

"I'm not sure how to ask you this, but I need to know. The other night, Paul grew teeth. I know it sounds nuts, but I swear I looked at him and he grew teeth. Do you do that? I'm—I'm not sure what's real anymore." Good. She was finally going to get to the bottom of this.

"You want to know if I have fangs. Is that it?"

"Yeah, I think that's what I'm asking. Was that all in my head?"

"No, ma'am. Paul and I have fangs. Feel better now?"

"Can you...do you think you could grow them? I need to see it again." In the future, Lenore would replay this conversation in her head and wonder what would have possessed her to press the point.

Richard seemed taken aback. "Are you serious?"

"I think so. I have to know what I'm dealing with here. I think that's fair."

He shook his head. "Okay I guess it's fair, but I need you to understand something. In the future—well, in the future if it's just you and me, and you know I'm hungry, asking me to grow fangs probably isn't a smart move, understand?"

She nodded. With that, Richard's lips curled back into what might be interpreted as a snarl or menacing grin, and Lenore watched in awe as his canines extended into sharp protrusions.

"Thanks. I appreciate it." She ogled his mouth in total fascination, feeling a bit reminiscent of second grade, watching her best friend pop her eyes out of their sockets.

Richard was actually smiling now, fangs exposed. "My pleasure." He closed his lips, and when he opened them again, his teeth were back to normal. Then he stood up and, offering Lenore a helping hand, brought her to her feet as well. He studied her upright figure with a bemused expression, exclaiming, "Nice outfit. I see you found Angie's favorite shirt."

Was she still wearing that you-call-me-a-bitch-like-it's-a-bad-thing shirt? "It's growing on me."

He looked at her thoughtfully for a moment and then said, "We might as well get this over with." Lenore's entire body tensed as if she were anticipating a particularly unpleasant procedure at the doctor's office. She shut her eyes tightly and gritted her teeth.

"What are you doing?"

She opened one eye to see Richard standing in front of her, clearing reveling in her confusion. "Aren't you going to bite me or something?"

He shook his head. "Not unless you want to wind up like that guy on my carpet. If I start biting you I probably won't be able to stop. Not to mention, it wouldn't leave you with two neat little pinpricks like you see in the movies. I'll rip you apart." Lenore gulped. "Walk with me to the kitchen, okay? We're going to have to go over some rules."

Lenore once again grew nervous as they approached the slaughter room down the hall. She slowed her pace and waited for Richard to enter the kitchen first before following behind. He stood in front of the sink, arms crossed, waiting for her to catch up.

"I'm not trying to trick you, you know. If I were going to take you to the other room, I'd just do it." He furrowed his brow and eyed Lenore with suspicion. "Something doesn't sound right about you. Your heartbeat's all fucked up. Do you have some sort of condition I should know about?"

"No." None that was any of his business, anyway.

She walked to where Richard stood and leaned weakly against the counter. He pulled a small plastic tube from his pocket and washed it with antibacterial soap in the sink. When he finished, he dangled it in front of Lenore.

"Do you know what this is?" he asked.

"No," she replied.

It looked like a catheter; something that might be hooked up to an IV bag. The sight of the tube brought back memories of her mother being treated for breast cancer.

"It's called a PICC line, but modified. So what we do is insert this

37

into your arm and tape it there. And then it's there permanently…for the rest of your life, anyway. There's a spigot at the end of the line. You pour blood out of that when I tell you to, and you don't stop until I tell you to. Understand?" Lenore nodded and Richard continued. "Once I start drinking, stay away from me until I'm finished. We can go over the other rules when I'm done."

Richard grabbed a needle from the counter, attached it to the line, and passed the combination to Lenore. "Do you know how to insert this?" he asked. She shook her head. "You need to find a vein—the one in the middle of your arm will do—and you insert the needle. Then, you push the catheter through, detach the needle, and we bandage you up." He pulled some medical tape from his back pocket.

This was insane. Lenore did not want to put that *thing* in her arm, and was particularly repulsed by the idea that it was not intended to come out. Where had that *thing* been, anyway?

"Is this sanitary? Did Angela have one of these?" Rinsing *that thing* in the sink moments beforehand could not possibly be medical procedure. Wouldn't they need to boil it or something? She turned the device over in her hands with skepticism.

"This *was* Angela's, as a matter of fact, and she would have had it in her arm by now," he replied. "Is there a problem?"

Ugh. What about AIDS? What else could you catch from contaminated blood? Probably several things. What did Richard care? Lenore did not want to upset him. "There's no problem. It's like an IV. That's basically what this is, right? Does it hurt?"

Richard grinned. "Compared to what we *could* be doing? No. Now get to it."

Lenore had no trouble locating the vein on the underside of her arm, but her hands shook too violently to properly aim the needle. After several unsteady attempts, she had pierced her skin in numerous places but had not managed to hit the vein.

Richard approached her, rolling his eyes. He grabbed the line. "Am I seriously going to have to do this for you?" he asked. He fingered the wounds on her arm. "I don't think you have any idea how dangerous this is. It's a good thing I'm not all that hungry or you'd probably be dead by now."

With one swift motion, he inserted the line and detached the catheter, which immediately began leaking blood all over the kitchen floor. He pulled out the tape and wrapped it around Lenore's arm to secure the device in place. Then he retreated to the other side of the room, saying, "Goddammit, squeeze the end of the tube so that you don't waste more blood! Raise your arm up, for Christ's sake!" Lenore raised her arm and tightened the spigot at the end of the line, preventing additional spillage.

"Now, go and get a glass from the cabinet. Not *that* cabinet. Two to the left. You got it. Fill up the glass and go sit at the table. Got it?"

Lenore grabbed a class from the cabinet and, despite the violent tremors in her arm, managed to set it down on the counter without shattering it all over the floor. Richard had inserted the catheter so quickly that she had only felt a slight pinch, but now as she attempted to manipulate the line, she noticed how sore the pierced area actually was, especially when she bent her arm toward the glass in front of her. After awkwardly positioning herself into a stance that did not aggravate the wound, Lenore released the tap and watched with disgust as her blood dripped into the container.

Richard looked on from afar and gave her a thumbs up when the glass was full. "Now go," he said, shooing her away as if she were a cockroach. Lenore went to sit at the kitchen table and watched as he drained the glass. When he was finished, he signaled her for a refill. How much blood could she stand to lose? They repeated the process twice more before Richard was finally sated.

Richard rinsed and dried the glass before putting it back in the cabinet. He then walked over to the pantry and grabbed a bottle of Gatorade, which he placed in front of Lenore before taking a seat at the opposite end of the table.

"Drink up," he said.

She looked at the bottle with total lack of enthusiasm. "I'm not a big fan of Gatorade."

"Suit yourself, but you need to get some fluids back into your system, and I don't have many other options besides water."

Lenore closed her eyes and nodded. She was tired now, and feeling a bit light headed. She grabbed the bottle in front of her with shaking hands and drank deeply. Somehow, Gatorade was not quite as disgusting as she remembered from her childhood, and the bottle was three quarters empty the next time it landed on the table.

"Feeling better?"

"Yeah, actually."

"So I think this went pretty well, all things considered. Now that you have the line in your arm this should be a piece of cake the next time."

"How often do we do this?" she asked.

"Well, the short answer to that question is whenever I feel like it, and that's about every few days, but it depends. Here's the problem, though...you're not producing blood at a fast enough rate to keep up with that schedule. If I do this every few days you're going to bleed to death. So I supplement. You get to take breaks."

Lenore was not encouraged by this information. "How often can you supplement? Can you do it with animals or something?"

"What? No. It's with people. If I could drink the blood of animals don't you think I would? Christ. Why would I go to all this trouble? And I supplement whenever I can."

"Does Paul do this?" She gestured toward the tube running out of her arm. "Does he have this arrangement with someone?"

"Like the arrangement I had with Angela and now have with you? No. Paul does something totally different."

"He said the other night that he doesn't kill people—"

Richard laughed and shook his head. "Paul's so full of shit. And I think that guy he let bleed all over my floor would probably disagree with him. He *tells* himself he doesn't kill people, though. And I guess for the most part that's true. Paul is all into this vampire club scene, and it's fucking weird. He goes out to these clubs and there are all these people there and they're dressed in black and shit and they *think* they're vampires—drives me crazy. Anyway, some think they're vampires and the other ones—they just want to be victims. The ones that want to be victims cut themselves in the back room and it's like an all you can eat buffet."

"You don't do that?"

"So there are a ton of problems with doing that, and what happened on Tuesday is a case in point. Paul's hungry, and then all of a sudden the victim guy who's just cutting himself for fun or whatever—well, all of a sudden it's not so fun and he's all over the floor. Paul has to go to these clubs *constantly* because he wouldn't want to show up hungry. Not to mention he's hanging out with these people, who are obviously bat-shit insane, all the time and pretending to be their friend so he can take them into a filthy back room and bleed them for a while." Richard clearly had strong opinions on this topic. "I think it's just a lot of work is what I'm saying—and I'm not saying that I haven't done it, because I have—but it gets old real quick."

Richard looked at Lenore now and smiled. "And I have to admit, the big reason I'm not into the club scene is because I like finishing people off all the way. I know it's awful, but I do." Lenore said nothing. What was there to say?

Richard clapped his hands, as if to signal the end of uncomfortable silence. "Rules," he said. "Let's go over rules. The house is open to you, but don't go into my bedroom. There's a guest room across from Angela's room. I'd appreciate it if you stay out of there as well. Okay?"

She nodded. "Okay."

He cocked his head to the side and narrowed his eyes. "I don't believe you, so I'm going to make both of our lives a little easier and tell you this right off the bat, I'll know if you go on those rooms. I can smell you. I knew you opened my computer the other day, for instance. It had your scent."

Lenore's eyes grew wide. She opened her mouth to speak, but Richard lifted his hand to stop her.

"It's fine," he said. "I'm not mad about it. I would have done the same thing. But you know better now, right?" She nodded. "Angela's room is your room now, so please keep it clean—especially the bathroom. No mess."

"So you have a bedroom? You sleep?" she asked.

"Of course I sleep."

"Do you sleep in a coffin or something?"

Richard snorted. "I sleep in a *bed*. This isn't Nosferatu." He paused for a moment and looked at the ceiling. "What else should I tell you? Oh this is important—when I'm hungry stay away from me. Don't make any sudden moves or I'll start chasing you all over the apartment. You haven't seen me really hungry yet, but you'll know when it happens."

Lenore was beginning to feel very strange and had some measure of difficulty keeping up with the conversation. She picked up the bottle of Gatorade and started drinking in an effort to combat her lightheadedness. Richard kept going.

"We can put together a list of things you'll need for your stay here like food, medications..." Why would he say medications? Why would he say medications unless he knew about the withdrawal? Lenore snapped back to attention and quickly attempted to change the subject.

"What is there to do around here?" she asked.

"What is there to *do*? Well, to put it bluntly, you're pretty much just here for one reason. Other than that, I don't care what you do. What did you do beforehand?"

Lenore thought about that question and had trouble coming up with an answer. What did she do other than work all day and watch television in the evenings? She almost never left her apartment unless it was to obtain food or prescriptions. Over the past three years she managed to lose touch with what few friends she did have from college. She supposed this life would appear lonely to someone looking in from the outside, but the hard fact was that she was too sedated most days to recognize her isolation.

After some deliberate thought, she said, "I guess I'll manage. The television works in Angela's room, right? I haven't tried it out yet."

Richard nodded. "Yeah it gets some stations, but you need to keep the volume off when I'm here and just set it to use subtitles. I hear differently than you and I can tell if it's on from anywhere in the apartment."

"Can I use a computer? I have a job and clients that are expecting—"

"I'm going to stop you right there. No. You're dead now. That's all over. Welcome to the afterlife." Hell was a well appointed kitchen.

"I figured it was worth a shot." The conversation was fading in and out again.

"I can't fault you for trying." Richard shot Lenore a quizzical glance. "Hey what are you doing?"

Lenore was not sure what he was asking her. She tried to respond, but found that her lips would not shape words and that her tongue was glued to the left side of her mouth. All that she was able to produce was a low moaning sound, which she was only partially aware may have been coming from her in the first place. A loud buzzing could be heard in the distance and there was also the sound of something hitting the table in front of her. Now everything was wet.

Richard stood over her, looking down. Was she on the floor? How did that happen? Richard put something in her mouth. Where was she? Her vision was now locked on her shoulder. No blinking.

Chapter Three:
Charles

Lenore felt something being pulled out of her mouth and opened her eyes to see Richard holding a damp wooden spoon. She was back on Angela's bed, but she was not sure how she got there. Had it gotten colder? No. She was wet. Disoriented and shivering, she looked down to see that her clothes were soaked from the waist onward. Richard walked out and quickly returned with a towel and another bottle of Gatorade. Something was wrong.

"What happened?"

"You mean you don't know? You had a seizure," he said. His words were tinged with excitement. "I've been around a long time but I've never seen one of those before."

Lenore rolled her eyes. It had happened. The withdrawal seizure. Fuck. Was the dampness on her jeans urine?

Richard unfolded the towel in his hands and passed it to Lenore, who immediately started wiping off her face. What was all over her chin? Had she been drooling? Richard then offered her the bottle of Gatorade, but she declined.

"So you know what's funny about your reaction to all of this?" he asked rhetorically. "It's that you don't seem very surprised. So I'm thinking to myself, you're either an epileptic, or you're going through a nasty withdrawal." Lenore was silent. "And you know what? I don't think you're epileptic. Am I right?"

Lenore nodded. She had hoped it would not come to this, but if she had her way, she would be home right now.

"So what's your poison?" he asked smugly.

"Xanax. Please...can you get me some more?" Lenore was disappointed to find herself waxing emotional. "It's—it's bad enough with everything else going on here, but I don't want to have another seizure."

Richard looked her over with a pained expression on his face. "I'm starting to think you're more trouble that you're worth, here. I'm not going to shell out money to buy you drugs."

Drugs? Xanax wasn't crack. Although if crack were available by prescription, Lenore was fairly sure she'd be on it.

"I don't mind getting you food," Richard said, "because if you don't eat then I don't eat, but for everything else you're on your own."

"I'm agoraphobic. I don't have a drug problem. The Xanax is for agoraphobia. I can't go outside without it and—"

"Let's get something straight. I'm not stupid. I know how much you took the other night. I could even smell it on you. So you know what's funny, though? It's that I didn't put this together until you had a seizure. I thought your heart sounded funny because you stopped smoking. I was going to offer to get you Nicorette gum or something. Shows how much I know."

"When I came to meet you on Tuesday, I brought three hundred dollars cash to buy those records. Is that still my money?"

Richard chuckled. "Are you still interested in buying my collection?"

"No—I mean for Xanax."

"Umm sure that's still your money, but I can't just waltz into a pharmacy and pick up a bunch of those pills for you without a prescription—"

"The bottle in my purse has three refills. Oh and there are two more prescriptions in the front pocket..." She stopped herself. This was not helping her case.

"No good. You're dead, remember? I have ways of covering you guys up, but I'm not trying to make things harder on myself with a paper trail. Besides, let's say that we got you some pills—what happens when your money runs out?"

"Get me the pills this one time and I'll wean myself off. I swear. Just get me as far as my money goes."

"Oh Christ, you're a mess. At least Angela was *clean*. This was a mistake. I'm going to have to find someone else."

"No! Never mind about the medicine. I'll get through this on my own."

"You've already *tried* that and now you're having seizures. I have neither the time nor the desire to coddle you through another five of these until you're back on your feet. I was completely fine with whatever your medical issue was beforehand—even though you refused to tell me about it—and I would have gotten you something from over the counter, but this is ridiculous."

"I'll stay out of your hair. Please don't find someone else. Please." Lenore paused for fear of crying. "Please don't take me to that room in the back," she whispered.

Richard sighed and looked at the purse on the floor. Saying nothing, he fished out the wallet and extracted the wad of cash inside. Shaking the bills in front of her, he said, "I'm not a thief. This is your money. You get to making a list of everything you need and I'll talk to Paul. He'll probably know someone who can get you those pills. You figure out how to get yourself off that shit for good, though, because there won't be any refills, understand?"

"That's fair. Thank you!" Lenore felt sick for thanking her kidnapper.

"Uh huh. Just so we have an understanding, if this type of thing happens again I *will* find someone else. And I'm not cleaning up after you. You get yourself cleaned up and then you go clean up the kitchen."

She looked at her clothes. "Where's the laundry?" she asked.

Richard grinned. "It's that room you don't want me to take you to. Put your clothes outside the door and I'll take care of the rest."

"Did Angela go in there?"

His grin widened. "You might say she never left."

"I mean to do laundry."

"Oh. No. It gets pretty messy in there. See that hamper?" He pointed to an overturned plastic bin on the floor. "Fill it up, leave it outside the door, and when I get around to it, I'll give it back to you with the clothes washed and dried. This isn't the dry-cleaners, though. If it doesn't look dirty to me I'll tell you to wear it again. You aren't here to impress anybody."

"Can I get clothes with the money?" Lenore needed some jeans that fit.

Richard rolled his eyes. "Look, I don't care what you spend it on. Work out a budget and I'll see what I can do." Then he gestured to Lenore's shirt and asked wryly, "What? Are wacky catch phrases out this season?"

"They're very last fall."

Richard nodded and turned to the door. "I'm heading out for a bit. When I get back, I expect the kitchen to be cleaned up and you to have a list together of everything you need. Food is on me, by the way, so if you're budgeting out the three hundred don't worry about the cost of food. And you know what? I just got an idea. You pack up all of Angela's shit you don't want. I'll have someone take it over to Goodwill and trade it in for some new clothes. That should help your money go further, what do you think?"

"That works for me."

"There's a desk with some paper and a pencil in the library. You can make your list there and *don't forget to clean the kitchen*. No mess." With that, he was gone.

Lenore watched Richard shut the door with a feeling of helplessness. What if she had another seizure in his absence? Perhaps it was better that way; another seizure in his presence and he was likely to kill her. She exhaled, noting that the taste in her mouth had not improved. Where was the bottle of Gatorade that she refused earlier? She found it on the nightstand and consumed the entire container before stepping into the bathroom.

After taking a quick shower, Lenore threw her urine stained clothes into the hamper and then went to the dresser to find another outfit. The venture resulted in another disappointing look through Angela's T-shirt drawer. Lenore eventually selected a red shirt with the words SHE DEVIL inscribed on the front. The "L" in devil was cleverly depicted as a tail.

She looked around her new bedroom and decided to pick up some of the mess. Lenore started by placing all of the books back on their shelves and then affixing the television back atop the entertainment center. She turned the television on for white noise and was peeved to discover that it only received four stations. Six, if you weren't picky about reception, and seven if you counted the home shopping network.

A game show roared in the background as she set to work sifting through a pile of clothes by the dresser. The apparel presented a logistical quandary. She did not want it, and therefore it did not belong back in the drawers; but it didn't belong on the floor, either. Lenore decided to abandon the endeavor until Richard returned, at which time she might ask for storage containers.

Lenore walked to the library to work on her list of necessities, which ended up being shorter than she had imagined. The invoice consisted mainly of toiletries, Xanax (not to exceed two hundred seventy-five dollars), and nicotine replacement therapies (not to exceed twenty-five dollars). Clothing could come entirely from good will, she reasoned, listing that her waist was twenty-six inches; shirts could be oversized for all she cared. Food was dry cereal, Doritos and toaster pastries, leaving her present diet unchanged.

When Lenore glanced over her completed list, she thought it might as well have said *I surrender*. The act of making the list in itself suggested she had given up on escape. When had she lost her nerve? Richard was out of the apartment—why wasn't she tugging at the front door? Why wasn't she exploring those rooms he told her not to enter? Because he would kill her. No, that wasn't it. *Because this was starting to feel normal.* And there was the real danger.

Was there some possibility of escape in the list itself? Weren't there certain household products that, when combined, could form explosives or deadly poisons? MacGyver would be out of there by now. She picked up the pencil and doodled a door at the bottom of the page, then erased it in frustration. There was a way out of this predicament, but she needed to stay alive long enough for the opportunity to present itself.

Sensing that Richard might return at any moment, Lenore turned her attention to the original task he requested of her, which was cleaning up the mess in the kitchen. She dreaded what she might find, still ambivalent about whether the liquid on her pants was indeed urine or perhaps, she hoped, some spilled Gatorade. As she entered the room, she concluded with disgust that it was probably a mixture of both. Taking a deep breath, she grabbed some paper towels from the counter and set them on the floor to absorb the grotesque puddle underneath the table. Then, using sanitary wipes from the sink cabinet, she mopped up the remainder of the mess. She hoped that Richard would find this satisfactory.

Lenore grabbed another bottle of Gatorade from Richard's pantry before heading back to her room to watch TV. She surfed through the stations, hoping that one of them might reveal what day it was, although she was not quite sure why it mattered. After about five minutes or so, she landed on a network news program that claimed the time was 11 p.m. on Friday night. Lenore grew depressed when she realized she had been there since Tuesday, and that no one was coming to save her.

The nightly news had passed into the late show by the time Lenore heard voices coming from down the hall. Richard called out, "Hey, Lenore. Could you come down here? *And turn off the goddamn TV.*"

Lenore clicked off the television and followed the sound of voices into the parlor, where she saw two men replacing the rug that had been removed after the Lance incident. Richard stood leaning against the pool table, watching with his arms folded and occasionally making helpful commends such as "Don't bang that shit into the wall" and "Make sure to keep it centered."

One of the men unrolling the new rug had a familiar face, and Lenore recognized him as Richard's friend, Paul, from the other night. The other man, who was probably six inches taller than his counterpart, wore a black trench coat, black pants and black boots, all of which matched a pony tail of jet black hair. When he turned to face Lenore, she saw that his eyebrows, nose and lips were decorated with several piercings. Was he wearing eye liner?

He looked up at her and smiled. "Well, if it isn't the new party favor," he said.

Lenore was immediately vexed. Why would he refer to her that way?

Paul sensed her irritation and tried to lighten the mood by saying, "Charles, this is Lenore. Call her by her *name*. Lenore, this is Charles. You two kids play nice."

From Lenore's vantage point, it was readily apparent that Charles did not move the same way that Paul and Richard moved, and that he was human, just like her. She thought back to her first encounter with Richard at the coffee shop and wondered how she had not instantly known that he was unlike other people. It all seemed so obvious now.

She watched in silence as the two men finished laying the rug. Once the room had been appointed to Richard's liking, Paul celebrated his accomplishment by plopping down on the sofa and resting his feet on the coffee table, which, at Richard's behest, had been repositioned four separate times until it was in the exact right spot.

Charles roamed the floor looking at this watch. "Relax," Paul said to him. "It's only 11:45." Paul turned his attention to Richard. "Are we all set here?"

Richard nodded, rolling one of the balls around on the pool table. "Yeah I think so. Lenore, did you make that list of what you'll need?"

Lenore pulled the list from her pocket.

Paul looked up from where he sat. "Hey, you can just hand that over to Charles. He's the one who's going to pick everything up for you."

She brought the sheet of paper to Charles, who grabbed it from her without deigning to turn his head.

Paul watched him look it over for a minute before asking, "Are any of those things going to be a problem?"

Charles pursed his lips. "Just the fucking Xanax, man. I don't know how much I'll be able to get for two seventy-five. I think I can take care of it, though, and she'll just have to make do with whatever I can get."

Lenore spoke up. "Whatever you can get will be fine. I appreciate it."

Charles did not acknowledge her and addressed Richard instead. "I don't know why you're bothering with her, though. This is a lot of bullshit to go through. I could bring someone else in here for you by tomorrow night."

"Oh, really?" Richard rolled his eyes a little as he said this, but Charles did not seem to notice.

"I got someone in mind. Don't waste your time with this chick."

"I might take you up on that, but I won't be hungry for a couple more days, so it won't matter until then. In the mean time she can spend her money." Richard disinterestedly spun the eight ball as if it were a top.

Lenore looked down at the floor. Perhaps she was not going to make it after all. Perhaps Richard was just killing time until the next feeding. A silent panic was descending.

Charles was not ready to abandon his argument. "Rich, this is bullshit. Just kill her and *take* the money. She don't want to be here. And I got better things to do than waste my time getting shit for someone who's gonna be dead in a few days. Lemme get one of my friends in here instead."

51

Richard slammed the ball to a stop. *"Goddamn it, Charles.* You get her the medicine because I fucking tell you to get her the medicine. However long I choose to keep her around is none of your goddamn business."

Charles went back to silently pacing the floor.

Paul grinned at Lenore from the sofa. "You guys are such asses. She's right *here.* Hey Lenore, I'm sorry Charles and Richard are being dicks. Just ignore them. How are you feeling? I heard you had a little episode."

"I'm much better, thanks." She could hear fear and agitation in her voice, and hoped it was not recognized as such by the other parties in the room.

Richard looked at Paul excitedly. "Paul, you would not believe this shit. She was sitting in the kitchen and then all of a sudden started going all like this." Richard started blinking and twitching furiously to act out the event, much to his friend's amusement. "I've never seen anything like it. You'd had to have been there."

"I'm glad you enjoyed it so much," Lenore said tersely. She walked to the wet bar and grabbed a glass of water to ease the taste in her mouth. Her hands shook terribly.

Paul chuckled. "Oooh, you've pissed her off now. No more seizures for you."

"Hah. Not if I can help it. You should have seen the mess she made. There was crap all over the floor." Richard gestured to his friend as though regaling him with the size of a particularly large fish.

"I'm telling you—just kill her," Charles said, shaking his head. "There could be someone new in here tomorrow no problems."

Richard turned to him with thinly masked irritation. "I heard you the first time, asshole."

Paul winked at Lenore. "I think Miss Lenore is going to work out just fine. No need to replace her. Hey Charlie boy, when do you think you'd be able to have her meds?"

"Prolly later tonight or tomorrow? There's someone I need to hook

52

up with at the Rose." Lenore would later learn that he was referring a vampire club. "I'm pretty sure it won't be a problem."

"Excellent." Paul rose from the sofa and started walking with Charles to the door. "Hey, Lenore, I'm glad you're feeling better. Try not to have any seizures until we get back. Rich, are you sure you don't want to come with us?"

Richard smiled, throwing his hands in the air. "Golly. I would, but I'm all out of eyeliner." This was clearly meant to be a dig at Charles, who muttered something to himself and kept walking.

Richard, who could not help himself, smiled and waved at Charles as he left. Lenore then heard the two men walk out the front door and lock it behind them. Paul must also have keys to the apartment.

Richard shrugged and looked at her. "So I think you're good to go."

"Yeah. Sounds good, I guess. I started going through Angela's things while you were gone. Do you think I could get some storage containers or something to put them in?"

"Oh, I totally forgot about that. I said we'd give that stuff to charity, right? I'll tell Paul's creepy manservant to bring some boxes the next time he comes by."

Lenore disliked the thought of dealing with Charles again, and must have made a face because Richard looked at her and asked, "What's that expression for?"

"Nothing. That's fine. I'll pack up her stuff when he comes back."

Lenore walked back to her room and planned not to leave until more Xanax arrived; any seizures in the interval were best endured in private. She grabbed The Lady or The Tiger and took it with her to the bathroom, where she lay in the empty tub (she did not want to soil the bed in the event of another episode) and attempted to settle in for the rest of the evening.

She must have dozed off.

Lenore awoke to see Richard standing over her, his face a mask of total amusement. "What are you *doing*?" he asked. Lenore looked around and realized that she was still in the tub. Thankfully, her pants were dry.

"I didn't want to wet the bed if I had another seizure," she said drowsily.

"Hmm." He nodded. "I guess that makes sense. Paul and Charles are back with your things. I tried knocking on the door but you didn't respond. I didn't mean to barge in on you." He offered Lenore a hand to help her out of the tub, which she gratefully accepted.

"What time is it?" she asked.

"Five a.m., Saturday. We need to hurry this up because I'm going to turn in soon."

Stiff and sore from lying in the tub, Lenore stretched in an attempt to straighten herself out. "So you're nocturnal?"

"Yeah, I guess. C'mon."

Paul and Charles stood in the foyer with two grocery bags at their feet. Both men appeared exhausted and eager to leave. Richard, despite being tired himself, forced Charles to go over each of the items on the receipt before reimbursing him for the purchase.

"Hey, were you able to get the Xanax?" he asked.

Charles reached into his back pocket and pulled out a little plastic bag filled with white pills. "Here's all I got. I was able to get sixty. It's normally five bucks a pill."

He handed the bag to Lenore, who sat on the floor to count the pills for herself. She noted that there were indeed sixty there, and more importantly, they were 1 milligram apiece; her standard dosage.

"This is awesome, thank you!" She popped four pills into her mouth and did something she hadn't done in years; she chewed them, and the bitter taste in her mouth felt a lot like ecstasy. Everything was going to be all right from now on. It was Lenore and Xanax against the world.

Paul started moving toward the door and said to Richard, "I think we're out of here. I guess I'll bring Charlie by tomorrow night with those boxes to pack up Angie's room." Then, looking at Lenore, he said, "Try not to take all those pills at once, kiddo. So long."

Richard closed and locked the door behind them. He turned to Lenore, stuffing his hands in his pockets. "I'm going to bed. When I wake up, I want everything in those bags put away and the empty bags in the trash. No mess." She nodded and watched as he walked down the hall.

Lenore sat on the floor for nearly ten minutes with her eyes closed, waiting for the Xanax to kick in. When it did, she experienced a tranquility that could only be described as the silence heard after the elimination of a perpetual drone; the receptors in her brain had finally stopped screaming. Now, at long last, she had her head on straight.

She drowsily eyed the grocery bags next to her, wondering what goodies lay inside. She carried the bags into the kitchen, where she then set about the task of sorting their contents into two distinct groupings: toaster pastries and non-toaster pastries. The toaster pastry grouping was attended to first, and Lenore consumed three packages before setting about the next task, which was dividing the Non-Toaster Pastry grouping into smaller subsets of itself, such as toiletries, Nicorette gum (which lay deliciously atop one of the bags), and the rest of the consumables. She made quick work of finding a home for all of the groceries in Richard's pantry before taking the remaining items back to her room.

The first thing Lenore did upon returning to her room was brush her teeth, and for a good ten minutes. Next, she put the bag of Xanax in the medicine cabinet for safe keeping. Finally, she ripped open the package of Nicorette gum and rewarded herself with a piece—instant relief. It occurred to her that some of her shakiness was probably from quitting her two pack a day habit. Perhaps Richard's initial diagnosis had not been too far off after all.

What was she supposed to do with herself now? She thought about taking another dose of sleeping pills, but decided it was a bad idea to continue using them to pass the time. Books and television were going to get old pretty quickly, she thought, but it was at least worth trying to get into a routine. Back at home, Lenore almost never left her apartment, going for days at a time without so much as opening the front door. She took a shower every morning, however, made coffee, got dressed, worked and settled in for the evening with a reality show or crossword. Were things so different now?

Lenore spent the rest of the day with the television on mute, watching soap operas via subtitle, and finishing the collection of short stories from Richard's library. She made it until six p.m. without becoming terribly bored, and to her surprise, without thinking about taking another Xanax (although she had plowed through three more pieces of Nicorette gum). As six rolled around, however, she felt shaky and decided to take another four pills. Only 52 now remained out of 60, and it had only been one day. At this rate, although dramatically scaled back from previous consumption, the medicine would not last more than a week. Like it or not, she would have to taper the dose.

Lenore brought the pills with her to the kitchen so she could take them with dinner. Soon after sitting down to a bowl of cereal, she heard Richard rumbling down the hall. He popped his head in the kitchen door and watched her eat for a while.

"You sound much better today," he said.

She nodded with a mouth full of Captain Crunch.

"So I told Paul to be here around seven with those boxes you wanted. Charles can help you pack up the room. Did you get enough food? I was expecting them to bring more stuff back from the store."

"I'm not much of an eater," she said. "I have to remind myself to eat or I forget about it. Sometimes I'll go a day before I remember."

Richard raised his eyebrows. "Really? Some days all I can think about is eating."

Lenore found this comparison in poor taste.

He walked off, saying, "Please wash your bowl out when you're through."

Half an hour later, Lenore sat in the parlor drinking coffee when the front door opened and Paul's voice yelled out, "Hey guys we're back with the packing supplies!"

She emerged to find Paul and Charles sliding several stacks of cardboard boxes into the foyer from the outside. The front door was wide open. She fantasized about evading her captors and scaling the paper hurdles in her path like the digital protagonist of a video game.

Richard appeared from somewhere in the back and studied the large stacks with skepticism. "Angela didn't have that much stuff. Don't you guys think that's overkill?"

Paul shook his head and locked the door, having carried in the last load. "We have to evict 112. It's been three months. I figured if I was going to get boxes anyway, we might as well have these just in case. I need you to contact the lawyer tonight and start getting the paperwork together on this."

Richard's arms folded. "Yeah that's not a bad idea. 502's been complaining about their AC unit again, by the way. I need you to take a look at that."

He looked at Charles for a moment. "Hey, take some of those boxes and get Lenore started packing up Angie's stuff."

Richard turned back to Paul. "I'm going to show you what I've got in the file for 112—the lady made a partial payment in January, but I don't think it's going to count for shit. Oh! And get this—we're being sued…"

Paul and Richard walked off to the library, leaving Lenore and Charles standing awkwardly in the foyer.

Charles looked irritated to be dealing with Lenore directly. "So how many boxes do you think you'll need?"

"Maybe three? It's mostly clothes, I think."

Charles nodded. He grabbed three disassembled sheets of cardboard and walked with Lenore to Angela's room. On the way, Lenore glimpsed Paul and Richard talking in the library and waving pieces of paper at one another. They must own the apartment building. Charles would know, she thought. Charles would know lots of things.

They each sat on her bedroom floor and began assembling the boxes.

"Do Paul and Richard own this building or something?" Lenore asked. "I heard them talking about evicting someone."

He did not look up. "Yeah, Rich technically owns the building, but Paul's his partner or something."

"Does Paul live here too?"

"He's got the penthouse. They've had this building since the 1920s." Charles concentrated on the cardboard puzzle in front of him, deliberately avoiding eye contact with Lenore.

She did not care. "Oh okay. Now that you mention it, I think Richard said something about his grandfather buying it back then or something—or maybe it was his great-grandfather."

Charles looked up from his task and began to speak slowly, as if addressing a child. "No. You don't get it. *Rich* has had it since the 1920s." Lenore thought that seemed unlikely.

"Okay...but the two of them manage the building together?" She tugged at a cardboard flap like it was besting her in an arm wrestling competition.

"Yeah, I think Rich takes care of the legal stuff and the accounting, and Paul manages the day to day. He's more of a landlord."

"Gotcha. I was wondering what Rich does. He seems to be gone a lot."

"Well, they're renovating some apartments right now. I've been helping them with painting and what not."

"So you work for them?"

"Nah I just help out."

Lenore looked at Charles as she folded. "So...so you're not like them. How did you get involved with...you know...with these guys?" She did a terrible job articulating the question, and could tell by the look in Charles's face that she had somehow offended him.

"What do you mean?"

"Well, you're not a vampire—you're like me—I mean what are you doing here?"

"I *am* a vampire, just a different kind. I'm a psychic vampire. I feed off other people's energy."

Lenore smiled, thinking he was kidding. "Bullshit. Grow fangs."

Charles glared at her. "I don't need fangs to feed off of energy, stupid. You're lucky I'm not feeding off of you right now, or you'd know what I was talking about." From the conviction in his voice, there was no sense in arguing.

She decided to change the subject. "Did you know Angela?" Lenore was almost finished assembling her first box. Charles had finished his second and rested his hands on top of it as if it were a coffee table.

"Somewhat. I brought her here and all." He huffed impatiently. "No offense, but this conversation is over. I'm not going to get too attached, if you get my drift. What did you want to pack up in here? Does everything go?"

She looked around the room and thought about how much more depressing (if that were even possible) it would look with all of the belongings removed. "Yeah, I guess leave the entertainment center and the clothes in the bottom shelf—just so I've got something to wear until new stuff arrives. The books can all go too. Hey now that I think about it, don't bother packing up the nail stuff on the vanity." With all this new found time on her hands, Lenore would command a pedicure that was the envy of the entire apartment.

Charles tipped the bookcase, emptying the contents into one of the moving boxes. "You got it."

Lenore began pulling items out of the top dresser drawer, refolding each one before placing it into the cardboard container. "So you brought Angela here? What made her want to come?"

"Are you still talking to me?" Charles asked, rolling his eyes.

He wasn't going to get off the hook that easily. "Yeah. Tell me about Angela. Why did she come here?"

Charles shook his head. "Whatever. You wanna talk? Let's talk.

59

Angela didn't want to come here. Not at first. I kinda talked her into it. I think she was being kicked out of her home or something. Didn't have anywhere else to go."

Lenore looked at Angela's sad possessions and wanted to hug them. "Wow. She...must have really trusted you."

Charles chuckled at this. "Yeah, I think she thought I was her boyfriend or something. I fucked her a few times in that bed you been sleeping on."

A vulgar image of Charles engaged in awkward coitus had entered Lenore's mind, and she would not soon be rid of it. She made a mental note to have the sheets washed, preferably boiled.

"Were you—were you upset when she died?"

"Nah she wasn't nobody to me." Sometimes a southern twang would slip out when Charles spoke. He sat on the floor, having finished loading the first box, and looked around. "Man, they really tore this place up the other day." He flicked out his tongue ring as if juicy flies were in the vicinity.

"Yeah what was it they were looking for again? I told Richard that you and I would keep an eye out for it while we packed up." She had practiced this line in her head ever since walking into the room and was thrilled to have so smoothly interjected it into the conversation. Whatever Richard had been looking for, it must have been important.

"Just anything with silver on it, I guess. I don't think there's any here, though. They would have found it." Thank you, Charles.

"I'll keep an eye out."

He smiled at her. "Oh, will you? You think that's gonna help your case? You know Rich is gonna kill you, right? It's only a matter of time. Whatever he's promised you, it ain't gonna happen. He isn't gonna let you go."

But Richard had promised her nothing. "What the fuck is your problem?" she asked.

"Just telling it like it is."

Lenore sat on the lowest rung of the totem pole and Charles was going to make sure she knew it. "Oh and you're immune, I suppose? Because you're some sort of bullshit feelings vampire and they've embraced you as one of their own?" He was silent, but still smiling. "Why don't you make yourself useful and get some tape so I can close these boxes?"

Charles did not move. "I really don't think that you're in a position to be giving orders to anyone, sweetheart."

"I'll do this myself. Just get out of my room."

Charles got up from where he sat and started toward the door. Before he left, however, he turned around and slid his forefinger across his neck, childishly insinuating that Lenore's time was near. She thought about returning this gesture with her middle finger, but was too busy wrestling an item from its drawer to be bothered trading insults.

Twenty minutes later, the dresser was empty, and Lenore walked out to ask Richard where she could find some masking tape. She found him in the library, still engaged in the same conversation with Paul from before. They had amassed several documents atop the coffee table and were now both staring at something on Richard's computer. Charles stood at the other side of the room, flipping through a National Geographic.

Lenore lurked in the doorway for a while, unsure whether or not to disturb them until she caught Paul's eye and he waved her in. "Hey there, kiddo. Are you all packed?" He shot a glance at Charles. "Weren't you supposed to be helping her?"

Charles shrugged. "She told me she'd do it herself. Wasn't much there."

Lenore did not care to explain why he left. "I'm all finished, but I don't have a way to close the boxes. Do you guys have any tape I could use?"

Richard turned around. "Yeah I've got some in the laundry room. Charles, help her drag the boxes to the front hallway and I'll seal them up before you guys leave." He went back to the computer and began typing, gesturing for Paul to proofread behind him.

Charles started walking back to Angela's room, but Lenore stopped him before he reached the door. "That's okay. I can drag them out myself. I'm good, really."

"Whatever you say." He went back to flipping through his magazine.

Richard bristled when he saw that Charles had stopped leaving. *"Dammit, Charles.* Go help her."

"She said she don't want no help."

Richard stopped typing and addressed the monitor. "I don't give a shit what she wants. We're working in here and I can hear you standing around breathing and turning the pages of that goddamn magazine. Get out of here and help her move those fucking boxes right now."

Charles nodded, putting the National Geographic back on the shelf. Then he looked at Lenore and grinned. "Hey Rich, I can mess with her a little back there, right? Do you care?"

Lenore shot Charles an icy glare and then turned to Richard. "Wait. What does he mean by that? I don't like the sound of that."

Richard was too engrossed in his present task to pay her any notice. Paul had noticed, however, and tapped his friend on the shoulder. "Hey, Rich? I think that—"

"Dammit, people. I'm trying to finish a fucking email. Shut the fuck up!"

Everyone, including Paul, stood in silence as Richard typed furiously on the laptop for several minutes. When he was finished, he slapped it shut and turned to the group with his eyes closed, taking several deep breaths before speaking. "Now," he said, "what is going on here?"

Lenore, with Xanax fueled composure, walked to where Richard stood and declared, "I am not going *anywhere* with Charles until I find out exactly what—" she held her fingers in the air for quotation marks,

"—'messing' with me means."

Richard rolled his eyes over to Charles. "Listen, leave this one alone. I know you had an arrangement with Angela, but I don't think she's going to be into that sorta thing." Lenore realized, to her horror, that *messing* with her meant exactly what she thought it meant.

She pointed her finger at Charles. "Hell no. No no no no no. *That* is never ever going to happen."

Charles flicked his tongue in her direction, like he was spitting acid. "Like you have a choice."

Was this really happening? "I *do* have a choice, and I would rather die."

Richard and Paul exchanged smiles behind her.

Lenore turned to leave, saying, "I'm going move those boxes now. I'll do it by myself."

"Have fun with that," Charles said menacingly. "Maybe I'll pay you a visit later on."

This needed to be nipped in the bud. She spun toward him, holding the catheter in her arm. "I will rip this out and bleed to death all over Rich's floor if you come anywhere near me. I swear to God." Falsely brave, Lenore met Charles's gaze and was determined to hold it for as long as possible. Any sign of weakness or submission would be exploited, and she could not afford to expose a single foothold.

Richard laughed, stepping between them. "Don't worry, Lenore. He wouldn't know what to do with a woman if he had one."

Charles's face turned bright red. "Oh yeah? At least I *can* fuck, asshole."

Lenore stumbled backward as Richard snatched Charles by his arm, pulling him close.

"Would you like to see how I fuck?" Richard asked.

Charles's lips trembled. "No," he said, looking to Paul for help. "Paul? Paul, please tell him to let go of me."

Paul, who up until this point had been a happy spectator, walked over to where the two men stood and made the timeout "T" with his hands. "If you guys keep playing rough like that, it's going to end in tears."

Richard loosened his grip, but did not let go. "I'm not putting up with any more of his bullshit," he said, yanking Charles around like a rag doll. "If he mouths off to me again I expect you to take care of it."

Paul shrugged. "Look, I'll get rid of him right now if you really think it's a problem. He said he could bring you someone next week, though—a full kill—so you need to make up your mind and let me know what you want me to do with him."

Richard seemed intrigued by Paul's last statement and sneered at Charles, who wriggled uncomfortably in his grasp. "You're going to have someone next week?"

"Yeah.I was...I was gonna bring someone by. Please...I wanna make it up to you."

"Yeah I'm sure you do," Richard said, releasing him with such force that Charles fell backward into the wall, knocking several books off their shelves. "Fine. He gets to live, but I swear I don't want to hear another word from him from now on." He looked down at Charles, who lay on the floor holding his upper arm in pain. "Get to cleaning up those books you spilled."

Chapter Four:
Paul

As Richard had predicted, Sunday night's feeding was a piece of cake. Lenore sat across from him at the kitchen table, drinking her post-hemorrhage Gatorade and wondering what would be on television later that evening.

He looked at her with his brow furrowed. "Your heartbeat's a little funky again."

"I've only taken five pills today. It's probably going to be this way for a while, but I don't think I'll have another seizure again, if that's what's worrying you." She fidgeted with the tube in her arm. "How do I take care of this, by the way? I've been scared to get it wet in the shower, but I assume I need to change the tape. I don't want it to get infected."

Richard snorted. "Yeah, we wouldn't want that. We've got a piss poor health plan around here, in case you haven't noticed. Although antibiotics are easier to come by than that other shit you're taking. Change the tape every few days. I think Angela was putting some sort of cream on it or something."

"Neosporin?"

"That rings a bell. Sure."

Over the next several days, Lenore watched Richard come and go amid a haze of late night television. Every time she heard him close the front door, the three locks turned in tandem, with no break in the routine. Making matters more interesting, Paul popped in and out of the apartment with his own set of keys. Eventually, one of them would forget to lock up, but she would need to be there to take advantage of the mistake.

For the most part, Richard and Paul ignored Lenore completely. She spent the vast majority of her time sequestered in Angela's room and was satisfied to limit her interactions with the pair to the accidental pass in the hall. And while Richard would brush past her without saying a word, Paul would attempt to engage Lenore in awkward conversation before continuing on his way. Nearly every exchange focused on when Lenore's clothes would arrive.

The clothes did eventually arrive that Friday (at least she thought it was Friday). Charles did not so much as look at Lenore as he dumped three bagfuls outside her door.

"Where do you want me to put these?" he asked, already turning to leave.

"Right there is fine."

"Yeah," he said, walking off. "Don't thank me or nothing."

"Thanks for being an accessory to my kidnapping, asshole," she called at his disappearing figure in the hallway.

After Charles was gone, Lenore brought the bags inside her room and enthusiastically rummaged through their contents. She was delighted to discover that nearly all of the items would fit and that none were damaged past the occasional stain or ripped hemline. There were jeans, dresses, T-shirts, and even a pair of pajamas.

Looking up from the pile of clothes, she spotted Paul grinning at her through the doorway. "So what do you think?" he asked.

Did he expect her to thank him as well? "They'll do."

"I'm really glad. We went to a lot of trouble to pick them out for you. I wasn't sure if you'd like them." Somehow, when Paul said "we", she did not take it to include Charles, who's contribution to the effort probably took the form of scowling somewhere in the back of the store.

"The PJs were a nice touch." She waited for him to leave.

Instead, he walked into her room and shoved his hands in his pockets, as if unsure how to proceed. "How would you like to get out of here for a little while?" he asked. "I talked to Rich and he said it's okay as long as I keep an eye on you."

Lenore never expected to see the outside of the apartment again. "Are you—do you mean it?"

"I mean it. If you aren't too tired, that is. I know you probably sleep at night."

Lenore wasn't too tired. Her biorhythms had started tapping to Richard's nocturnal beat. But why would Paul want to take her anywhere? Why would he risk her escape? She eyed him skeptically. "Where would we be going?"

"I was going to take you to a place a couple blocks down. Get you something to eat. Are you game?"

She thought about it for a few seconds and nodded. If Paul were going to kill her, why take her out of the apartment at all?

"Great," he said, stepping back out of her room. "Get dressed and I'll meet you up front. Actually, I'm going to drop Charles off and I'll come back for you. It shouldn't take me over twenty minutes or so."

Lenore closed the door behind him and then searched through her new wardrobe for a change of clothes. She settled on a dress with long sleeves to hide the catheter in her arm and slipped it on over her body, enjoying the feel of something besides Angela's oversized tees. Checking herself out in the bathroom mirror, she decided on a whim to blow dry her hair and apply some of the makeup that atrophied at the bottom of her purse. None of this was intended to impress Paul, but Lenore did not know if or when she would leave the apartment again and was determined to make the most of it.

On her way to the front hall, she glanced in the library and saw Richard who sat hovering over his laptop at the epicenter of four separate piles of documents. He looked up as she walked by and gave a one hand wave, suggesting hollowly that she "have a good time." He mumbled "agoraphobic my ass" before returning to his papers.

Fleetingly, it occurred to Lenore that she and Richard had not engaged in their blood letting ritual since that Tuesday, and that he was due.

As she waited in the foyer, Lenore contemplated plans of escape. Once outside the apartment, she would tell Paul that she needed to use the bathroom and would find a phone instead. Or perhaps she would just scream once they got up to the street. Or perhaps she would flag down a passing car. The possibilities beyond the front door seemed endless.

Nearly ten minutes passed before the bolts turned and Paul stepped through the entrance.

"You ready to hit the town?" he asked.

"Yeah, sure," Lenore replied, rising from where she sat.

He ran his hand through his hair. "Before we do, and I don't want this to come out as a threat, but you know I can catch you, right?"

She stared at him, perplexed.

"I'm going to show you something," he said. "I'm not doing this to freak you out, okay? Stay right where you are."

Lenore watched with suspicion as Paul walked to the far end of the room. "Get ready, now, and keep your eyes on me." She obliged, and shrieked when an instant later felt him behind her, his arms clasped tightly around her waist. It was as if he had teleported across the floor. "Do you see?" he whispered in her ear. "I can move very fast when I want to. If you try to run, I'll catch you. I want to make sure you understand that, or this little outing is going to go badly for both of us. Well, mainly for you."

Paul released Lenore's trembling figure, but slowly, allowing her to regain balance.

"Don't do that again," she said, her voice faltering. "Don't ever touch me again."

He took two steps back. "Jeez. Relax. I'm not going to hurt you. I don't want to *have* to hurt you, though, and I would if you tried to run away. Oh wow you're mad at me. Do you still want to go out?"

She closed her eyes and nodded, but escape seemed like a cruel joke now. Paul would catch her if she found a phone. He'd catch her if she started screaming. He'd catch her if she ran to a car. He'd catch her. And he'd drag her back.

"You know," he said casually, rocking on his heels, "you clench your teeth when you're upset. Look at you. You're all *tense*. Smile. Please smile. Or at least say something. I feel like a jerk right now."

Reconciliation was not Lenore's forte. "I'm over it, okay? But I would have taken your word for it. You didn't need to pounce on me like that. I mean...God...don't you think I know where I stand these days?"

"I know you do, and I apologize," Paul said, looking at the floor. "I really think it'll do you some good to get out of here for a while, though."

He led her to the front door and turned the handle. When he swung it open, a cool evening breeze wafted into the foyer, fanning Lenore's dress against her legs. She closed her eyes and took a deep breath before stepping over the threshold into the night air.

"Wait here," Paul said, turning the bolts behind him.

When he finished, Lenore followed him through the dank entryway, stepping past a homeless man who had created somewhat of a nest for himself within the basement hall. Paul reached into his pocket and handed the old man a twenty dollar bill, saying, "Stay warm tonight, sir," to which he received a toothless grin and hoarse "God bless you." The walkway ended with a half flight of stairs leading up to the street. Lenore remembered descending them nearly two weeks prior, thinking she might as well have wandered into a glue trap.

Climbing the final step, she asked, "Does that kind of thing happen a lot? I mean where a homeless person moves into the basement like that?"

Paul grinned, hopping onto the street. "It happens all the time, but I don't think Rich minds so much."

"So where are we going?"

"I was going to take you to a diner that's about two blocks down. If that's okay with you, that is. Frankly, it's the only place I know in the area that's open all night."

"Yeah that's fine with me. I don't know this part of the city very well."

"All right, awesome. I hear this place has pretty decent food. It's probably been a while since you had anything besides cereal. According to Rich, that's all you eat. Oh and toaster pastries. He said you love toaster pastries."

The two a.m. streets were barren, except for the occasional passing car, but far from silent. The hum of neon lights sang in the background, along with the collage of sounds from residents of the nearby apartment buildings, many of whom were up talking, crying, fighting, or just watching TV. A siren rang out in the distance, and a dog began howling in harmony.

Paul looked over at Lenore. "Aren't you cold? I should have told you to take a jacket. I don't think it's getting out of the forties tonight."

"I'm a little cold, but I'm just kinda enjoying being outside," Lenore said, trudging along with her arms folded. "It's refreshing."

Paul only wore a white T-shirt and jeans himself, but seemed quite comfortable in the night air. He was a man in his element and, like the elongated shadow he cast in the light of the street lamp, appeared larger and more powerful in the darkness. "Well, we're not too far off. You see that light over there? To the right? That's where we're headed."

He led her to a small diner, which was unobtrusively tucked into the corner of an old brownstone. Although the sign on the door said "OPEN 24 HRS", they were the only customers, and sat themselves at a booth near the back before attracting the notice of the only waitress on staff. She threw two menus down on the table before retreating to the back to do whatever it is that night shift waitresses do.

Lenore flipped through the menu for a minute or two before closing it and placing it back down on the table. Paul never opened his, but stared at the artwork on the cover as if it were on the verge of speech.

When the waitress returned, Lenore ordered coffee for herself—leave the pot—and steak and eggs with pancakes on the side.

"How are you holding up?" Paul asked, watching Lenore pour five packets of sugar into her coffee.

"I'm not sure how to answer that question," she said honestly.

He frowned at her, folding his hands. "I know this situation sucks for you."

"I guess it's better than being dead," she replied, desperately thinking of ways to change the subject.

"I'm not so sure about that. I think Rich put you in an extremely difficult position. If it were me, I would've just killed you and gotten it over with."

Lenore looked around the restaurant, wondering if anyone in the back could hear their conversation, before meeting Paul's eyes again. "Rich offered to do that, like he'd be doing me a favor or something."

"Well, that's just my point," he said, leaning back in his seat. "It's an unfair position to put someone in. Who's going to be like 'yeah just kill me'? I sure as hell wouldn't. But in the long run it's fucking horrible. Poor Angela was stuck in that apartment for *fifteen months*." Lenore winced, to which he raised his hand apologetically. "Hey. I'm not trying to upset you or anything."

"No, it's fine. I mean, it's not *fine*, but I can't cry about it anymore. And I've done a *lot* of that this past week. Rich mentioned there have been others, though. How long did they last?"

"Oh no one in recent memory has lasted as long as Angela. That shit was a marathon. I guess a few months or so, maybe? He'll have someone, and then he'll get tired of them—or hungry, or whatever—and then decide that it's a bad idea altogether for a while, but he always goes back to keeping a live body on retainer. I think he gets nervous if he doesn't have a backup plan. This isn't one of Rich's habits that I'm a big fan of, by the way. I don't have a problem with him eating, but I don't like that he drags it out like this. It's almost cruel. You know what's interesting about your situation, though? To me, anyway?"

Lenore was still trying to digest her new life expectancy. "What's that?" she asked absently.

"It's that Rich hasn't promised you anything. I think he's actually been pretty honest with you—from what he's told me, anyway. See, everyone else so far has wanted to be *turned,* like they'd signed up for an internship or something. Not you, though. You've walked into this with your eyes open, at least, even though I personally think it was a bad decision"

Lenore sipped her coffee. "Have you ever heard of Quantum Immortality?" she asked.

"I don't think so. Is that a band or something?"

"No not at all. I'm probably not going to explain this very well, but it's this idea that the universe splits every time there's a decision. So if you were playing Russian roulette with half the rounds loaded, fifty percent of the time you'd die, but the other half of the time, you'd make it. The universe splits for every outcome. Anyway, if you kept playing, the universe would keep splitting, and your likelihood of surviving would become infinitesimal, but there would have to be one scenario, one perfect universe, in which you wouldn't die—where you'd play forever."

"Okay. I think I get it."

"Well, my point is that there has to be a universe where I get out of this. If I chose to die upfront, I'd be giving up on that. Does that make any sense to you?"

"Hah, that's an interesting idea. I'll give you that. Very Pollyannaish. All this over some old records, huh?"

"Yeah, tell me about it." She sighed.

"Are you a die hard music fan or something?"

Lenore shook her head. "No not at all, but I'm really into mechanical things. I got myself an old phonograph and I thought it would be fun to have some records for it."

Paul frowned. "Mechanical things?"

"Yeah, specifically windup devices. They fascinate me. I think it's cheating if something has to have electricity to run. If something needs electricity, it essentially has to have batteries or an outlet at all times. Otherwise, it's broken. But that's not the case with a gramophone, for instance. You can take it anywhere, and it works when you wind it up. It's perfect. I collect perfect things."

Paul was still frowning. "You're kinda *weird*," he said.

Lenore looked down at the table and blew her hair out of her eyes. "I know. I'm not trying to bore you."

"Quite the contrary. So what did you do before...all this?"

"I worked from home. I was a software engineer for a small consulting agency. It was pretty cool because I got to set my own schedule and no one bothered me until something was due."

Paul brought his hands together and grinned. "Hah. I knew it. I knew you worked with computers. I could just tell that about you. Family?"

Lenore slouched in her seat. "My mother passed away about four years ago."

"No father?"

"He left my mother when I was eleven. We don't really keep in touch."

"Jesus. What happened to your mother? Do you mind me asking?"

"Breast cancer," said Lenore, closing her eyes from the pain of the words.

Paul knitted his eyebrows sympathetically. "How long was she sick?"

"For about three years. I fought with her a lot toward the end because she stopped taking her medicine. She might still be alive if she'd kept fighting."

His lips formed into a half smile. "In her perfect universe?"

Lenore nodded, swallowing a gulp of coffee. "Exactly."

"Is that when you started taking Xanax?"

"That's a completely separate issue," she said, shaking her head. "I've got absolutely no excuse for how many pills I was taking, but I *am* agoraphobic."

"Oh yeah? What caused that?"

"You mean the agoraphobia? Nothing really *causes* it. I think I had my first episode was when I was around fourteen, maybe? My mother took me to see a Broadway show. We're sitting in the audience, and I get this thought in my head—more of a fear—that all of a sudden, for no reason, I'm going to jump onto the stage and start singing with the rest of the cast."

Paul started laughing.

She smiled in spite of herself. "I know it sounds nuts, but I was paralyzed. I made her take me out of there immediately, and that was the start of a long trip downhill."

"So does Xanax completely cure your condition?"

"Oh no. Not at all. But it takes the edge off. Most of the time when I go out, everything's fine, but the times when I *have* panicked have been so traumatic, that it's like I'm frightened of the panic attack instead. I'm frightened of being frightened. And I get into this cycle where I'll be out and wonder if I'm going to panic, and that *causes* me to panic. Xanax breaks the cycle, because I don't worry about panicking so much to begin with. I know this makes no sense."

"You know, I think there's a strange logic to it. No one's ever explained it to me before. I just thought it had to do with germs."

Lenore poured herself another cup of coffee and looked up at Paul, who fidgeted contemplatively with the fork in front of him. "Can I ask you a ton of vampire questions now? I don't want to be rude, but I'm dying to."

Paul shot back his trademark grin. "Ask away. I hate the '*vampire*', though. I don't even know what it means. It sounds like '*I vant to suck your bloood*' or something. So stupid."

"Oh really? *Really*? What do you call it, then?"

"I don't know. Why do I need to call myself anything at all? Oh, wait. You know what else irritates me, while we're on the subject? Don't call yourself 'human', like implying that I'm *not* human. We're both human. I've just been turned, and you haven't been turned. It's as simple as that."

"Turned and not-turned." She paused and mouthed the terms to herself, trying them on for size. "Okay, here are my questions. You can't transform into anything, can you?"

"What? Like a bat? How would that even *work*?"

"What about sunlight?"

"We don't like it." What did that mean, exactly?

"Stake through the heart?"

"Oh the death ones are tricky. I mean, I'm not dead so how would I know?"

"Silver?" Silver had to be important. Important enough for Richard, of all people, to make such a mess in an effort to find it.

"Ugh. You want to know about silver." Paul rolled his eyes and groaned, like she had just asked him for his checking account number. "We're allergic to it, but I wouldn't say we can really be *hurt* with it. Not badly, anyway. Hey do you remember what my hand looked like on the night that you met me?"

Lenore thought back to the burn on Paul's forearm. "Yeah. It was burned, right?"

Paul placed his fully healed appendage on the table for examination. Only a faint scar remained. "It wasn't really burned. It was just irritated is all. Angie came at me with a silver knife that night, and I think she was pretty disappointed when I didn't burst into flames or something. Silver's about as dangerous to us as poison ivy."

"I see," Lenore said, sharing in Angela's disappointment. As far as she knew, poison ivy was only deadly if inhaled.

Paul pursed his lips, thinking. "Look, Rich goes ape shit over the silver thing, and I think he blows it completely out of proportion, but if you want to stay alive past the next feeding, don't mention silver to him. Not as a joke, not as a question, just don't even say the word."

Lenore nodded, stirring her coffee out of habit. "Can you read minds?"

"Let's find out." Paul lifted his spoon and pointed it at her, assuming the demeanor of a game show host. "Think of a number between one and ten. Got it? Nine?"

She shook her head. "Horrible. Not even close."

"Cheater," he said. "I'll bet you weren't even thinking of a number in the first place."

Lenore smiled involuntarily. "How did you know?"

"Maybe I'm psychic. Or maybe I've played this game before, and I never think of a number either." This information would turn out to be quite useful later on.

"I'm moving on to my next question. Do you use the bathroom?"

Paul dropped the spoon and snickered. "What are you, five? Who asks that?"

Lenore shrugged and stuck out her tongue.

"Okay, check this out. If I eat food it comes out the other end, but I don't have to eat food, so I don't. I guess the short answer would be no."

"Really? I'd probably still eat, just for fun."

"Nah it's not the same because it isn't really *food* anymore. Like, it would be like shoving this napkin in your mouth and trying to swallow it." He lifted the napkin in front of him for effect.

"But, *I* look like food to you?"

Paul took a deep breath. "It's a lot more complicated than that. You only look like food to me when I'm hungry. And it's not even the way you look, it's the way you *sound*. Especially when you're scared and your heart starts racing. It drives me crazy. All I can think about is making it stop."

Silence.

He leaned forward. "Have you ever seen those old Tweety Bird cartoons where the cat will be talking to the bird and then all of a sudden he's talking to a big chicken leg? Because that's all that's on his mind?"

The waitress burst out of the kitchen holding two plates, and Lenore moved her hands off the table to make room for her order. As the waitress turned to leave, Paul troubled her for an empty cup, presumably to share in Lenore's pot of coffee.

When the waitress was gone, however, he slid the cup across the table and said, "I hate to do this to you, but all this talk about eating has made me really hungry. Can you hook me up?"

Unsure of how, or if, she could decline, Lenore reluctantly began rolling up her sleeve. What would happen if she refused? Paul might be friendlier than Richard, but he was still just as likely to kill her.

"I hope I haven't made you uncomfortable," he said, watching her fill the container. "This isn't why I brought you out here, you know. I'm not trying to take advantage of you or anything."

Nodding insincerely, Lenore looked at the food in front of her and discovered that she had lost her appetite. Richard would still need to be fed when she returned. How much blood could she stand to lose in one evening? To Lenore's consternation, she found herself on the familiar brink of tears.

"You're clenching your jaw again," Paul said. He sipped her blood slowly as if it were a hot beverage. "Are you pissed off at me *again*? I thought this had been going so well."

Tears were starting to emerge. "I think I want to go back," she whispered, hastily wiping her eyes.

He shook his head. "I don't think you want to go back there right now. Rich is killing someone tonight. I thought you'd want to be out of the house for that type of thing."

Lenore stared blankly at her pancakes. There was a guilty relief in the knowledge that she would not have to feed Richard upon her return.

"Well?" he asked. "Was I right? You don't want to go back there, do you?"

"No," she replied, tears stifled. And then a thought occurred to her. "Does this have anything to do with the homeless man in the basement?"

Paul chuckled. "Totally. I was wondering if you'd put that together. Rich is like one of those trapdoor spiders. You know the ones I'm talking about? They build these caves." Paul cupped one hand on the table to represent a cave. "And then insects come walking by." He walked the fingers of his other hand around the cave entrance. "And then when one gets too close, WHAM." The cupped hand grabbed the fingers and carried them down beneath the table.

"I just don't understand. You gave him twenty dollars. Why would you have done that?"

"Oh. It's this game that Rich and I play. He'll give me the twenty back later tonight. It's like a little joke that got started a while back. I know it sounds immature."

"It sounds mean."

"Jesus. That probably wasn't a good story for mixed company. Look, we're already killing people. You throw practical jokes on top of that and it's like pissing in the ocean. Besides, I probably made that guy's night when I gave him the money."

Silence.

Paul rolled his eyes in frustration. "You need to lighten up. You realize that if Rich doesn't feed off other people you're going to die, right?"

She nodded.

"Then chill out. You don't know him, and neither do I." Paul resumed his amiable countenance, taking another drink of blood. "This really bothered you didn't it?" he asked, gesturing to the cup in hand. "I won't ask you for more."

Lenore despondently ran her finger over the outline that the catheter made through her sleeve. "I'm less worried about it now that I know Rich is supplementing tonight."

"Ha is that what he's calling it these days?" Paul slammed his hand on the table. "That's too funny. I couldn't figure out what your problem was, but you thought you were overextending yourself, huh?"

"It's more than that," Lenore said, determined to maintain composure. "I was really enjoying our conversation, and I guess just being out of the apartment. It made me forget my situation for a while, which is stupid because that's all we've been talking about. But I felt like it wasn't happening to me—like it was happening to someone else—and that I was just having coffee with a friend. But then you asked me to fill your cup and I remembered that you're *not* my friend, and that this *is* my life. And I realized that you're just..." She looked up at him and scowled.

"Just what?"

"You're just playing with me."

Paul's grin widened, and Lenore felt as though she might fall in. "Sure. Maybe a little. But what else am I supposed to do with you? It isn't like I've lied to you, and I hope I haven't given you a false sense of security. I'm playing, but I'm playing *fair*, so to speak."

"What am I supposed to do with that?"

"You play back," he said, reaching over the table and punching her lightly on the shoulder. "I get you out of the house when Rich kills someone, and you fill my glass. Everyone's a winner. That's not such a bad game, right?"

She eyed the half filled cup of blood on the table. "How am I supposed to recover if you're bleeding me?"

"Well, that's the trick, isn't it? But—and I mean this with all due respect—you don't really think it's going to matter, do you?"

Paul was right, of course. It wasn't going to matter. Richard would probably kill her long before she ran out of blood. "Does he know?" she asked.

"Who? Rich? That I'm feeding on you? Oh, I think he has a hunch. He wouldn't care, though, if that's what you're getting at. Not unless I killed you, and you can rest assured that I won't."

"I see," said Lenore, thinking back to how Charles first referred to her as a party favor.

Paul winked at her from across the table. "Hey, cheer up. I don't know if this'll make you feel any better, but I want to tell you something. I enjoy you." He smiled playfully. "And not just because you're delicious. I think you hold your own. I think you're going to be okay." He studied her for a while before continuing. "I'm going to pay you back for the drink you gave me. What if I got you more medicine? That would help you out, wouldn't it? One less thing to worry about? I can keep you supplied for the remainder of your time here. How does that sound to you?"

Lenore raised her eyebrows. "It sounds like you're trying to hand me a twenty dollar bill."

Paul looked surprised for a moment and then laughed, catching her reference. "That's *exactly* what I'm trying to do. Will you accept it? I can't let you go, obviously. I can't even kill you at this point—you belong to Rich—but I can get your medicine. What do you say?"

"I'll take whatever I can get. Thank you." Lenore's Xanax starved receptors stood in ovation. She felt her appetite return and grabbed a container of syrup from the condiment stand, drowning her plate of pancakes and attacking it with gusto.

"Awesome," Paul said, clasping his hands together. "I'll talk to Charles. We'll set it up. Ha, why are you making that face? Not a fan of Charlie-boy, huh?"

"You know I'm not," she replied.

Paul watched her wrestle a bite of pancake from the top of the stack. "Well, you're in good company. Rich can't stand him either. And don't take the way he's treated you personally. He's been supplying Rich's donors for years now, and I think he's upset that you didn't come through him."

Lenore chewed pensively. "Why's that?"

"You're messing up the dynamic. He probably thinks of you as competition."

"Competition?" Lenore wrinkled her brow. "Oh, he wants to be turned."

"Of course he does. Jesus. Just look at him."

"Do you ever turn *anyone*, or do you just string people along? It sounds like you guys make a lot of empty promises."

Paul's lips curled into a half smile. "I'll let you in on a little secret about turning someone. They almost never survive. I don't know why some people make it and some don't, but it's practically a death sentence. I don't turn anyone I couldn't stand to lose, and Charlie's a pretty good Renfield—I'm totally making a reference to Dracula's assistant here—"

"I got it," she said, wiping some syrup off her chin.

"Okay, just checking. He's constantly running errands for me during the daytime. And then at night he's kind of a god in the club scene, so he brings a lot of people my way."

"Yeah Rich mentioned you're big into vampire clubs. That's how you know Charles?"

"Uh huh. There's a big weird hierarchy there. It's like a pyramid, almost." He drew an invisible pyramid on the table surface with his forefinger. "At the bottom are all the people who are more or less transient, and are just there for the *feel* of the Goth or S&M thing—and don't ask me what sex has to do with any of this, because I honestly don't know. Anyway, then you get people who are even more into it, and they're regulars and show up all of the time, and they might engage in a little deviant activity here and there, but not much. They're just experimenting. *Then* you get the hard core crowd. They're the ones who claim to be psychic vampires, or sanguine vampires, and they're bleeding each other and fucking each other and pretending to suck each other's energy and what not."

"I think Charles told me he's a psychic vampire," said Lenore, who was too busy eating to look up from her plate.

Paul smirked. "There's no such thing. Psychic vampires are part of

81

the subculture, though, and it's a pretty easy thing to claim. I mean, how can you prove he *didn't* drain your aura? Anyway, there are an elite few that actually have contact with the real thing, and Charles is in that crowd. Now, if you go to these clubs, and you're lucky—or maybe unlucky, depending on how you see things—you work your way up this little ladder and there's a tiny possibility that you'll be turned, but it comes with a price. You're constantly finding us food. People go missing from the scene all the time, and no one does anything about it. I usually don't kill anyone, though. Charles will bring a couple of people to the back and I drink from them and then that's it. They even seem to enjoy it."

"That doesn't sound so bad, actually," Lenore said. She grabbed another morsel with her fork and thoughtfully used it to mop up some syrup. "I'm surprised Rich isn't more into it. When he described it to me, he made it sound like a trip to the dentist's office."

"He says it gets old—which it does—I'll give him that. He doesn't have any interest in interacting with people who are so much younger than he is. That's really the crux of it."

Vigorously munching on the last of her pancakes, Lenore emptied the pot of coffee into her cup. "How old are you, anyway?"

Paul gasped in mock offense. "What a rude question. But I'll tell if you'll tell. Fair's fair."

"I'm twenty-seven," she said, shrugging, "but I'll be twenty-eight in a couple months. May 16th. Save the date."

"I just might do that."

"Well?"

Paul bit his lower lip and smiled. "Why don't I tell you how far back I go with Rich instead? Are you curious?"

"Sure." Lenore leaned forward, elbows on the table, giving him her undivided attention.

"Rich used to run a speakeasy out of that basement in the 1920s, and I was his bartender. We were...turned at the same time, so to speak. He's seven months older than I am, and—believe me—he was never a nice guy. I never figured I'd still be working for him after all these years."

"I'd been wondering why he has a bar in his living room."

Paul stared at the table for several moments, smiling, lost in reverie. "Old habits die hard," he said finally. "I still love making people drinks, in case you hadn't noticed."

The waitress returned with the check soon after and asked Lenore if she wished to pack her steak and eggs, which she did. Watching Paul attempt to calculate fifteen percent of $17.50 in his head left Lenore under the distinct impression that his vampiric powers did not include a knack for restaurant math. He finally muttered something under his breath and left twenty five dollars on the table.

Getting up, Paul said, "We should do this again. Charles is bringing someone over for Rich in a few days. I can get you out of the house for that too if you'd like."

"That would be really nice," she said, grabbing her meal.

Lenore walked back to the apartment in silence, and briskly, as the wind had picked up and she was succumbing to the cold. When she reached the basement stairs, however, she was overtaken by a strong impulse to run. Death was at the other end of that passage; it was only a matter of time. Maybe if she started moving toward the stairs she could double back and possibly flag down a passing car. Maybe if she timed it right.

"I know what you're thinking," Paul whispered, turning to her. "I can hear your heart pounding. Please don't make this hard on me. Don't make this hard on yourself." He took her by the hand. "I have to take you back down there. I know you don't want to go back, but this isn't the last time you'll see the outside of that apartment. I'll get you out again soon, okay? Rich just fed—you're in no immediate danger—but you could screw that up if I have to drag you through the door kicking and screaming, understand?"

Unable to speak, she mouthed the word "yes" as he pulled her toward the entrance. Slowly, they descended the steps together, and

Paul did not let go of her hand until they had reached the very bottom. The homeless man from before, along with his sad puddle of belongings, had vanished without a trace, leaving behind a horrible emptiness where he once sat against the wall.

Richard met them in the front hall with a blood stained twenty dollar bill in his hand, a smile on this face. Lenore briefly thanked Paul for dinner and then stepped out to spend the rest of the evening sobbing in bed.

Chapter Five:
Dinner Theater

Four days passed with nothing but the television to keep Lenore company. In college, she would have considered Richard the perfect roommate; he was clean, quiet, and never around. Under present conditions, however, the arrangement had its drawbacks; Richard was nowhere to be found, and Lenore was running out of food. Crumb filled containers were all that remained of the cereal, toaster pastries and chips from the previous grocery run, and Lenore was now reduced to eating packages of Ramen noodles that sat in the back of the panty and claimed to have expired in June of last year. She decided that her best chance of flagging Richard down would be to sleep in the library next to his laptop as he was sure to check email.

After half a days waiting, the plan bore fruit. "Hey Rich, I'm out of food," she said, uncurling on the sofa as he walked in.

"What do you want? More toaster pastries? I told you I didn't think you got enough food. Make a list and we'll give it to Charles when he comes by later. Do it somewhere else, though. Get out of here." Richard would not look at her and walked to the other end of the room as if avoiding solicitation.

There was something off about him.

He was hungry.

He was hungry and warning her away. How much danger was she in, exactly? After four days, probably a lot. Lenore thought about how boa constrictors will starve themselves before a large meal. Richard was getting ready to eat something big. What had she been thinking waiting around for him like that?

Slowly, she stood up and started backing out of the room, careful not to make any sudden moves. "He's bringing someone by tonight, right?" she asked, hoping to remind Richard that she was not on the menu.

"He'd better be, for your sake. Now go." When he spoke, she saw fangs.

From the dubious safety of her bedroom, Lenore sat paralyzed, listening to Richard ravenously pace the hall. She stared nervously at the clock on the wall, wondering when Paul and Charles would be by with a human sacrifice. What if Richard couldn't wait that long? He seemed entirely too far gone to be satisfied with a helping from her intravenous tap. A panic was taking hold, exacerbated by the knowledge that Richard could probably hear her heart racing like a dinner bell from outside the door. Xanax. She needed to take some Xanax, if only to slow it down. In spite of careful tapering, only eleven pills remained. Nonetheless, she grabbed four and started chewing. Paul said that he would bring more, he just had to.

Forty-three minutes later, and much, much calmer (had she passed out for a minute there?), Lenore heard a knock at the door. What if it was Richard coming to drag her to the laundry room? More knocking. If he *were* coming to kill her, would he bother to knock at all?

"Lenore? *Lenore?* Fuck it. I'm not standing here forever. Paul says he's got something for you. He's here with Charles...take it or leave it, I don't give a shit." His footsteps faded in the distance.

Paul looked genuinely happy to see Lenore when she joined them in the parlor, and he broke away from his conversation with Richard to greet her at the door.

"You okay?" he asked. "I hope you weren't freaking out or anything. I know we cut this a little close, but you're home free now." He motioned to a young woman sitting next to Charles on the sofa.

The newcomer, who could not have been a day over twenty five, sat quietly, hands folded, looking terribly confused. Periodically, she would turn her head to Charles as if on the verge of a question, but he would not return eye contact. Richard eyed her carnivorously from the pool table, and Lenore wondered if his subject had transmogrified into a giant chicken leg.

"Walk with me," Paul said, wrapping his arm around Lenore and leading her into the hallway. He put his finger to his lips, urging her to keep their conversation quiet, lest she compromise the awful conspiracy unfolding in the parlor.

"So that girl, she's—"

"She's dinner, yeah. Don't worry about it. I know I said I was going to get you out of here, but I think I'm going to sit in on this one. I'm feeling a little peckish."

"I thought you said you didn't kill people," she whispered. Was that really even true? Perhaps it was just something she wanted to believe.

Paul made a face. "Oh boy. Look, this doesn't count. She's already dead. I mean, Rich is going to kill her no matter what I do. I might as well eat."

Lenore found this statement absurd; akin to eating a cheeseburger and claiming vegetarianism on technicality of who killed the cow.

"Besides," Paul said, as if reading her mind, "I said I *usually* don't kill people. Big difference."

"Yeah," she muttered absently. Sure. Why not?

"I got you more Xanax, by the way," he whispered excitedly, reaching into his jacket and placing a bottle of pills in her hand. "That's 180 pills. Should last you a while. Ha and it's a good thing too. You look like you've had a few this evening."

Murderer or not, Lenore could have hugged him. "Thank you so much!" And yet, at this exact moment, for no discernible reason, she wanted to throw up.

"Shh not so loud, kiddo. Now get out of here. You don't want to stick around. Rich can get pretty sadistic when he's hungry."

"I sure can, can't I?" Richard emerged from around the corner and blocked Lenore's path. He looked at the pills in her hand. "Oh, I'm sorry. Am I interrupting your little drug deal?"

Lenore slid the medicine into her pocket.

Paul frowned. "We're all finished, Rich. She was just going back to her room."

Richard grinned, fangs exposed, unmoving. "I can see that. But I think she should join us in the living room. Let's make this interesting. Let's introduce her to Charles's friend."

"Don't do this, Rich. Let her go."

But Richard had already taken hold of Lenore's wrist. He walked her back into the living room and planted her in front of the sofa. Paul followed, shaking his head.

Richard released Lenore's arm and addressed the girl who sat before them. "Stacy, I'd like you to meet Lenore."

Stacy nodded, nervously fidgeting with her hair.

Charles started inching away from where she sat, as if it was on a fault line. He exchanged glances with Paul, who raised his hand reassuringly. Something bad was about to go down.

"Lenore, meet Stacy," Richard said.

Lenore looked down at her feet, shuffling them along the new carpet. What was going on?

Richard shouted into her ear. "*I said, meet Stacy. Say hello.*"

"Hi, Stacy," she mumbled.

"That's better," he said. "*But look at me.* Stop looking at the floor. Are you calm? You seem pretty calm. You've taken your medicine, right?"

Lenore nodded, squeezing the container in her pocket.

"Good," he smiled. "I want you calm for this."

"What are you doing, Rich?" Paul asked, walking toward the bar. He leaned against the counter with his arms folded. "Where are you going with this?"

Richard grinned at him. "Let's do something we haven't done in years. Dinner theater."

Lenore did not like the sound of that.

Paul rolled his eyes. "I thought we don't do dinner theater anymore. I thought we quit that."

"I'm bringing it back. I think I have an interesting new spin on it."

"What's dinner theater?" Charles asked. He had managed to distance himself from Stacy by an entire sofa cushion, and was still maneuvering.

"You don't have to worry about it," Paul said, shaking his head. "You aren't playing." He turned to Richard. "He isn't playing, right?"

"He doesn't have to play. This game will be ladies only. He should stick around, though, because he has a stake in it." Richard grinned at Lenore, clasping his hands. "So let's get started. Lenore, do you know what Charles told me? He thinks that I should give your job to Stacy, and that instead of killing her tonight, I should kill you instead."

Stacy whimpered, wringing her hands. "What's he talking about, Charles? You said they were going to turn me." She grabbed his arm. "What's he talking about?"

Charles wrestled free of her grasp. "There's been a change in plans," he said. He walked over to Paul and stood beside him.

The girl on the couch frowned as she watched him leave, and pawed the empty air where he once sat as if she might catch him still. "You said they were going to turn me." She bent over, producing a wet gulping noise that Lenore at first mistook to be coughing. When Stacy lifted her head, however, Lenore realized that she was sobbing. Interestingly, Stacy did not scream. Probably because she knew no one would help her.

Richard eyed the vacancy on the sofa with glee. "Lenore, can you please take a seat next to your competition? That should make things a lot easier going forward." He shoved Lenore toward the empty spot, where she reluctantly sat down. "That's better. Now I can see you both.

89

So, Lenore, what do you think of Charles's suggestion? Do you think I should give the job to Stacy?"

Xanax replied. "Maybe you should give the job to Charles, since he seems to have taken such an interest." Fuck Charles.

Richard slapped his hand on his knee. "What an excellent idea, and very generous. You want the job, Charles?"

"I ain't food," Charles said from behind his bodyguard.

Richard chortled venomously. "Like hell you're not." He turned his attention back to the Lenore. "Unfortunately, it doesn't sound like Charles wants the job, but I like the way you think. Stacy wants the job, though, don't you, Stacy? You don't want to die tonight, do you?"

Stacy shook her head, choking back tears.

Satisfied with this response, Richard continued. "So Lenore, in the interest of being an equal opportunity employer, I'm going to give Stacy a shot at replacing you." He closed his eyes. "I'm thinking of a number between one and ten."

Lenore clenched her jaw. "No, you aren't." Fuck Richard.

"Excuse me?" Richard's fanged grin widened.

She dug her fingers into the upholstery, imagining it was Richard's face. "You've already made your decision."

Richard brought his hand to his mouth facetiously. "Why, Lenore. This is exceptionally poor sportsmanship. We'll have to start with Stacy instead and come back to you later. Stacy, pick a number between one and ten."

It took nearly a minute for Stacy to sob a comprehensible response. "Seven."

Paul chuckled and nudged his human companion. "They always pick seven."

Lenore watched their exchange with a mixture of abhorrence and envy. It wasn't fair. Charles should be the one sitting in the hot seat. Charles should be the one picking a number. Charles should be the one dying in the laundry room.

Richard snapped his fingers in her face. "Goddammit. Stop looking at them. Look at me. Pick a number. Don't make me pick one for you."

Her mouth curled into a half smile. "I'll pick a number if Charles plays."

Charles shot Lenore an icy glare. "Give up, you stupid bitch. I ain't playing."

"Oh yes you are!" Richard cackled. "Get over here! We need an extra player!"

Charles did not move and whispered something to his protector.

Paul placed his hand on his friend's shoulder, shaking his head. "You can't make him play, Rich. That's out of the question."

"He had no problem putting *their* lives on the line," Richard said, motioning to Lenore and Stacy. "He's playing. I insist."

Paul pursed his lips, mulling it over. "Okay, you've got a point there. But you have to replace him if he loses." He waved Charles toward the sofa.

Charles winced, and grudgingly went to sit between Lenore and Stacy as if they were a pair of lepers. Lenore could feel his long legs shaking beside her, and noticed that his mouth was locked in an involuntary grimace. The frown of someone about to cry. Good.

Paul grinned at Richard. "You turn into such an asshole when you're hungry."

"You're having a good time, though. Admit it."

"I'm definitely entertained."

"That's all that's important." Richard smirked at his new contestant. "Charles, will you pick a number, please?"

Charles looked over to Paul.

"Pick a number," Paul said.

"I don't want to pick a number!" His eyes filled with tears. "You can't do this to me, Paul. I'm not food! I've done everything you've ever asked me to do. I brought Stacy here. I got Lenore her pills. You can't do this to me."

Richard frowned at him condescendingly. "Charles, I'm disappointed in you. You're looking at this all wrong. We're teaching you a valuable lesson here...it's..." Richard looked up, trying to determine what valuable lesson they were actually teaching Charles.

"Empathy," Lenore chimed in.

"Empathy!" Richard cried, as if he were calling bingo. "Thank you, Lenore! You just scored fifty bonus points! It's empathy. Yes, empathy is a valuable, valuable lesson."

Paul snickered, gripping the counter behind him as if it were a seat on a roller coaster. He looked like he was enjoying the ride. "Jesus Christ, you two are so full of shit. But that doesn't change things. Charles, pick a number."

Charles sobbed a little. "One."

Richard smiled. "Holy shit, are you crying? Did you just say one?"

Charles nodded.

"Okay, great," Richard said. "Now it's back to the high-off-her-ass Miss Lenore. Pick a number, Miss Lenore. I got Charles to play. Don't go welching on your promise."

She gritted her teeth. "Seven."

Richard shook his head, making a buzzer sound. "*Eh.* Nope. Try again. Seven's taken. I believe the hysterical Miss Stacy already went with seven."

The hysterical Miss Stacy whimpered in agreement.

Lenore crossed her legs and leaned back in her seat. "Then you'll just have to choose. I'll live or die with Stacy. Charles lives or dies on his own."

Richard bit his lower lip to stifle a grin. "This is highly unusual," he said, facing Paul. "I'll have to consult with the judges to see if it's allowed."

Paul giggled, pulling away from the counter. "I think she's calling your bluff, Rich. And I think I'm going to allow it." He walked over to the sofa. "I'm sorry, guys, but Lenore just won't play fair. I'm going to have to disqualify her. Lenore, you are excused." Paul extended his hand and helped Lenore to her feet.

She followed him to the wet bar. "Well played," he whispered, patting her on the back. "Can I make you a drink?"

"No."

"Do a shot. I think I'm in trouble when this is over. Do a shot for me."

Richard continued to antagonize the pair on the sofa, who had drifted apart from one another with almost magnetic repulsion. "And the number I was thinking of was...it was seven! Stacy won that round, Charles, but lucky for you, we're going with the best two out of three."

"Tequila," Lenore said, wincing at the belligerent rampage.

Paul placed a shot glass on the counter and filled it to the brim. "Done."

Lenore swallowed it down.

"Good girl." He signaled the ring leader on the carpet. "Hey, Rich? You don't need Lenore anymore, right? She can go back to her room, right?"

"Nah, let's make her stay," Richard said. "Hey Lenore, want to see what happens to the loser? How would you like a free empathy lesson?"

Paul shook his head. "I think you've dragged this out long enough." He raised his voice and spoke with authoritative flair. "Charles, you have been disqualified. You are excused."

Charles nervously looked at Richard, who motioned for him to stay put.

"We still have two rounds left!" Richard protested.

"*No*," Paul yelled. "*Game over. Stacy loses.*" Stacy began wailing, and he slammed his hand on the counter. "That is my final judgment. Charles, get up. It's over."

Charles shot from his seat like a man out of a cannon and landed beside the pool table. He leaned against its edge, wiping the sweat from his forehead with trembling hands. Lenore noticed that he would not meet Paul's gaze; he looked over to Stacy instead. Perhaps Charles had learned empathy after all.

Paul placed his hand on Lenore's shoulder, interrupting her analysis. "Go," he whispered. "I'll handle Rich."

She hesitated, eying the quivering girl on the sofa. "You're going to kill that girl now, aren't you?"

He nodded, licking his lips. "Get out of here if you don't want it to be you."

Lenore wandered trance-like back to her room, cupping the bottle of pills in her pocket as though it were a blue ribbon from the state fair. Now with the Xanax economy in full swing, she chewed two more tablets in an effort to make peace with what was about to take place. Did this make her an accessory to murder? What, if anything, was her responsibility to a total stranger? Even if she had wanted to help Stacy, what could she do?

Screaming in the hallway.

Angela had screamed like that. Undoubtedly, and soon, Lenore would be dragged to the same fate. Would she scream too? Would Paul join in if he were feeling "peckish"? Would Charles stand by and watch, mocking her? It was only a matter of time. Terrible images crowded Lenore's mind like weeds overrunning a garden. Images of Stacy being ripped to pieces. Why wasn't the Xanax working to make it all go away? How many pills would she have to take until the rest of the apartment faded into oblivion?

More screaming.

Lenore was helpless to make it stop. Exasperated, she shoved her fingers in her ears and repeated to herself *this will be over soon.*

And it was all over soon.

When the hall grew quiet again, she looked up to see Paul standing in her doorway. He stepped into her room, characteristically chipper, wearing a fresh set of clothes and his million dollar grin. "I wanted to swing by to see if you were okay," he said. "I could hear you talking to yourself in here."

Badly shaken, Lenore did not speak for a full minute. When words did finally find her, they emerged with Xanaxy cool. "I was trying to block out the sound of the screaming."

He nodded. "You're really upset, huh?"

She met Paul's eyes, noticing with revulsion that speckles of blood decorated his left cheek like so much poorly applied rouge. "Yeah, Paul. Yeah, I'm really upset."

"I knew I should have gotten you out of here for this," he said. "I had every intention." He cocked his head to the side. "What happened, though? You seemed okay when you left."

Lenore curled up on the bed, hugging her pillow. "I guess it didn't seem real until she...um...she started screaming."

Paul groaned. "You know, I could rattle off a dozen ways that she had it better than you do right now. She probably had a really good life. The last half hour just sucked. You, on the other hand, who knows how much of your life is going to suck because of this bullshit."

She threw her pillow down on the floor. "Thanks, Paul. Wow. That really cheered me up. You have a gift."

He opened his mouth to speak.

But Lenore interrupted him. "Don't pretend to care. I find it insulting."

Paul looked around the small room for a place to sit down, but could not seem to find one. He leaned against the entertainment center instead. "Fine. But you shouldn't pretend to care either. It doesn't become you." Lenore raised her eyebrows. "I don't think for one second you give a rat's ass about that girl. And I know I'm right. Do you remember the first thing you did on the night that I met you —when you walked into Rich's living room and saw the dead guy on the floor?"

"No. What does this have to do with—"

"You turned the fuck around, that's what you did. Most people would have been concerned or offered to call 911 or something, but not

Elena Hearty

you. No, you made straight for the door, and you can blame it on the medicine, but the more I get to know you, the more I think that's just who you are."

"Seriously? Is this how you're trying to comfort me?"

"Who said I was trying to comfort you? I don't think you need comfort. I think you need to realize how tough you are. You need to turn on some of that wonderful detachment from the other evening."

"Yeah? Well, it's pretty hard to feel detached when I know I'm probably next. I felt horrible for that girl. I *empathized,* and that's something you couldn't possibly understand."

"Oh, Jesus. Empathy again?" Paul threw his hands in the air. "Let me tell you a little something about empathy. Empathy is an inherently selfish emotion. You didn't feel sorry for Stacy when you heard her screaming. You felt sorry for *yourself.* I'm probably the only one here who actually felt sorry for her."

"Oh really? Is that why you killed her?"

"No, but it's why I brought that stupid game to an end."

"You could have ended it a lot sooner."

"You're right, I could have." He let out a deep breath. "Believe me, I regret the game. That's part of why I'm here. I wanted to apologize to you. If I'd known Rich was going to pull a stunt like that, I wouldn't have asked him to call you out of your room in the first place."

Lenore closed her eyes and nodded.

"You were right, though. Rich wasn't thinking of a number."

"Yeah. No shit."

"You weren't ever in any real danger."

"It was still degrading."

He smiled, shaking his head. "Not the way you played it." He shifted his weight back onto his feet. "Hey, you want to get out of here for a while? It's pretty early. Let me buy you a cup of coffee somewhere."

Lenore unconsciously reached for the catheter in her arm. "Why?

96

You've already fed."

"Oh no. It's nothing like that I swear. No ulterior motives this time. I feel pretty bad about what happened this evening. Charles still isn't speaking to me and I could use someone to talk to."

"It isn't my job to make you feel better."

"I'm not asking for you to make me feel better. Just distract me for a while. Couldn't you use a distraction too? If you sit in this room you're just going to mope around."

She squeezed her eyes together and then glared at him. "What are you trying to pull here? You think you're going to walk in here with blood all over your face and pretend to be my friend?"

Paul scratched at his cheek and smiled. "That was pretty much the idea, yeah."

"No thanks. I'm lonely, but I'm not lonely enough to think that you're my friend." She pointed him toward the door. "Thanks again for getting me those pills. I'm sure I'll be paying you back later."

Paul frowned, walking toward the exit. "Hmm that was unexpected. I thought we got along."

"Well, maybe that's part of the problem. I don't want to get along."

"No. That's not the problem," he said, stopping at the door and turning to her. "I'll tell you what the problem is, though. You're over-thinking this. Did it ever occur to you that you were trapped before you even came here? That you'd thought yourself into a corner and were scared to leave? Look, we both know what's eventually going to happen to you. For all I know I'll be there. But you aren't going to die *tonight*. If you don't feel like getting coffee, then at least walk up to the street and smoke this pack of cigarettes with me." And, like a magician raising her chosen card from the deck, Paul produced a pack of Marlboro Lights.

It had been a while.

Paul blew awesome smoke rings, like the caterpillar from Alice in Wonderland. They stood next to each other on the street in front of the apartment building, backs against the wall, like two kids skipping class.

"Hey you've gotta be freezing," he said, handing her his jacket.

"Won't you be cold?" she asked. "Do you even feel cold anymore?"

She transferred her cigarette from one hand to the other as she slipped her arms through oversized sleeves. There was something strange about the way his jacket felt against her torso. The fabric contained not a trace of body heat. It felt cold, as if it had come off a hanger instead of a man.

"Not really, actually. I think I operate at a much lower body temperature than you do."

"So, what makes you the way you are? Do you know? Is there a medical explanation?"

"No clue."

Paul watched Lenore try to blow a smoke ring. The experiment failed miserably, resulting in amorphous white cloud. He disapprovingly shooed it away with his hand. "No, you're doing that all wrong, kiddo. You need to get your tongue into it." He demonstrated.

"So where's Rich tonight?" Lenore asked. "He's never around."

Another failure wafted toward Paul.

"He's in the building. We're renovating all of the apartments on the second floor. He's tiling a bathroom tonight. You know that he and I run this place, right?"

"Yeah, Charles told me."

"We own the next building over too." He pointed to one of the faceless apartment complexes along the street. "I should probably be helping Rich out up there, but I'm irritated with him right now."

"Over dinner theater?"

Paul nodded. "Yeah. He knows how I feel about dinner theater. He knows I don't do that type of thing anymore."

"But you used to." Lenore did not phrase this as a question.

"Yeah. I wasn't always such a nice guy."

She smiled at him. "You don't say. Did you know that girl?"

"Who? Stacy?"

"Who else would I be talking about? Had you met her before tonight?"

Paul narrowed his eyes. "Why do you ask?"

"I want to get a feel for how much you play with people. Did she think you were her friend?"

Paul opened his mouth to speak, and then closed it again. "That is a loaded question. I think you're trying to make me feel guilty or something, and I don't like it."

"Just tell me if you knew her," Lenore said, tapping the ashes off her smoke.

He jerked his head in annoyance. "I'd met her a couple of times, yeah. But I wasn't *friends* with her or anything. Jesus. If you want to know if I tricked her or something the answer's no. I don't trick people. I play fair, remember? She was Charles's friend. Either way, it's over and I'm not sorry about it. I enjoyed it." Paul took a step toward Lenore, starting to smile. "*Especially* when she started to struggle. Her heart was racing." He placed his hand over her chest. "I'd enjoy killing you too. That's just what I am."

Lenore recoiled, dropping her cigarette on the pavement.

"Is that the answer that you wanted?" he smirked. "Because I can keep going."

"Are you trying to scare me? Because—"

"I *know* I'm scaring you, Lenore. I can hear your heart. Not to mention you're doing that jaw thing again. What's funny about you is that you're so *used* to being scared, you've actually got a pretty decent poker face. But I know better. I don't want to scare you, though. I honestly don't."

"Yeah, I think you did just now," said Lenore, who realized she was still retreating only when the heel of her foot touched the wall.

Turning his back to the wind, Paul lit a cigarette to replace the one that she dropped. "It's not like that, you know," he said, handing it to her. "I'm just being honest with you. But it *was* a loaded question. Did you want to know the answer or not?"

Biting her lower lip, she nodded. "It really bothered me that you fed off her."

"I know it did. But she was already dead."

Lenore wondered if she fell into that category.

"Does Charles do that a lot?" she asked. "Bring people over, I mean. I thought you said Rich mainly goes after people who wander into the basement."

"It depends. Charles has to find someone who meets the right criteria, and that doesn't come by too often."

"Do you usually...participate?" Lenore looked at her companion apprehensively, hoping that he would not interpret this as another loaded question.

Thankfully, Paul did not seem offended. "You know, I was thinking about it, and if Charles brings someone by I usually do. I hadn't given it much thought until tonight. But I think the reason is that if I'm tagging along—and I have to tag along, because Charles doesn't ever come by without me, in case you haven't noticed—"

"I've noticed."

"Anyway, if I'm staring at the person for all that time, just knowing they're going to be dinner, knowing they're already dead, I get hungry and want a piece. I know how shitty that must sound to you."

"What are you guys doing with the bodies?"

"Why would you want to know that? It's just going to upset you." Lenore would spend many nights crying alone in her bedroom, staring up at the carcass infested lighting fixture on her ceiling, thinking that Paul was right.

"I can handle it."

"Have it your way. So get this—this is ingenious—Rich has a

walkway that leads straight from the laundry room to the furnace for the entire building. As Rich would say, 'no mess.'"

That's not so bad, Lenore thought, but could not have anticipated the ways in which this fact would seep under her skin and eat at her from the inside. Later, much later that evening, she would look down at her body and think with no small amount of self pity that it would soon be reduced to a pile of ashes. Awful questions would gnaw at her the next morning as she stood in the shower. Why bother taking care of her body at all? Every hair on her head, every tooth in her mouth, every memory that remained of her mother, all destined for the furnace.

Paul turned the pack of cigarettes over in his hands, eying the Surgeon General's warning under the street lamp. "Did you ever worry about cancer? With smoking, that is? I'm surprised anyone smokes anymore, to tell you the truth."

"When I started I was fifteen—"

"And you still can't blow a smoke ring?"

"—and you just don't worry about cancer when you're fifteen. I always meant to quit, though, but after watching my mother die as young as she was, I didn't see the point. I mean, she never smoked, ate healthy, and something still got her. Something's gonna get everyone."

"I think that is an enlightened point of view." Paul ran his nails along the wall. "Dammit. I can't believe I made Charles pick a number tonight. He won't even look at me. He won't even let me apologize."

"You really care about him, don't you? You aren't playing with him. Not the way you're playing with me."

Paul nodded. "He's like a little brother to me. I shouldn't have put him on the sofa with you and Stacy. It was wrong of me to look at him that way."

There was an unspoken corollary to this statement that Lenore found unnerving; *she* belonged on the sofa with Stacy.

"He deserved it," she said finally.

"Oh? Well, he certainly doesn't think so. He's going to blame *you* for this, you know."

"So what? He's had it out for me since I came here."

"No. It's different now. You've made him your *enemy*. For instance, you're out of food, right?"

"Oh yeah. I'm supposed to make a list."

"Well, you can forget about giving that list to Charles. Do you think he's going to get you food now? Think again. And do you think Rich is going to do it? Why would he bother? Why wouldn't he just replace you with someone else, and get Charles to go to the store instead?"

Lenore was silent. None of these consequences had occurred to her, and she wondered if Paul could discern her apprehension. Would Richard kill her immediately, or let her starve for weeks on end before finally finishing her off? It was time to ask for help. "Will you go to the store for me?"

"*Of course* I'll go to the store for you. You've got a raw deal as it is."

Lenore let out a sigh of relief.

"But that isn't the point," Paul continued. "You don't want me to be the only person who's keeping you alive because—no offense—I'm not getting anything out of this relationship. Pissing Charles off wasn't a wise move. You should have thought twice before dragging him into that game."

The memory of Charles crying on the sofa brought a smile to Lenore's face. "I would have pulled you in, too, if I'd thought I could get away with it."

Paul blew another smoke ring and grabbed at the center like a child chasing a bubble. "I would have played, you know. I think I enjoy playing with you."

Chapter Six:
Low

Paul raised his glass. "I propose a toast," he said.

Lenore looked up from her scrambled eggs and smiled. "You're going to toast me with my own blood?"

Paul shrugged. "I'm open to alternatives. Want me to bleed that waitress over there? You distract her and I'll slit her wrists with this butter knife." He wielded the blunt object menacingly.

"That's okay," Lenore grinned, readying her cup of coffee. "What's the occasion?"

"Haven't you guessed? Rich isn't supplementing tonight. Didn't you wonder why I was getting you out of the apartment anyway?"

"I just figured you were hungry."

Paul frowned. "No. Jesus Christ. You know, I actually *do* like hanging out with you. Do you really think I'd do this every week if I didn't like you? You aren't *that* tasty. I didn't even feed on you last time—or the time before, now that I think about it."

Somehow, Lenore did not remember it that way, but what was the point in arguing? "Okay, okay. So what's the fuss about?"

"It's your birthday, stupid. May 16th, right? Happy birthday, Lenore."

Lenore raised her cup, but did not feel like celebrating. This meant that she had been at Richard's for over three months, and freedom was starting to feel like a distant memory.

Once again, Lenore siphoned her essence into a glass on the counter. And once again, she stood back, waiting for Richard to signal the next round. He surprised her by taking the glass over to the sink and rinsing it out instead.

"I guess you're letting me off easy today?" she asked, puzzled. "You usually have three."

"Not this time," Richard said abruptly. "You're low."

It had been a few weeks since Richard's last supplement, but Lenore felt fine.

"How long can we go on like this?" she asked, alarmed. She thought back to her birthday dinner with Paul, where he requested that she fill his cup three times.

"Not long. You're in trouble if I can't find a supplement. I hate to do it, but I'm going to have to ask Charles for help. *Fuck*. This is going to be so awkward." He said the last part to himself.

"Maybe someone will come down to the basement," she offered helpfully, but who was she trying to reassure? Richard would be fine, regardless. Fine enough to drag her to the laundry room and burn her remains in the furnace.

"That's tricky this time of year. It isn't as cold as it was when you came here. People aren't coming down the way they were."

Sometimes, Richard would lure cold stragglers into this clutches by placing a space heater near the basement steps. Lenore wondered if he might be willing to explore more aggressive options, like a house made out of gingerbread.

"Don't worry about it," he said, drying the glass and placing it back in the cabinet. "I'll talk to Paul and he'll set it up with Charles. I'm sure he'll work it out. I'll email him about it right now. Relax. Stop grinding your teeth."

Paul stopped by a few hours later, interrupting Lenore's thrice daily coffee routine in the parlor.

She looked up as he entered, shaking three sugar packets into her cup. "I didn't hear you come in," she said.

"Yeah I'm pretty sneaky like that," he replied, pulling up a stool. "How are you feeling?"

"Just fine. Why do you ask? Is this because Rich said I'm low?"

"Jesus. Can't I ask how you're doing without you getting all weird about it?"

"You didn't ask how I was doing. You asked how I was *feeling*."

"Ha. Good point." Paul swiveled in his seat. "I haven't even talked to Rich yet, as a matter of fact. I came to see you first. He wouldn't need to tell me you're low, though. I can just tell. Like how vultures know when something's dying, pardon the comparison. You've lost a lot of blood. You're in trouble."

But she felt fine, maybe a little tired. "Rich needs a supplement."

Paul laughed. "Get ready. I'm about to blow your mind. YOU need a supplement. These people are no longer dying for Rich, they're dying for you. You're practically one of us now." He shot her a smug grin.

"Are you going to help me or not?" she asked, ignoring him.

"I don't know," he said, looking down at the counter, tracing granite patterns with his fingers. "I've just about run out of favors with Charles. He told me flat out that he won't get you any more medicine. The last two bottles came directly from me. Making matters worse, he's been pushing to replace you with his new girlfriend. He isn't going to bring someone in here if he thinks it'll buy you more time, not when he wants you out the door."

Since when did Charles have a girlfriend? Lenore pictured Morticia Adams. "Why would he want to sign his girlfriend up for this?"

"He's got this idea in his head that we'll eventually turn her. I can't bring myself to tell him that we won't."

Lenore would never understand what prompted Charles to keep chasing that carrot, or what prompted Paul to dangle it in front of him in the first place. "Can't...can't you get someone? Do you have to go through Charles?"

Paul's ever present grin widened. "Now hang on for a minute there. You realize what you're asking me to do, right? Everyone up to this point—Rich was going to kill them anyway, so you aren't responsible for their deaths—but here's where it all changes."

"What are you talking about? Rich emailed you, right? *He's* the one asking."

Paul shook his head. "Oh no, kiddo. I'm not going to make it that easy on you. I didn't come down here to talk to Richard. I came down to talk to *you*. I want to hear *you* ask."

She looked pained. "Why are you doing this to me?"

"Because you and I have something terrible in common," he smiled. "We have to kill people to stay alive. I want to know what you decide to do about it."

Lenore took a long sip of coffee, processing his words. "No. It's different. You're putting me in this position."

"Oh you must think I'm the devil now, huh? Well, I have several things to say to that. First, I didn't choose to be in this position either, but that's life. Also, you're the one asking *me*. It isn't the other way around. Even if we pretend this is all Rich's idea, chew through the candy coating and you'll hit a bitter truth. Someone's dying for you, someone who wouldn't have had to die otherwise. And I'm not trying to make you feel bad about it. I'm the last person on earth who would do that, but I think you can stand to take some of the responsibility."

She stared at him icily, placing her cup on the counter. "Fine. I'm asking you to find someone else."

"Excellent." He brought his hands together dramatically. "Then we have a deal, but before we sign any paperwork, let's get a few things straight."

"Like what?"

"You're helping."

Lenore's mouth fell open.

And Paul chuckled, scratching his head. "Now, how does that saying go? Give a man a fish and he'll eat for a day, teach a man to fish and he'll eat for the rest of his life? Something like that. Anyway, here's what we'll do. We're going to take a little field trip, you and I, and you're going to find a man and bring him back here. It's easy for women, trust me. It's as simple as asking someone to walk you home.

Her eyes grew wide. "Don't do this to me. You know I can't agree to that. Paul, please don't do this. Please don't play this game with me."

"What makes you think this is a game? Killing is nasty business. It isn't a game at all. And I refuse to pretend that you're some helpless damsel in distress. You're smart enough to know what you're doing, and to deal with the consequences." Lenore stood in silent contemplation, nodding once before Paul continued. "Do you know why Angela stuck around as long as she did? It wasn't by coincidence. She went out and lured men back here for dinner."

Lenore's hands formed into fists. *"I'm not Angela*, Paul. And I'm never going to agree to this. Not to buy myself another week. Once I go down that road, there's no going back."

Paul drummed his fingers on the counter like a pianist trying to tap out a melody. "You know, I don't get you at all. I don't understand why you were comfortable asking me to find someone, but the moment you have to get your hands dirty, you bail."

"I buy my meat at the grocery store."

"The grocery store's closed, kiddo."

"So that's it then." A panic had started to arise, but was bedded back down by the six Xanax racing through her system. "Oh God, Paul. I don't want to kill anyone..."

"Well, I think that's probably a good thing, don't you? Cheer up. Nothing's going to happen for the next few days. I'll give you the opportunity to change your mind, and I hate to say it, but I think you will. I told you before, I think you're pretty good at looking out for yourself." He looked up at the ceiling for a moment, crafting his next sentence. "I want you to know something. It's not like I *want* you to die, do you understand? Quite the opposite. I think we'd actually have a really good time hunting together, if you'd give it a chance."

Hunting together? Lenore shook her head in disbelief. "I'm through talking to you. I'm going to talk to Rich."

"You're going to talk to Rich." Paul repeated her words as if they were in some ancient Greek dialect.

"Yeah. I don't like the option you're giving me, so I'm making a new one."

Paul leaned backward in his seat, crossing his arms in amusement. "All right. I'll buy a ticket for this ride. What are you going to say to Rich?"

"I'll ask him to man up and go to the clubs until I'm back to normal."

"And you seriously think he's going to agree to that?" Paul whispered, turning his head to make sure they were alone. "Why would he do that for you? You're disposable to him."

Lenore smiled. "That's why I've got nothing to lose. What's the worst thing that could happen? I piss him off? He's going to kill me anyway."

Paul raised his eyebrows excitedly. "Can I come with you? Can I watch?"

"Sure. Come on. He's probably in the library."

Richard was indeed in the library, hunched over a pile of documents. He did not look up as they entered, but instead grabbed what looked like a contract from the edge of the desk and held it up in the air.

"Paul, you need to sign this. It's from the attorney."

"Yeah, thanks Rich. I'll look it over in a bit."

Richard turned to face them now, the corner of his mouth lifted in a half smile. "So you guys know I could hear every word you said in the other room, right? I mean, Lenore probably wouldn't have known that, but Paul—seriously—why bother whispering?"

"Jesus Christ. *I know you can hear us.* But give the girl an illusion of privacy. What the fuck is wrong with you?"

Richard snickered, shuffling in his seat. "So am I supposed to act surprised now? Okay. I'll act surprised. Do the two of you want to walk in again, or should we just take it from here?" Richard cleared his throat and proceeded to speak in cue card monotone. "Well if it isn't Paul and his moribund friend. To what do I owe the honor of your visit?"

Paul shook his head, smiling. "Cut it out, dickhead. Will you or won't you?"

"I'll do it. I'll 'man up,' to use Lenore's eloquent phrasing."

Paul stared at him, agape. "*What?* You *hate* the clubs."

"Not as much as I hate Charles, and I think this should really piss him off." Lenore thought she had never seen Richard look so happy.

But Paul looked deflated. "Jesus. I should have known. You're so fucking predictable."

"Aw. I'm sorry. Am I messing up Lenore's indoctrination? From what I could tell, it wasn't going very well to begin with."

"She would have come around," Paul said, shooting her an appraising glance.

"Yeah," Richard snorted. "She sounded like she was about to crack any minute. You had her right where you wanted her."

"You didn't even give it a chance. You have to let them sweat it out a little. It's better in the long term if she—"

Richard stiffened. "The long term? I don't have time for the long term. I'm hungry *now*, Paul. So let's run the abridged version by her. Lenore, how would you like to head out to a bar, seduce a strange man, and bring him back here to die?"

Lenore smiled involuntarily. "No thanks."

Paul raised his hands in exasperation. "You're not even—"

"Shh," Richard said, waving his words away. "I'm getting to the

109

sweat-it-out part. We'll do that right now. Lenore, I will kill you if you don't bring someone back here. Does that change your mind?"

"No," Lenore said, still smiling.

Richard pointed to his friend gleefully. "See? See? Are you satisfied now? She isn't going to do it. She'd rather die. And you know why? Because she isn't bat-shit insane like the other creeps you bring around here."

Paul rolled his eyes. "Well, now you're just being—"

"Did you really think I'd tell Lenore that I'd prefer to kill her than hang out with you for a few nights? Why would I do that?"

Paul studied his friend for a long time, as if Richard might sprout wings or manifest a beak. "All this from the man who brought us dinner theater?"

"Oh please. That was *months* ago. And I was only kidding. You knew I was only kidding, didn't you, Lenore?"

Lenore examined her fingernails. "You're a real card, Rich."

"Shut up." He turned to Paul. "How much of an asshole do you think I am?"

"I don't know. Let's see." Paul rubbed his chin, giving the question grave consideration. "I'd say you're a really big asshole."

"*Me*? The worst thing I'm going to do to Lenore is kill her. At least I'm not buddying up to her so I can use her as bait. You think you did Angela a favor by getting her to do that? You drove her insane is what you did. I know you think they're all your little friends, and you want them to have something in common with you, *but they aren't like us.* They aren't meant to do that. That's not what they're *for.* It's confusing for everyone involved. Christ. Take Charles, for example. He doesn't even know what he *is* anymore."

Paul stood in silence.

"Find something else to have in common with Lenore. Why don't you develop a dependency on pain killers or something?"

Paul stood in uncomfortable, extremely annoyed silence.

Richard powered through it. "She's working out pretty well. I'm not trying to replace her. Especially not with one of Charles's minions. Not to mention, have you noticed how Charles-free the apartment's been lately? I think I've got Lenore to thank for that. We bring another one of his friends in here and he's just going to start hanging around all the time again, irritating the shit out of me."

"Okay...then you'll come out with us tomorrow?" Paul asked, still in shock. "We'll...umm...we'll swing by and pick you up."

"That's fine," Richard said, getting back to his paperwork. "Now, can I assume we're done here? Paul, I need you to stick around and go over these documents with me. Lenore, if you want to stay, do it quietly."

She did not want to stay, and instead headed back to where coffee was waiting. Lenore added an extra packet of sugar to celebrate her victory, because although she would never admit it to Paul, she knew she would have changed her mind.

Richard insisted on a light feeding before venturing out with Paul and Charles, who waited patiently for him in the foyer. "If I go in hungry, I could lose control," he explained, walking Lenore into the kitchen. "Listen, when you fill up the glass, do it slowly. Bend the tube so that only a little comes out at a time. If I think you're getting too low, I'll tell you to stop, understand? And then when you're done, go lie down, okay?"

"Yeah," she said, nervously rolling up her sleeve. How low was she, exactly? What invisible symptoms warranted such precautions?

As Richard pulled a glass from the cabinet, Lenore noticed Charles appear in the doorway. "What's he doing here?" she asked.

Richard turned around, slamming the glass down in annoyance. "No idea. Goddammit, Charles, what are you doing here? Why aren't you with Paul?"

"Paul went upstairs for a minute. I thought I'd keep the two of you company."

Lenore shook her head. If she were sitting on a plane and looking out the window, she would see Charles ripping at the wing. "Rich, I don't want to do this while he watches. He gives me the creeps."

Charles leaned against the entrance with his hands in his pockets. "It's a free country, honey. Besides, I won't stay long—just wanted to see what all the fuss was about. You do look a bit peaked." He turned to Richard. "Rich, this is bullshit, man. She's dying anyway. Just finish her off. I'll introduce you to my new girl tonight. She's psyched to be your donor. She don't have a problem pulling people in, neither. You'd never go hungry, I guarantee it."

"I've heard you…several times. Now please leave while Lenore and I finish up in here."

"Seriously, this is bullshit," Charles said, retreating down the hall. "She don't even want to be here."

With Charles comfortably out of the room, Lenore leaned over the glass on the counter, bending the catheter in her arm before releasing the spigot. Although Richard customarily waited several feet away during this phase of the procedure, he stood beside her now to monitor the ebb of blood into the container, allowing it to reach the three quarter mark before instructing her to stop. He then told her to stand still, and slowly, as if trying to pet a wild foal, reached out and placed his hand around her neck. For a brief moment, their eyes met, and there was a terrible connection.

"You'll live," he said, releasing her. "Go sit down, now." Richard drank as she stumbled toward the table.

For the first time after a feeding (not counting the seizure-feeding), Lenore felt fatigued, and buried her head in her arms. Richard slid a bottle of Gatorade in front of her before walking out of the room. She wondered if she were starting to taste like Gatorade; it seemed to be the only fluid her body could keep in steady supply.

Five minutes passed with her head on the table. Lenore could hear Paul reenter the apartment and talk of heading out soon, right after Richard shot another email to the attorney.

The sound of footsteps echoed in the kitchen and stopped beside her. "How you feeling, sweetheart?" Charles asked.

She looked up, eyelids heavy. "Not so hot. What do you want? I thought you guys were leaving."

"Yeah, we are, but I thought I'd hang out with you for a minute...one last time. You think you got it made with these guys, huh?"

Had Charles looked at her lately? Did it *look* like she had it made? Suddenly, the kitchen had turned into middle school, and the boy in gym class was torturing her for no reason. "If you have a problem, why don't you go and bitch to Rich again, because I think that's really starting to work out for you. I think he's really starting to listen."

"There's more than one way to skin a cat, Lenore. Keep that in mind."

"What does that even *mean*?"

Charles ignored her question. "You given any thought to what's gonna happen when these guys lose interest? They're gonna find a new way to play with you, and you might not like it so much. Now, Rich ain't gonna tell you this, but I think you should know—sometimes he likes to pop people's eyeballs out of their sockets before he runs them through. Just for fun. Ask Paul if you don't believe me. Haven't you ever wondered why Paul's so bent on getting you out of the place when Rich kills someone? It's 'cause Rich does it slowly. He has a real good time with it."

Lenore tensed. Although Charles was clearly trying to manipulate her, it was working, and she sensed he was telling the truth. She thought back to how long Angela screamed.

Charles smirked at her with his arms crossed. "Now I figure you got yourself a shit ton of Xanax. Why don't you do yourself a favor and take enough so you never wake up? Rich ain't gonna make it easy on you. He don't make it easy on anyone."

Lenore had nothing to say, but conjured up a satisfying mental image of ripping Charles's eyeballs out, and then stuffing them into his simpering pie hole.

"Good talk, sweetheart," he said, walking off.

"Good riddance," she mumbled, setting her head back down on the table and closing her eyes.

Seconds later, someone patted her cheek.

"Lenore? Lenore? You okay?" Paul leaned over beside her.

Now Richard was coming in.

And Charles, looking predictably pissed off. "I thought we were gonna go, Paul. I told Deirdre we'd be there at ten."

Paul lifted two fingers for silence and grabbed Lenore's neck the same way that Richard had minutes before. "Rich, she doesn't sound too good. How much did you drink?"

Through closed eyes, Lenore imagined Charles's excitement.

"Not that much. Have you seen how small the glasses are? I didn't even fill it to the top. I think she sounds okay...a little irregular, maybe."

"Nah, Rich. She isn't breathing right. She's going into shock."

"Well, here's part of the problem," Richard said casually. "She hasn't even touched the fucking Gatorade I brought her."

There was more patting on her cheek.

"Lenore? Hey Lenore, you need to drink that Gatorade. You need to get some fluid in you." She looked up to see Richard twisting off the cap (as if unhinging an eye from its socket) and waving the bottle in her face. "Drink up," he said. He made her take three large gulps before placing it back down.

It was freezing in there all of a sudden. "I'm cold," she murmured, closing her eyes. She felt nauseated.

"This is bullshit," Charles declared. "Just kill her. What happens if she dies while you're out? Then it's a waste."

From the silence in the room, Lenore could tell they were taking his point into consideration, and to her detriment, it was a sensible argument.

"Yeah, I dunno. I still think she sounds okay. I think she just needs to get back her electrolytes and shit," Richard said, waxing scientific.

Lenore pictured him in a lab coat, removing people's eyeballs with a scalpel.

Paul came to her rescue. "Rich, why don't you go on ahead? I'll hang out with her and make sure she's okay. I fed the night before last. I can always go tomorrow instead."

"Whoa. I'm not so sure I like that idea. What happens if she dies? If you finish her off you owe me."

"I'll just give you Charles if that happens," Paul said amicably. "Calm down, Charles, I'm just kidding. Rich, do you have your cell phone on you? I can text you to come back if it looks like she isn't going to make it. I think you're right, though. I don't think she's going to die, she just needs to pound some Gatorade. I'll watch her."

Charles opened his mouth to speak, but Richard cut him off, sneering, "Wait. Let me guess what you're going to say. Hang on, it's coming to me. 'This is bullshit,' right? Am I right?"

Charles was silent.

"Okay," Richard continued. "It looks like it's just you and me tonight, so don't piss me off. And if I hear one more thing about your slut girlfriend I swear to God I'm going to kill her. Paul, do you need anything before we go? You've got this?"

"Yeah, I've got it."

Lenore heard the sound of the two men shuffling out of the kitchen, and then the front door opened and shut, and then the deadbolts turned. It was freezing in there. Paul removed his jacket and hung it around her back.

"Hey, you," he said softly, taking a seat in front of her. "How are you feeling? I need you to finish this bottle of Gatorade and then I'm getting you another one. Then you need to go to bed."

She looked up at him and weakly shook her head. "I don't feel like drinking. I feel like I'm going to throw up."

"Well, your whole system's off. It's going to get worse if you don't drink. Just take a few sips."

She did.

"Easy does it. Remember a few weeks ago at the diner when you referred to the waitress as 'crack head chick'? You look just like that. You should see yourself." He smiled.

"Am I dying?" she asked, shivering.

"I don't think so. If you wake up tomorrow morning you're going to be fine. You could probably use some sugar, though. Where does Rich keep your toaster pastries?"

"Pantry," she replied, pointing.

"Take another drink," he said, walking over. He studied the container on his way back. "What the fuck is riboflavin? No wonder you're all fucked up. Back in my day, we didn't pump ourselves full of all these chemicals. You'd get a loaf of bread and it was just flour and sugar and water. Now there's all this shit with yellow number five. No wonder everyone's got cancer." He opened the foil wrapper and handed her a pastry. "Just take a bite. That's it. Chew. Excellent. Now take another sip of Gatorade."

"If I start to get worse are you going to kill me?" she asked, too groggy to be afraid, just curious.

"I don't think you're going to get any worse. If you do, you'll pass out and won't have any idea who pulled the plug."

"That might be nice." She closed her eyes again for a second, picturing it.

Paul shook his head back and forth. "Heeey, let's not talk like that. And don't tempt me. You look particularly yummy when you're all sick and helpless like this. You need to take another drink. I need to see you finish that entire bottle."

He watched in silence as she took several belabored sips from the container, stopping occasionally to rest her head against the table. After several minutes of this routine, the toaster pastry started to work its magic, enabling bolder sips as time went on. Soon, the bottle was empty.

Paul returned with another. "Finish this one, too, and it's off to bed. You look better, though. You sound better, anyway."

She nodded, and with growing alertness had started pondering the things Charles said to her before walking out the door. *Rich is going to rip my eyes out.* "I think I need to take some Xanax."

"No, I think that's a particularly bad idea right now. Take some in the morning."

"Seriously, Paul. I'm starting to panic. I need something to take the edge off." *Rich is going to rip my eyes out.*

"You know what? Panic. Go nuts. I'd love to see it. You're always so doped up on that shit I'm curious to see what it's protecting you from. Besides, you don't take Xanax, the worst that's going to happen is you panic. You *do* take it, and I'm not sure how it'll affect your condition. It's not worth it."

"First off, that's ridiculous. You've seen me upset before. Second, I...can't function right now. I feel like I'm dying." *Rich is going to rip my eyes out.*

"You're pretty damn close," he said, giggling. "I'm kidding. You're not really dying. I think you're in the clear so long as you drink that bottle and get some sleep. So chill out. Doctor Paul says you're out of the woods." He grinned. "But maybe Doctor Paul should stop drinking so much from you on our trips to the diner."

Lenore unconsciously brought her hands to her eyes. *Rich is going to rip my eyes out.* "Paul, please."

"I told you, you're going to make it. What's the matter?"

"I don't want to talk about it."

"You on the rag or something?" Paul's smile faded when he saw that she was starting to cry. "What's the problem?" His eyes narrowed. "Shit. Did Charles say something to you? He did, didn't he? I know he

117

came by the kitchen, but Rich and I were talking about legal stuff, so I didn't hear what he said. Whatever it was, he's full of shit. Don't let him get to you."

"Rich is going to rip my eyes out."

"That's the most ridiculous thing I've ever heard," he said, leaning back in his chair. "Charles told you that? You shouldn't listen to him."

She noticed that Paul was not smiling. "No, it's true. He said I could ask you and you'd tell me it was true."

"That he rips people's eyes out?"

Lenore nodded tearfully.

Paul took a deep breath. "Lenore, I swear to God, he isn't going to rip your eyes out. Okay? I can't fucking believe Charles told you that."

"It's true, though," she said, looking for validation.

His response hinged on a long uncomfortable silence. "It's true," he whispered. His brows knit with frustrated compassion. "Look, I won't let that happen to you. And it's not like he does that every time. I can't imagine he'd do it to someone he *knows*. Shit. I'm going to get your pills. Where are they?"

Between tears, Lenore told him they were on her nightstand.

When he returned he handed the bottle to her, saying, "I guess if these kill you it'll look like an accident. I've got my story straight, at least." She chewed four, letting the bitter powder dissolve under her tongue.

Minutes later, she had stopped crying.

"Are you better now?" Paul asked.

"Yeah. Charles suggested I take the whole thing," she said, caressing the bottle. "It's not like that hasn't occurred to me off and on since I came here, but after the eye comment I'll have to give it more thought."

Paul ran his hands over his face. "Don't say that type of thing in front of me. I'll be forced to take the bottle away. Rich is all weird about me getting you these pills for that very reason. If you kill yourself he doesn't eat." He touched the corner of his eye thoughtfully. "Listen, a couple of things, now that you're calmer. First off, I'm not going to feed on you anymore. I shouldn't have been doing that in the first place, and I'm sorry. When I get you out of the apartment, we're just going to hang out as friends. Does that sound good to you?"

Lenore nodded.

"Second, you absolutely positively do not need to worry about Rich...messing with your eyes. I won't let that happen, okay? Case closed?"

"I don't think there's anything you can do about it."

"That's where you're wrong. When he takes you to the back room I can be there...I know that sounds bad...I wouldn't—I wouldn't join in or anything."

She pictured Paul seated in a folding chair behind a pane of glass, attending a state execution. "I really wouldn't want you there. I've been pretending you're my friend. It would mess that up to think you're going to be there. I can't pretend that hard."

Paul looked up at her. "Well, that's serious business then. I've been pretending you're my friend too. I don't have many, you know. Just you, Charles and Rich. You're the only people who know what I am."

"Was Angela your friend?"

"You'd better believe it. I wish the whole thing with Angie had ended differently. I really do. I didn't click with her the way that I click with you, though. *I* think we click, at least."

"You haven't known me that long. I'm pretty sure it'll get old. I'm locked in a basement all day."

"What? Like it hasn't been getting old with Rich? I've known him for nearly 100 years now, and he's pretty much locked in a basement all day himself."

She shot him a wan smile. "So, of your two friends besides me, one wants me dead and the other is going to kill me."

"One big, happy family, right? Charles is pretty much in the same boat, by the way—maybe even worse off. Rich wants him dead, and I'm sure you do too, if I'm not mistaken."

"I wouldn't exactly throw him a life preserver."

"Yeah, he's been acting out. I don't know what to do with him. I've known him for twelve years, though. Makes it difficult. He came to me when he was only seventeen. Anyway, you're Rich's to kill—no doubt about that—and Charles is mine. He just doesn't know it. Once you get involved with us, you don't exactly die of natural causes." He looked over at the wall, lost for several moments in silent preoccupation, before turning his attention to Lenore's bottle of Gatorade. "This shit can't be good for you either," he said, shaking the bottle. "I'm going to get you some multivitamins or something. I'm so out of touch. People back in my day never took vitamins. But they're good for you, right?"

"Yeah, I guess. Get me Flintstones vitamins."

"What are those? Like, the cartoon show?"

"They're vitamins, but they're like candy. They're awesome. Wasted on children."

"Okay, I'll see what I can do. Now finish that drink and you need to go to bed. And take it easy for the next few days—no heavy lifting." When Lenore had emptied the second container, he walked her down the hall to her room, and sat quietly at the edge of the bed until she fell asleep.

After a long while, the door cracked open, jolting Lenore from fitful slumber. Through half closed eyes she saw Richard standing beside the bed, placing another bottle of Gatorade on her nightstand.

"Hey, I didn't mean to wake you," he breathed. "You feeling better?"

"Yeah," she replied, shifting under the covers. "Did Paul leave already?"

"He left a little while ago."

"Did you feed at the club?"

"Some. It wasn't that bad. Easier than replacing you, that's for sure. I could have done without Charles's yapping all night, though. He's really trying to kiss my ass over this new girl, and now that I've met her, I can see why. He'll never pull anything like that down again. Bitch must need glasses...and a hearing aid. Anyway, he says he can bring me a supplement on Thursday. It isn't going to help his case, but I won't turn it down, either."

She nodded. "What day is it? I lose track of time."

"Sunday. Sunday morning."

"That's five days. Are you going to go back to the club in the mean time?"

"I don't think so. I can make it for five days. I could make it for weeks, probably." He smiled. "You're the one who wouldn't make it. After a while I wouldn't be able to stop myself from killing you." He looked at the floor uncomfortably. "So while we're on the subject, I want you to know something. It is not, nor has it ever been, my intention to rip your eyes out. I think when you first came here I said I'd make it quick and that hasn't changed. Paul told me you were really upset, and I thought you'd want to hear that from me firsthand."

God bless Paul. She lifted her head from the pillow and nodded, unsure of whether to thank Richard for his promise to murder her quickly. Had it come to this? Was she so resigned to being a victim that a painless death looked like a favor?

Richard continued. "And listen, I know you can take care of yourself, but Charles is a serious douche bag. Let me know if he harasses you again and I'll take it up with Paul. It's not like you'd be bothering me, either. I'm always looking for an excuse to get rid of him. Anything you could do to help my case would be appreciated."

"Will do." Wheels were turning.

"Great. Get some sleep and let me know if you need anything. It's my fault that you got sick, so just say the word and I'll come running."

Chapter Seven:
The Laundry Room

Lenore spent the next two days sleeping, interrupted only by trips to the bathroom, swills of Gatorade and some overzealous monitoring from Richard, who would open the door every few hours to peek in, waking her every time. On Monday night (at least she thought it was Monday), the door opened again, but this time Paul walked through carrying a bottle of Flintstones vitamins.

Holding the container in his hands, he eyed the label with suspicion. "These are disgusting," he said before handing them to Lenore, who had recently stirred to watch television.

"What is it with you and nutrition labels?" she asked, removing the plastic seal. "Food isn't that bad for you, you know. Don't you realize how much higher the life expectancy is these days compared to when you were born?"

"Hah. I guess so. Either way, I got you like three bottles of this stuff. The other two are in the kitchen. You have to chew six or something to get an adult dosage."

She smiled at him with her eyes narrowed. "I think you just made that up."

"So I did. So I did. That sounded plausible, though, didn't it? I was thinking of telling you to grind them up and snort them, but I thought that might be too over the top." He ran his fingers through his hair and whispered. "Hey, I shouldn't have to tell you this, but stay away from Rich. He didn't have too much to drink at the club on Saturday, and now he's trying to make it 'til Thursday night. That's a long time without food. I'll be in and out, but stay in your room as much as you can."

"You act like that's a big change from what I normally do."

"Well, the last few times I've stopped by, you've been out in the apartment. Don't go to the kitchen. Bring all of your food in today. I'll walk out with you to get it. No trips to the living room for coffee. Just hang out in here."

"*I can hear you in there, fuckheads!*" rang out from the walls. "*Paul, stop whispering like I can't hear you!*"

Paul slapped his hand to his forehead. "Fine, Rich, now shut up. Let me rephrase. Lenore, Big Brother wanted me to tell you to stay in your room for the next few days. He'll stay away from you, you stay away from him. He'd tell you himself, but he's already hungry."

"*Thanks, Paul. Now I need you to look over these permits with me.*"

The universe kept getting smaller.

Confined to her bedroom, Lenore busied herself with the antiquated video game systems that occupied the underbelly of Angela's entertainment center (and took pills, lots of pills). As promised, Paul stopped by a few times, even joining her in a spirited game of Tetris on Wednesday night before heading off to fix someone's air conditioning unit. Richard, for his part, kept his distance, but Lenore could hear him hungrily pace the halls at night, and at those times she would feel like the last feeder fish in a piranha tank.

Thursday came and the pacing got worse, taking on the alarming characteristic of long pauses outside her door before resuming course. During those moments, she would imagine Richard on the other side, fangs exposed, just waiting for her to slip up and start running. Where were Paul and Charles? The clock on the wall kept ticking, and the pauses grew longer and longer until Richard had stopped outside her door completely.

"Hey Lenore. Hey, why don't you come out and wait with me? Charles should be by any minute. He said he'd be here around ten."

The clock on the wall said 11:15.

No amount of Xanax would have stopped Lenore's heart from pounding when she heard Richard speak, but she tried to sound calm. "That's okay, Rich. I think I'll just stay here. I'm going to bed."

The door opened, and revealed something that looked like a ravenous cat wearing a man's face. "Oh no, I insist. Why don't you come out and wait with me?" Richard's movements had adopted a predatory harmony with her own; when her head tilted, so did his, if she leaned left, he leaned right. Fangs.

This was tricky territory. If Lenore argued, Richard might use that as an excuse to kill her on the spot. "Rich, are you sure that's a good idea?" she squeaked. "I thought you said we should stay away from each other."

"It isn't going to help at this point. I can smell you. I can hear your heart. But I'm not out of control yet. I'm so hungry, though. You have no idea. If I don't have someone to talk to, I'm going to go nuts out there by myself. Please come out and talk to me. If I'd wanted to hurt you I would have done it by now."

Richard's words rang true, and even if they were not, the lockless door between them offered no protection.

"Okay, Rich. I'll be out in a minute. Let me get dressed, though. I'm still in my pajamas." Really, Lenore was stalling for time, and when Richard closed the door to give her some privacy she ambled out of bed slowly.

"Talk to me while you get dressed. Talk to me about anything."

Lenore pulled on her jeans. "What do you think I have to talk about? You've got me locked in here all day. All I do is watch TV, read through your books."

"I know, I know. Do you remember the first book you took from my library?"

"No. What was it?"

"It was The Lady or The Tiger."

"Oh. Yeah I do remember that, actually."

"So, which is it?"

"Which is what?"

"Did she pick the lady or the tiger?"

"I have a different take on that story, Rich. I think in an infinite universe—"

"Oh, Paul mentioned something about that to me. That you have some weird theory about the universe."

"It isn't *my* theory. It isn't like I came up with it."

"Well, whatever. It's a fucking cop out. If you could only make one decision, what would it be?"

She donned an old sweater. "The lady. The lady is the better choice. And not only because everyone lives. It's better because she leaves the possibility open for the situation to correct itself. Maybe the princess's cruel father dies later and she reunites with her lover after all. Maybe she sees him on the side, even though he marries someone else. The tiger, on the other hand, that closes off all further opportunity. It's giving up too easily."

"That's a very level headed decision. I don't think the character is supposed to be level headed."

"She probably needs some Xanax." And so did Lenore. She chewed four pills.

"Are you done yet? I can hear you eating something."

"I'm done," she replied.

The door swung ajar, and Richard motioned for Lenore to follow. A wave of fear descended when she walked toward him, and a powerful instinct had begun to take hold, the animalistic drive to flee when confronted with a natural predator. Every joint in Lenore's body was poised to *run*, and ignoring that instruction felt as unnatural as trying not to breathe. *Fight or flight*, she thought, remembering an old term from high school biology.

"Where did you want to wait?" she asked, short breaths

undermining the calm in her voice.

"I guess by the front door," he said, walking. "Charles is over an hour late. He knows how long it's been for me. I don't know why he's pushing it."

"Maybe he's doing it on purpose," she offered, and then the impact of her words hit home. *There's more than one way to skin a cat.* Lenore's mouth ran dry.

"What? To piss me off? That doesn't make any sense. He's been kissing my ass lately."

Her eyes grew wide as she realized the horror of what was taking place. "No. It makes perfect sense. He's starving you out to get rid of me. Then he replaces me with the new girl."

They had reached the foyer, where Lenore took a seat on the shoe bench. Richard waited at the door.

"Don't be paranoid. He'll show." But there was doubt in Richard's voice. "He'd better fucking show," he muttered. "Let's keep talking. So let me tell you about this bitch that's suing me."

An uneasy hour passed as Richard outlined the legal case against him, which Lenore found fairly interesting. A woman in the building was recently diagnosed with mesothelioma, and claimed that her condition was caused by improper asbestos removal from her unit nearly twenty years ago. Making matters more interesting, the tenant had been hit with financial troubles lately and coincidentally brought suit around the same time that the rent checks stopped coming in. Richard was busy calling her every name in the book when the door opened behind him.

Paul stood contritely in the entryway, and Charles was notably absent. "Hey guys. How's it going? I went to the club but Charles never showed. He just texted me to say that he can't make it tonight. Says he's sick with the flu."

Richard looked like a pressure cooker with the lid screwed on too tight. "*Bullshit.* That is such bullshit! The flu's going to be the least of his problems when I get my hands on him."

"Shit happens, Rich. You don't know that he's lying," Paul replied, locking the door behind him.

"We aren't selling copiers, *Paul*. You don't just call out *sick*. That little prick is manipulating me. Don't you see what he's trying to do?"

"I know what it looks like, yes." Paul frowned at Lenore. "What's she doing out of her room? What's going on here?"

"Nothing so far. We're just talking."

Paul positioned himself between them. "Hey kiddo, what's up? You okay?" She shot him an unenthusiastic nod, and Paul turned his attention back to his friend. "Can you make it another day? I can find someone myself if you give it another day."

"Paul, I'm eating tonight."

So that was it, then. Richard was going to kill her.

Time stood still.

When Lenore's mother wrestled with terminal illness, there was a great deal of talk about preparing to die. *The five stages of death* were tossed around a lot in the conversation, with emphasis on the final stage: acceptance. It was vital, said that doctors (not to mention Lenore's therapist, boyfriend, next door neighbor, roommate, etc.), that her mother reach acceptance. Well, this never made a lick of sense to Lenore, because looking at it from the outside, acceptance seemed to sound an awful lot like giving up. And in an infinite universe, one should never give up. But now, as her death loomed near, Lenore realized that she had been missing the point. Acceptance was about control. It was about replacing hope with strength.

Lenore planned to face death with unflinching stoicism. She would not scream. She would not cry. She would not grovel or beg. *Death with dignity*—that was another term that was tossed around a lot when her mother was sick, but she understood that one right off the bat.

Time resumed.

"Jesus Christ, man. You can make it another day. You're not *that* bad."

"Whatever happens, you can blame it on that Kentucky fried Goth of yours."

"Just chill out. Give this another day. You don't want to make this—"

"Paul, this is what she's *for*," Richard said, gesturing to Lenore. "*This is why she's here in the first place.*"

"No. That's not cool, Rich. None of this is cool. She's sitting right *there*. She can *hear* you." Paul looked frantically over to Lenore, who watched him quietly from where she sat.

Richard threw his hands in the air. "Well, what should I do then? I suppose you'd like me to tell her that everything's going to be fine, and then fifteen minutes later, I'll yell, *surprise, Lenore!*"

Lenore jumped a little in her seat.

"*I hope you like surprises! I was just kidding earlier. You're really fucked after all! I'm coming to eat you!*"

"Now hang on, let's all just—"

"*Oh, you're so full of shit, Paul!* Just a month ago or so you were telling me how I should put her out of her misery, then the other night you tell her that you won't bother to keep her alive unless she fucking kills someone, and now you're all pissed off that she's going to die. *Look at her.* She doesn't even look upset about it anymore. This is what you do to people. You play and play and play and play and it's *not a game.*"

Paul grew very quiet and stared at his feet. "Okay. You're right. You're right. I fucked up. If I didn't want her to die I should have gotten someone the other night. This is my fault."

"Well there you go. I'm not the bad guy here." Richard folded his arms conclusively.

Paul started speaking to his friend as if trying to coax him down from a ledge. "No, you're not the bad guy here. It's me. I'm the problem, but I'm going to fix this. I'll go find Charles. I don't know where he is, but I'll find him. We'll be back with someone. I'm coming back. I'll even take her with me, that way—"

"*No.* She stays here with me," Richard hissed.

"Rich, come on, man. Don't do this. Let her come with me. I was planning on getting her out of here anyway when your dinner arrived. What's the difference, really?"

"You know the difference as well as I do."

Defeated, Paul took a deep breath and turned to Lenore, placing his hand on her head. "I'll be back, kiddo. I promise I'm coming back."

Lenore thought about how Paul had kissed Angela on the forehead that first evening, right before telling her goodbye.

Paul looked over to Richard. "Hey. Just please remember what we talked about. Do that for me at least?"

"You have my word. She's got some time."

And Paul bolted out the door.

Lenore gazed at Richard, wondering how they would spend her last few hours. And Richard looked back at her, possibly wondering the same thing.

"Well," he shrugged. "I think you were right. I think Charles has it out for you. I'm going to kill him, if it makes you feel any better. Paul's just going to have to deal."

She nodded, knowing that she would not live to see it. "What was Paul talking about when he left? He said, 'remember what we talked about.' What did that mean?"

"He wants me to go easy on you. I told him I would." Richard looked at her for a long while. "Do you want a cigarette? I stole your pack of cigarettes the night you came in, but I'll let you smoke one now if you want, to pass the time."

"Yeah," she said. "That would be nice I think." For the time being, Lenore was wonderfully calm. This was total surrender, and felt like sinking into a warm current after a long and tiring swim.

"Okay, great. Now where did I put them is the question...aha I think I know. Hang on one sec." Richard used his vampire superpowers for the mundane task of running down the hall and back, returning with a half full container of Marlboro Lights. "I can't let you smoke them here, though. But I'll let you smoke them in—"

The laundry room, Lenore thought.

"—the laundry room. Otherwise it's going to stink up the place."

But they both knew why they were really heading into the laundry room.

"Do you have a light?" she asked, standing up.

Richard produced a lighter. "Yeah, I think I took this from you too. Ladies first."

And she accompanied him down the hall, still strangely at peace with the idea.

When they stopped in front of the blood-door, Lenore's resolution wavered. "Rich, maybe we could do this out here instead. I don't want to see what's in that room."

"Relax. You're just going in for a cigarette while we wait. You've got some time."

Lenore's resolution took a U-turn.

"Paul's not coming back, though. I don't think Paul's coming back," she said, retreating a few steps.

Richard took a deep breath and placed his hand on her shoulder. "Lenore, I have to take you in here. Don't make me chase you. If I start chasing you right now I will kill you. Paul has all night to come back. I promise. But you need to wait with me in here."

With that, Richard opened the door to the laundry room, and Lenore stepped inside.

The universe kept getting smaller.

Richard shut the door behind them. The wash room was dark, and he pulled a chain to illuminate a single exposed bulb on the ceiling. Dim light bathed their surroundings, revealing a washer and dryer, a sink basin, a folding chair set against the wall, and cement floors with a drain in the center. A hose was piled in the corner, which Lenore presumed was used to wash blood down the drain when Richard

130

finished with a victim. *No mess.* A corridor wound off into the distance—the path to the furnace.

"Have a seat," Richard said, handing her the pack of cigarettes.

Lenore sullenly obliged and sat in the chair, staring at the floor, specifically the drain. A human tooth lay unceremoniously atop the grate. She brought her hand to her mouth, stifling a gasp.

"Aren't you going to have a smoke?"

"I don't know, Rich. I don't feel like doing anything right now. I'm shaking too bad to light one anyway." *Please don't cry. Please don't cry. Don't you cry, Lenore. Be strong.*

"You've got time. You need to relax."

"How am I supposed to relax in here? There's a tooth on the floor. There's a f-f-fucking tooth on the floor. Oh God." *Eyeballs. Rich rips people's eyeballs out. Just for fun.*

"I'm going to go easy on you, just relax."

If Rich told her to relax one more time she was going to lose it. "Oh God. Why don't you go easy on everyone? Why do you rip people's eyeballs out?"

Richard shrugged. "Not that it's any of your business, but it's a little fetish of mine and I'm not going to apologize for it. You try killing people all the time and keeping it interesting. Would it make me a better person if I killed everyone quickly? Would it even matter at that point?"

More things were coming into focus now, such as the chunk of hair underneath her foot. What human remains were ingrained in the chair on which she sat? Which parts of her mortal coil would work their way into the upholstery? "Oh God I'm going to throw up."

"Christ. Do it in the basin. And *run the water.*"

She followed his instructions.

Richard grabbed a paper towel from a roll atop the washing machine and handed it to her. "Here. Clean yourself up."

She wiped her mouth with the towel. "Where do you want me to put this when I'm through?"

"I guess in the trash can over there. Oh no. Wait. You know, on second though there are probably a bunch of things that you don't want to see in that can." He grinned. "Just give it to me. I'll throw it away for you." He walked over to where she sat and grabbed the vomit covered napkin from her hands, proclaiming, "Disgusting," before carrying it like a dead fish over to the bin.

"Sorry." But she said this out of reflex.

"Oh don't apologize," he said, leaning against the dryer. "You know, I'd say something like eighty percent of the people that I bring in here throw up. It happens all the time. It's not like there's a prize at the end for *not* throwing up."

Lenore lit her cigarette after several attempts with trembling hands. "So what happens now?" she asked.

"I guess now we wait...until either Paul comes back or I decide I can't wait any more. You can relax, though. I'm not going to jump out at you or anything. It won't be a surprise." Richard looked up at the ceiling, as if the right words were written behind the lighting fixture. "What I'm trying to say is, I'll tell you if I decide I can't wait anymore, so that you can prepare for it. Unless that's not what you want. Do you want me to tell you or not?"

"I don't know," she whispered.

He smiled reassuringly at her. "I don't know what I'd want either, to tell you the truth. I've never given anyone that option before. I've never been in this position before, with someone in a holding pattern like this."

She took a drag on her cigarette. "How long were you planning on waiting?"

"For Paul? I few hours, I guess. This is a pretty miserable situation for both of us. I'm really hungry. And I doubt Paul's going to bring someone back with him. I mean, he doesn't know where Charles is, and even if he finds that lying son of a bitch I don't know how they'd get yet another person back here in time."

"I agree. It seems unlikely." What was the point in waiting around?

"Thank you," he said, vindicated. "This is probably putting both of us through a lot of unnecessary pain and suffering."

Her eyes snapped back to the tooth on the floor. Richard had killed someone and now all that remained of that human being was inconvenient debris lying on top of the grate, ready to be washed down the next time that the hose ran, which would most likely be that night. Someone had worked hard to grow that tooth, and brush that tooth every day. Most likely, that person was congratulated by their mother or father when the baby tooth fell out that had held its place. Running her tongue over her own teeth, Lenore hoped they would all make it with her to the furnace.

Horrible thoughts wriggled inside her head. No matter how she conducted herself in her final moments, there was no dignity in this sort of death. Richard thought of her as meat, and was preparing her for slaughter. At this point, it would be a relief.

Lenore braced herself. "I...um...I want to be brave. God. I don't know how to say this. I want some..." Her mouth distorted into a frown.

Sobbing. This wasn't how it was supposed to be. She wanted to die calm.

Arms folded, Richard shot her an appraising look. "You know, you guys all act the same at the end. It's always a lot of begging and blubbering. Doesn't matter how strong or cool and collected someone is, you get them in here and—"

"*Dammit, Rich, I shouldn't have to be good at this.* Do you think you're any better? You think you'd act any differently?"

"I don't know. That's a good question. I thought *you* would, though. You're the fucking Xanax queen. Plus, you were calm on the way down here. I'm just surprised is all. You're cracking at the last minute. I thought you'd go all the way."

"What? I'm supposed to act calm now to impress you? Go fuck yourself. You don't know what this feels like." She buried her head in her hands.

"I do, actually. I really do. I wasn't trying to offend you. I'm just talking. I told Paul you had some time. I'm trying to give it to you."

"I should have brought my pills with me. I don't know why they aren't helping."

"So I can tell you why they aren't helping. It's because you're fucking addicted to them, that's why. I can't imagine being so dependent on something. They run your fucking life."

"Oh no, Rich," she said, lifting the tube in her arm. "I think you can imagine." Taking a few deep breaths, she tried to calm herself, and felt the earlier outburst abating. Maybe she could give stoicism another go after all.

"Fair enough." He frowned. "Either way, that shit couldn't have sustained itself."

"Did you talk to Angela like this before you killed her, or did you just do it right away?"

"Don't ask me that. I don't want to talk about Angela."

"What do you want to talk about?"

"I want to talk about Charles. I fucking hate that piece of shit. How do you think I should kill him? Let's go through all of the gory permutations. That might keep me busy for hours."

"I don't know, but when you kill him, tell him it's for me."

"What?"

"Like, in the movies. When one guy punches the other guy, and says, 'and this is for so-and-so.' I want you to say, 'and this is for Lenore.' Throw a punch for me."

"Love it. I'll do that. Swear to God."

Richard spent the next half hour or so itemizing his plans for Charles, and the list of options read like a Grand Guignol. All matter of organs and appendages were to be removed in painstaking detail before Charles would finally be allowed to expire. And then there were the sadistic choices that Richard would offer him, such as selecting a limb to be torn off first. Lenore found herself nearly smiling at a few of Richard's more outlandish proposals. There was something so unapologetically dark about the man that it was almost impossible to not to be entertained.

Finally, when there was a sufficient break in the conversation, and when Lenore was feeling particularly calm, she looked up at Richard and said, "Hey, I don't want to sit here all night."

"I can't let you out of here."

"I know."

"What are you trying to say?"

"Just do it."

"Are—are you serious?"

"Yeah," she said. "Do it before I lose my nerve. I don't want to die in hysterics—and that isn't something to impress you—it's for me."

"Lenore, I'm not *that* bad. You've got some time. I could probably even go another night, to tell you the truth, but it's the principle of the thing." Richard looked at his watch. "Paul's going to be pissed if he gets back and you're dead...he hasn't even been gone an hour yet."

But Paul wasn't coming back, and Lenore was through with false hope. There wasn't a perfect universe, there was only this universe, and she needed some control. She needed some dignity. "You can tell Paul it was my decision. He'll understand."

Richard raised his eyebrows and nodded. "Okay. He...um...he really liked you, for what it's worth. I liked you too. I'm sorry about all of this. Last chance to change your mind. Are you positive? You need to be positive because once I start, I'm not going to stop."

She stood up. "Yes."

"Okay. Then come here." They met in the center of the room, and he placed his hands on her shoulders. "This should be fun. I don't get to do this every day."

"What? What do you mean?" she asked, looking around uncomfortably.

"That you're—you know—not struggling or trying to get away. Should make it pretty interesting. Probably a lot easier for both of us." He ran his thumbs over her sweater.

She winced. "This...this shouldn't be fun. You promised not to hurt me."

"I won't hurt you—well, I'll *try* not to, anyway—but that doesn't mean I can't enjoy it. I want you to do something for me. I'm trying to remember something. Take off your shirt."

"No. Why? Don't make me do that," she said, trying not to cry.

"What do you care at this point?" He started removing it for her, and Lenore stood there, letting him. After all, how could she possibly stop him? Richard threw her sweater onto the chair, and ran his fingers over her collarbone, her breasts, and then the back of her spine. "I love women, Lenore. They're so beautiful. I can't enjoy women the way that I used to, but I remember how it felt. I love the way you curve...you're shaking."

And she was. "Your hands...they're freezing."

"That's okay," he smiled, cupping her waist with both hands, pulling her closer. "You're going to make me warm." His forehead touched her own. "Any last words?"

"I'm scared," she whispered, closing her eyes.

"Hey," he replied softly, touching her cheek. "We're all scared." Then he stroked her hair for a moment before twisting it back with his hand and pulling it away from her shoulders. "I think you're going to do great, but stop squirming like that. If you keep squirming like that I'm going to wind up snapping your neck."

There was a commotion in the hall, and the door burst open.

Paul looked angry at first, and then settled into a comfortable, medium-sized grin. "Am I...interrupting something?" he asked wryly, as if he had caught the two of them making out behind the bleachers.

Richard still held Lenore, and turned his head in anger. "*Yes.* Actually, yes. You *are* interrupting something. I'll be finished in a little while, please wait outside."

"Can't let you do that. I've got something better—worth the wait."

"Charles? He's here...I can smell him."

"Better."

"Better than Charles?" Richard loosened his grasp on Lenore.

"His girlfriend, Deirdre. You were right. He wasn't sick. I found the two of them smoking behind Thorn." (Thorn, Lenore knew, was a Goth Industrial club)

Excitedly, Richard left for the hallway, and Paul's grin appeared to follow him out the door. Eyebrows knitted, he frowned at Lenore, who shivered in the corner, arms folded to conceal her naked chest.

"What was Rich...what was he doing to you?" he asked, grimacing. "Why's your shirt off? Why would he take you back here? I said I'd get Charles. Jesus Christ. I couldn't have been gone for more than an hour. Didn't anyone believe me? Doesn't anyone listen to me?"

She opened her mouth to speak, but stopped. A few seconds later, she tried again, "Paul, please. Please don't look at me like this."

He turned his head. "Jeez. I'm sorry. Where's your shirt? Is it in here? I can get it for you if it's not."

"It's over on that chair. I'm going to get it. Just turn around, please. Don't look at me." Paul obeyed, and Lenore swiftly redressed. "You can look now."

"Are you okay?"

"Yes," she said coolly. And now that her shirt was back on, she was. But no—it was more than that. Lenore had faced death on her own terms and came out unscathed. There was nothing that Richard could do to her at this point that had not been done before.

"We're getting out of here. You can spend the night at my place. I'm sorry you had to see this room. I'm like fucking sick over this. I've fixed your problem, though, you'll see."

Lenore followed Paul into the kitchen, where two doomed lovers sat at the table. Charles's girlfriend was visibly upset and sobbed quietly in his arms; he held her hand fiercely and promised to make everything all right. Deirdre struck Lenore as exquisitely beautiful, and not in a cartoonish Elvira sense. Her plain features possessed an almost perfect symmetry, the hallmark of physical attractiveness.

Standing behind the table, and looking like he had just bought a new car, was Richard, who antagonized the tragic pair mercilessly. He shot Lenore a triumphant grin when she entered the room. "Hey Lenore, look who's feeling better? It's Charles. He's made a miraculous recovery and has decided to join us after all."

She grinned back at Richard, feeling that things were different now between the two of them; their scene in the laundry room would remain in the laundry room, paused and momentarily forgotten. For now they were in alliance, united against a common trench coat wearing fiend. "No kidding," she said, playing along. "What a relief. You know, I've heard the flu can be fatal."

He grinned at her meaning. "Aha! That's very true. Especially the fallacious flu, and I've heard that's been going around this time of year. Can't be too careful. Speaking of which...Charles, you cad. Suppose you were contagious? You may have risked your poor girlfriend's life, just by hanging out with her tonight."

Deirdre began whimpering, and Charles reached over to massage the back of her neck. "It's okay, Dee. Everything's going to be okay."

Richard chortled menacingly. "Fat fucking chance." Then he placed one hand on the shoulder of each, pulling them all together in a sarcastic embrace. "We're going to have so much fun tonight. We're going to play a lot of games. Lots and lots of games. Paul *loves* games. It's a pity he won't be joining us."

Charles's jaw went slack. "Paul? What does Rich mean by that? You're not leaving. You can't just leave us here. You can't do that. Deirdre didn't do anything. Paul, she hasn't done *anything*. You can't do this. *Paul. She hasn't done anything.*"

Paul shifted uncomfortably to avoid Charles's gaze, looking to Richard instead. "You can kill her," he said, pointing to Deirdre, "but don't kill Charles. He's mine, and I'm going to dispose of him in a manner that I see fit."

The girl in Charles's arms began screaming, and Lenore felt truly sorry for her.

"*Come on. Deirdre hasn't done anything. You guys can't do this.*"

Richard walked over to the counter to grab a roll of paper towels. "He'll be breathing when you get back. That's all that I'm going to promise you."

"*Paul. Listen to me, you can't do this to us. We trusted you when you brought us here*"

"Fair enough. Listen, Lenore's staying over at my place tonight. She doesn't need to be here for any of this."

"*You can't just leave us here.*"

Richard tore several towels off the roll and wadded them together before forcibly shoving them into Charles's mouth, causing Deirdre to scream uncontrollably. Richard shook his head and stuffed her mouth as well before resuming conversation with Paul. "I'd think Lenore would want to stick around. She's got as much stake in this as I do. Lenore, do you want to stick around and mess with Charles all night? You are cordially invited—I'll give you a front row seat to the show."

"No thanks," she said. It was difficult to tell for sure, but Richard actually looked disappointed. "Throw a punch for me, though."

"I'll throw several." He looked over to Paul, scratching his head. "You're going to bring her back tomorrow or something? I'm not sure how this little sleep over is supposed to work."

"Yeah tomorrow's good. Email me when you've had so much fun that you can't stand it anymore."

"Will do. Hey...do you want to make a trade here? Lenore for Charles? He's going to be pretty damaged when you get back and—"

"Just stick with the original plan."

"I'm just offering—"

"Yep. I know. Answer's no. Have fun."

Chapter Eight:
The Penthouse

Paul did not speak to Lenore again until they were inside a rickety old elevator heading up to the penthouse. "What the fuck was that? I want to know exactly what happened back there."

"What do you mean?" she asked, catching her reflection in the mirrored wall. She understood now why the doorman had sneered at them as they walked through the lobby. He probably thought Paul was bringing home a prostitute, a crack-head, or—more likely—some unflattering combination of the two. The past week had done nothing for Lenore's personal hygiene, leaving her face gaunt from lack of sleep and nutrition. When was the last time she even bothered to shower? She pondered that question as she looked down at her vomit stained sweater, noticing for the first time since putting it back on that it was inside out. Lovely.

A light overhead marked their passage over the fifth floor.

"You know exactly what I mean," Paul said, forcing her back to attention. "Why was Rich about to feed? I can't believe he didn't wait. I can't even tell you how pissed I am right now." And Paul did look pissed. He leaned forward, nose almost touching the door, hands stuffed rigidly in his pockets. Lenore noticed with some level of satisfaction that his jaw was clenched.

She met his eyes in the mirror. "Rich was going to wait. I told him to go ahead with it."

"You have got to be fucking kidding me," his double scowled. "Are you out of your mind? I was coming right back. I *told* you I was coming right back. Why would you do something like that?"

"I don't want to talk about it," she whispered, eyes on the ground.

Paul spun toward her, and the box that held them swayed with his weight, causing Lenore to stumble backward into the wall. "Oh? Well I fucking do."

"You're the one who's always telling me that I'm just dragging things out," she said, trying to regain balance.

Paul hovered over her like a menacing storm cloud, waiting to erupt. "Fine. I don't have a problem with that in theory or anything, but don't you think you could have had your big realization *before* I went out and got Charles? There's going to be some serious fallout over this. I really stuck my neck out for you tonight."

She shot him an icy glare. "Sorry to have inconvenienced you."

The lights flickered for floors ten, eleven, twelve.

"You want to die that bad, huh?" he asked, turning back toward the exit. "You know, I haven't eaten in a couple of days. Maybe I'll just finish you off when we get inside. I'll bet you'd make a pretty tasty snack."

Lenore gritted her teeth. "Go ahead."

"Oh really?" he smirked. "Great. Are you going to let me take your shirt off too?"

"Oh my God. You're jealous."

Floor nineteen illuminated, silently interrupting their conversation. The elevator stopped and the doors opened.

Lenore stood at the entrance to apartment P19 as her host fumbled with the keys. Paul turned the handle, muttering. "Unbelievable. *Everyone's* pissing me off today."

She followed him inside, wondering if it might have been a wiser choice to remain with Richard instead. At least he seemed to be in a jolly mood when she left him.

"Welcome to my humble abode," Paul said, dropping his keys on a marble stand by the door. Then he turned to her, half smiling. "So

141

where should I kill you? Should we go in the living room where it's more comfortable, or in the kitchen where it'll be easier to clean up the mess?"

"Right here is fine," she replied, unsure if she was calling Paul's bluff or if it was the other way around. She wondered how far the game would go before someone finally yelled chicken.

Paul cocked his head to the side, arms folded, perhaps wondering the same thing. "Nope. Let's do this in the living room. I'll feel all rushed out here." He started walking and motioned for her to follow. "We wouldn't want it to be over too quickly."

Lenore closed her eyes, so that she could roll them. "No. We certainly wouldn't want that."

Paul was not much of a decorator. Or a housekeeper, for that matter. The inside of his apartment was barren in most places, with no carpets or area rugs to break apart the bamboo floors, and it was clear that the walls had never been painted. The only exception to the Spartan décor was the mess in the living room, which swirled around a small television and sofa like rings about a domestic nucleus. Strewn with the remnants of a serial hobbyist, the area contained loosely organized stacks of crosswords, jigsaw puzzles, video games, music equipment, models and sketch pads. Interestingly, atop one of the pillars sat a rotary phone.

"Oh, we're nipping that in the bud right now," Paul said, having noticed the object of Lenore's attention. He walked over to where the phone sat and started to unplug the cord from the wall, but then paused for a moment before stopping altogether. "No. You know what? I'm not going to do that. You know what I'll do to you if you go near that phone, right?"

Lenore nodded.

"Well, the same goes for the front door. I'm not going to bother locking it. Just don't go near it."

She shrugged. "I'm not stupid, you know. You don't have to insult me."

142

"Well, you were looking at that phone awfully hard." He took a step toward her and then shook his head. "You can sit down if you want."

Lenore took a seat at the edge of the sofa, sliding a pile of magazines off the cushion to make room. She grabbed the topmost periodical and began leafing through the pages. It was a comic book.

"So you told Rich you were calling it quits, huh?" Paul asked, removing his jacket and tossing it on the floor. "Maybe this isn't your universe after all?" He kicked his shoes into a corner, where they joined a larger mound of discarded apparel.

"Maybe not." Lenore looked around the room uncomfortably, as if there were some other conversation she might join.

"What made you change your mind?"

Lenore took a deep breath. "You saw where he was making me wait, Paul. I'd never felt so...God. I didn't realize. He—he tears people apart like they're nothing, and then he washes them down that drain. There's no..." She trailed off, afraid to finish the sentence, afraid of the emotions it might wring.

"Dignity?" Paul asked, as if plucking the word from her mind.

"Dignity," she whispered. "I wanted some dignity. Stop beating me up for that."

Paul's stance softened, and he came to sit beside her, causing an avalanche of comics to topple onto the floor. "I'm really sorry you had to see that room. But you knew I was coming back for you."

"No I *didn't*," she said, sliding away from him. "Why *would* you, Paul? You guys kill people all the time. Why would I be any different?"

He lifted his eyebrows and smiled. "Well, that's easy. You're different because I *say* you're different. You're different because you're my friend."

"Like Angela?"

His head jerked back. "Now why would you bring her up?"

"You just handed her over to Rich that night."

"And you thought I was doing the same to you? Jesus Christ,

that's so stupid. Angela came at me with a *fucking knife*, Lenore. How was I supposed to protect her at that point? If you come at me with a knife—fair warning—you're on your own. Other than that, I'll see to it that you stick around."

"Oh yeah? For how long? How long are you going to see to it?" Lenore pictured herself twenty years older, a tube still running out of her arm.

"I don't know," Paul said, springing from the sofa. "A *while*. Let's leave it at that." He stopped in front of her with his hands on his knees. "Look, I don't want to walk into Rich's place and find out that you're dead. That would be so depressing. Who would I take to the diner? Who would kick my ass at Tetris? Who would bore me to death with logic problems and the history of vacuum cleaners, of all things? You're just about my favorite person these days, Lenore. I feel like I'm just getting to know you."

"If you really feel that way, you should let me go."

He raised his hands in frustration. "I can't let you go."

"You mean you won't."

"Fine. I *won't* let you go. Not even if I traded you for Charles."

"Don't talk about me like I'm property," she said, shuffling her foot along of the mess on the floor. "I don't appreciate it."

"Oh grow up. What do you think this is? Do you think you have rights? More importantly, do you think *Rich* thinks you have rights?"

Lenore's eyes locked onto Paul's. "I want to know what you think."

He ran his hands over his face. "Oh man, here we go. What do *I* think? I think I am what I am, and you are what you are, and we should both try to remember our places. Crap. That didn't come out right at all..."

"I think it probably came out perfectly."

"No, no," Paul said, shooing the words with his hand like an improperly formed smoke ring. "Let's try that again." He closed his mouth for a moment, and opened it again after much deliberation. "I respect you as a person. And I think of you as my friend. But you belong to Rich, and if I traded you for Charles you'd belong to me. And I'd do whatever I wanted with you. I certainly wouldn't let you go."

Lenore turned her attention back to the magazine in her lap and stared intently at an ad for collectible action figures. "That didn't sound any better the second time around."

"Yeah, I should have quit while I was ahead...or less behind." Paul lit a smile, which was quickly extinguished by Lenore's silent fumes. "Oh get over it. You know too much. You've *seen* too much. I know it sounds melodramatic, but it's true. We can't just pack your bags and call you a cab and say, 'Goodbye, Lenore. Sorry about the kidnapping.' I shouldn't have to spell that out for someone as smart as you."

"So back to the trade. What does it mean, exactly? Is it just who gets to kill me?"

Paul grinned. "Oh, that's certainly part of it. But I wouldn't do that right away. I'm not through with you quite yet."

"So what *would* you do with me?"

"I don't know. I hadn't thought about it. I guess I'd keep you up here."

"Would we have an arrangement?" she asked, motioning to the catheter in her arm.

"Oh, definitely. You'd have to earn your keep. But you could ditch the tube. It isn't my style. With Charles gone I guess I'd need a replacement, but I don't think you're cut out for the club scene, no offense. You don't strike me as much of a people person."

Lenore looked embarrassed for a moment, like Paul had guessed what color underwear she was wearing. "I know I'm not," she sighed. "I can't help it."

"Why would you want to *help* it? I think it's great. I think you're like those perfect machines you're so fond of collecting. Just look at how well you've adapted to your present situation. Take Lenore away from the world, and she still works. I think that's huge. There's something to be said for not needing to be plugged in."

Lenore smiled at Paul, wishing she had something wonderful and insightful to say to him in return. But what was there to say? Hey Paul, you're not as mean as that other vampire. I think it's awesome that you only kill people some of the time, when you can justify it to yourself. Nice comic book collection.

Paul continued. "I think what I'd have you do would probably be a lot easier than what Charles does, anyway. Women have a particularly easy time luring men back to—"

Their conversation was starting to sound awfully familiar. "No way. Forget it. You know how I feel about that idea. Besides, wouldn't you have to start killing people again?" For someone who claimed not to take lives, Paul seemed fairly open to the alternative.

"Well I can't just keep you here as a pet." Paul shook his head. "You know what? This is stupid. There's no point in arguing about it because I'd never make the trade to begin with. I'd never sell Charles out like that, even though I'm sure he thinks I've sold him out already. Everything's fucked now, you know. Rich expects me to kill him."

"But you won't?" Lenore wondered if Paul could hear the disappointment in her voice.

Paul shrugged. "I don't know what I'm going to do, to tell you the truth. I'm buying time right now while I figure that out. The way I see it, I've got two options. The selfish choice would be to let Rich have him. That' perfect for me because I don't want to kill Charlie and I'd get you in the deal as a bonus. I could probably even talk Rich into letting Charles be his donor. He might not have to die right away. But none of that's really in *Charlie's* best interest. The best thing I could do for *him* is to kill him myself, but that's almost too horrible to think about. I—I wouldn't eat him, you know. I wouldn't want to...to enjoy it."

Lenore nodded, thinking she would not have to eat Charles to enjoy killing him. "You said you've known him since he was seventeen?"

"Yeah."

"How on earth did you get mixed up with a seventeen year old?"

Lenore tried to imagine a scenario in which the answer to this question was not totally creepy, and found herself drawing a perpetual blank.

"I hang out around high schools." Paul said this with such deadpan that Lenore at first did not know what to make of his statement. Then he started snickering. "I didn't know Charles was seventeen when I first met him. He was just another guy hanging out at the clubs. You know that Rich used to come out with me, right?"

"No, but okay."

"Well, the whole reason I got into the club scene was so I didn't have to kill anyone. Rich was the opposite, he went there looking for full kills. He just loves finishing people off."

"I'm aware."

"Finding full kills in the club scene can get complicated, though, because these people have jobs, social lives, etc. It isn't easy to make them disappear. So it's kind of like a challenge. It's kind of like a game. You have to convince the person to cut all ties, to essentially do all of that work for you."

"How?"

"You promise to turn them. You earn their trust and tell them that they're special, basically."

"You've done this?"

"Yes, of course." Paul met Lenore's eyes, grinning. "I hope you don't think less of me."

"I don't really think that's possible."

"What a relief. Anyway, I'd say something like, 'Lenore, you fascinate me. You are too beautiful and unique to grow old and die with the rest of these mortals. I wouldn't be able to bear it. Let me turn you.' And, of course, I've just told you exactly what you want to hear, and you're chomping at the bit."

"And I run out and cancel all of my credit cards and quit my job."

"Oh, it's so much worse than that. Cut ties with your family, your friends, and then I want you to lay low for a few weeks. It's such a scam. These poor people give up everything to die for us. Rich was amazing at running this game on people. He can be pretty charming when he wants to be."

Lenore raised her eyebrows in disbelief.

"Just trust me on that." Paul chuckled, reading her expression. "Anyway, Rich told me to come down to his place one night because he had two full kills—a guy and a girl—trapped in his basement. I figured they were dead anyway, so I might as well eat."

Over the past few months, Lenore had noticed that many of Paul's stories started out this way, and that '*I figured I might as well eat*' was tantamount to '*once upon a time*'.

"When I got down there, Rich had already killed the girl, and there was Charles, sobbing over her in the laundry room. And I realized they were just kids. I don't kill kids. Neither does Rich, for that matter, but we have differing opinions on how young is too young."

"Hang on. What's your limit?" Lenore pictured Paul carding his victims, demanding a valid photo ID.

"My limit?" Paul shrugged. "I don't know. It's not like I have a specific age in mind. *Seventeen's* a little young to die, don't you think? Anyway, Rich and I got into a huge argument about what to do with Charles, and I convinced Rich to let me have him. I told Charles we'd turn him, but he was too young, and to give it more time. I told him he was in training, basically."

"Wait. He was cool with you after you killed his girlfriend?"

"He was upset, but—in his mind, at least—she just didn't make the cut. I think he was happy to sacrifice her, to tell you the truth. Charles has followed me around ever since that night, and I've taken him under my wing. Rich has never liked him, though. Every year, Charlie gets older and Rich asks me if he's still too young to die. I joke around about killing him all the time, but I'd never actually do it. After twelve years, he's become like family to me. I can't turn my back on him."

Staring at the patterns on the sofa cushions, Lenore privately

148

concluded that Paul's story was marginally less creepy than what she had originally anticipated. Or maybe it was more creepy. The jury was still out.

"No matter what I do, I'm going to lose him," Paul went on, his face crumbling. "I can't believe how badly I fucked him over tonight. I wish there was some way to make it up to him. He's like my brother. He's like my baby brother. Whatever he's become, it's my fault. I made him this way."

Paul met Lenore's eyes, frowning, waiting for her to respond. Unfortunately, if he was looking for either sympathy or compassion, she was fresh out of both. "What do you think *he'd* want you to do?" she asked finally, settling on the most neutral response imaginable.

The question hung in the air for several seconds, prompting the cogs in Lenore's mind to start tackling the problem themselves, even though she had no real interest in finding the answer. What *would* Charles want? What had Charles wanted all along? She smiled when she realized that it was probably something to her benefit as well.

"He'd want me to let him go," Paul said, interrupting her revelation. "I wish that was an option. Kill him or give him to Rich. They're both such shitty options."

"Then make a third," Lenore said, wide eyed, marveling in the elegance of her own solution.

He paced in front of the sofa. "There *isn't* a third."

"Yes, there is. Turn him."

"How is *that* a third option?" Paul asked, nearly slipping on a magazine as he paused in front of her.

"Wouldn't that be a good way to make it up to him? Isn't that what Charles has been waiting for? Isn't that his dream?"

"Yeah, but Rich would never go for it. Not in a million years."

Lenore leaned forward on the sofa. "Didn't you say it was a death sentence? Rich hates him. Don't you think he'd risk it?"

Paul furrowed his brow. "That's an interesting angle, I'll give you that." His lips formed a half smile. "I take it that's why you're so keen on the idea?"

"I want him dead. I don't think you'll go through with it otherwise."

"Fair enough. But what if it works?"

"He'd have what he wanted. Why would he bother me anymore? Either way, you'd have to replace him with someone new. Hopefully you'd find someone who's willing to go to the store for me, who's willing to find supplements for Rich when I'm low."

"So everyone gets what they want here? Rich plays the odds that Charles won't make it, Charlie gets his shot at immortality, and you win either way?"

"Yeah, I think that sounds about right."

Paul shook his head. "Do you know anything about turning someone?"

Other than that Charles would almost certainly die? "No." Everything else was likely to qualify as a minor detail.

"Well—let me just tell you—it's messy, and it takes about a week. Lots of people have to die. We're talking five or six victims here, minimum. Do you want all that blood on your hands? It's a little much for even *me*."

Lenore frowned. "Why do you need all those people?"

"Because Charles would need to feed almost constantly in the beginning, or he starves to death. That's why people usually don't make it. They can't keep up. I've seen people drink and drink and drink and they *still* can't get enough blood into their system to survive. Jesus Christ, it's a nightmare. And then there's me, of course. I'll have to give Charlie some of my blood every few hours or so, and then I'll need to feed. I'll go through two or three victims on my own. It's like a horrible cycle of death." Paul chuckled. "Now that I think about it, Rich could probably get into the idea."

Lenore made a face. It did sound awful. And it did sound like something Richard would enjoy.

Paul smiled at her. "Doesn't sound like such a great idea anymore now, does it? Do you want to be stuck in the basement while all of that is going on around you?"

"Why would you do it at Rich's place? Why wouldn't you do it up here?"

"Furnace."

Lenore nodded. Perhaps it was even better that way. Charles dying in the basement, completely at her and Richard's mercy. The idea had potential.

Paul pursed his lips. "I think I might run this idea by Rich after all. It's not a bad compromise."

A terrible thought crept into Lenore's mind. "If you went through with it, you'd have to promise me that I wouldn't be—that I wouldn't be *used* for it. If Charles runs out of blood—if you run out of victims—I don't want to be thrown in to keep him alive."

"You won't go to Charles. I'd kill him before I let him have you."

"I don't want to go to you, either." Lenore stared at the ground, picturing herself atop a stack of bodies in the laundry room, collateral damage in the wake of her elegant solution.

"Hey, look at me, kiddo." Paul said, placing his hand on her shoulder. "I wouldn't do that to you. You know I wouldn't do that to you, right?"

"You aren't the same person when you're hungry. Neither is Rich."

"Jesus, give me a little credit here. I'm hungry right now and I'm not touching you."

"But you're thinking about it."

"I *am* thinking about it," Paul said, turning away from her, glancing around the room as if a more suitable topic might spring forth from the pile of clothes on the floor like a benevolent geyser. "Hey, you know what I did?" he asked finally, gesturing to his TV. "I recorded that movie you recommended to me the other day. The one about the guy and his old mother and the zombies? You want to watch it with me?"

Lenore nodded, smiling, grateful for the change in subject. "I think you're really going to like the lawnmower scene."

But she was asleep long before the lawnmower scene, and woke to the feel of warmth on her skin. Lenore stirred to see Paul sitting beside her, sleeping, using the far arm of the sofa as a head rest. Beams of light poured in through his oversized living room windows, bathing them both in the a.m. sunrise.

"Paul?" she whispered.

He squinted his eyes and looked up at her. "What?"

"I thought you couldn't stand the sunlight. Should I cover you up or something?"

"I said we don't *like* it," he replied, lifting his head. "It's irritating is all—like silver—but my windows are UV coated. I get sun in here all the time."

"Oh," she mumbled, jealous. This was the first time she'd seen sun in months. For all she knew, she might never see it again.

Paul shifted into a sitting position, smiling at her. "If I had started bursting into flames or something would you have tried to help me?"

Lenore thought about it for a moment and nodded. "You saved my life last night. I would have returned the favor."

He shook his head, still smiling. "I think that's got to be the dumbest thing I've ever heard. If you ever get the chance to get away, you take it. But thanks, I appreciate the thought." Paul pulled his cell phone from his pocket. "Rich has probably texted me from his laptop by now."

Lenore closed her eyes, sliding back into the sofa. "I don't know how you guys ever managed before modern technology," she yawned.

Paul chuckled. "It was a pain in the ass. Rich would literally knock on my door if he wanted to tell me something." Paul keyed several buttons before shutting his phone again, saying, "We need to get back down there. Rich has sent me about fifteen texts." He grimaced. "And a couple of pictures that he took with his web cam."

Lenore was pretty sure she didn't want to see the contents of those messages.

They took the utility stairs to the basement so that Paul could avoid the sun. An eerie silence hung in the air of Richard's foyer, only disturbed by the sound of Paul locking the front door behind them.

"Where are they?" Lenore whispered, afraid to break the stillness.

Paul took a few steps forward, craning his neck. "I can hear Charles breathing in the laundry room," he said, starting briskly down the hall.

Lenore followed, but stopped at the fork in the corridor, saying, "I'm not going to hang out for this, but good luck. I'm going to take a shower."

"*Oh no you're not,*" rang through the walls. "*Please join us in the laundry room, Lenore. Charles has something he would like to say to you.*"

Lenore and Paul exchanged an eye roll as they headed toward the sound of Rich's voice.

The blood door hung wide open and looked to have been repainted over the course of the past several hours, with fresh crimson beads starting to dry around the handle. Richard stepped around from behind it, looking like the gory punch line to an old joke that Lenore remembered from childhood. What's black and white and red all over? A vampire, after feeding on a victim and burning the body.

"You guys missed out on all of the fun," Richard smirked, rubbing some ashes between his thumb and forefinger. "Deirdre turned out to be a lot spunkier than I'd given her credit for." He turned his head toward the inside of the laundry room. "Didn't she, Charles?"

A low whimper emanated from doorway, and Richard smiled, waving Lenore and Paul inside.

At first, Lenore could not make out Charles's location in the dimly lit space, but finally glimpsed the figure of a man curled up in the corner. He was breathing slowly, covered in grime, and appeared unable to move. Something looked strange about the way he was positioned on the floor.

Richard beamed at her. "Hey roommate, Charles has something he's been wanting to say to you. He'd get up, but I've dislocated all of his limbs, so you'll just have to excuse him." Richard kicked the mound of flesh in the corner. "*Well? Let's hear it, Charles.*"

The mound moved a little. "S-s-sorry. I'm s-sorry."

"That's more like it," Richard said, looking deeply satisfied. "Charles wanted to tell you he's sorry."

Lenore questioned his sincerity.

Paul frowned at the broken man on the floor. "What's all over him, Rich? He looks terrible."

"Oh, that? That's Deirdre." Richard started to chuckle a little to himself. "She didn't survive the flu after all. I had to..." He broke off, laughing at his own joke, too merry to continue. "I had to..." More guffaws. "I had to burn the body so as not to spread the contagion. It's starting to look like the fallacious flu is fatal after all. Try saying that three times fast!"

Paul nodded wearily. "Yes, I enjoyed all fifteen of your text messages telling me about the fallacious flu. It's getting funnier every time."

Richard snickered, undeterred. "Did you get that pic I sent you?"

"Which one? The one with Charlie wearing Deirdre's eyeballs?"

He cackled. "Yeah, that's the one! I'm thinking of having it framed. Don't worry, Charles. I'll print you a copy. I'll get wallet sized."

Lenore started backing out of the room, watching for pieces of Deirdre in her path. Thankfully, no one stopped her, and she could still hear Richard ranting to Paul as she walked into the kitchen for a package of toaster pastries. Apparently, Richard planned to enter several photo contests, and would have calendars made.

What would go great with the toaster pastries? Coffee. Coffee, then a shower. No. A bubble bath. But first coffee. No, first Xanax. Lenore walked down the hall, repeating the sequence in her mind as if it held the combination necessary to diffuse a nuclear time bomb: Xanax, coffee, bubble bath.

Ten minutes later, Lenore sat in the parlor sipping coffee as Paul and Richard entered the room, engaged in heated debate.

"So, let me get this straight," Richard said, spinning to a stop in front of the sofa. "After all the bullshit Charles has put me through, you thought I'd jump at the chance to grant him eternal life? Have I got that straight? Are you out of your mind? When did we start handing out door prizes for fucking me over?"

Paul looked over to Lenore, raising his shoulders in an I-told-so-you fashion. "Just hear me out, Rich. He's done a lot for us over the years. Just give him what he wants and he'll be out of your hair for good. We both know that he probably won't make it."

Lenore met Paul's eyes and nodded encouragingly.

Richard watched their silent exchange with his brow furrowed. Then he smiled, wide eyed, at the two of them. "Well, what do we have here? Could it be? Lenore's in on it! The monkeys have taken over the zoo! Who's idea was this, anyway?"

Paul raised his hand to his temple, as if trying to ward off an impending migraine. "It doesn't *matter*, Rich. It's the best solution. You know I'm not going to give Charles to you. And I'm definitely not going to kill him. Not without giving him a shot."

Richard pointed to Lenore accusingly. "And *you're* okay with this? Charles tried to *kill* you."

She swiveled in her seat, facing Richard head on. *"Think it through, Rich."*

Richard stared at her blankly for several moments. "Why would Lenore be okay with it?" he muttered to himself. And then a wave of realization broke upon his face. "Hey, Paul? Get Charles out of here. Take him back to your place for a while."

"What? Right now?"

"Yeah," Richard replied, still staring at Lenore. "Why don't you give me a chance to think it over. It just occurred to me that this might work after all."

Paul looked surprised to have gotten this far and gaped at his friend, unable to contain his excitement. "Okay, I'll get him out of here right away. You really think you might go for it?"

Richard nodded, shoving his hands in his pockets. "I'm not sure yet, but it isn't like Charles is going anywhere. God knows he won't be able to walk for the next few days."

Loud screams echoed throughout the apartment as Paul popped Charles's limbs back into their sockets.

"Hey, roomie? Can I come in?" Richard whispered, disrupting the sanctity of Lenore's bubble bath. He stood hovering in the doorway, like a child awaiting entrance to his parent's bedroom.

Lenore shooed him away with a loofah. "No!"

"Can I talk to you from right here?"

"Fine. What is it?"

"Paul left with Charles a little while ago. I wanted to talk to you in private about this turning idea. Why are you all for it? What's going on inside that sedated little head of yours?"

"I think you've already figured it out, Rich," Lenore said, closing her eyes and sinking back into the tub.

"We're going to kill Charles, aren't we?" he asked, grinning.

Lenore nodded. "We're going to kill Charles and make it look like an accident. He's probably going to die anyway. Let's make sure that he does."

Richard's grin widened, threatening to surpass the confines of his face. "How?"

"No clue. But I'm sure you'll have fun coming up with a plan."

The grin retreated. "But Paul's going to be here the entire time. How am I supposed to kill Charles right under his nose?"

"How am I supposed to know? You're the murderer, not me."

"Yeah, but I'm not some sort of ninja assassin," Richard replied, shaking his head and taking a step forward. "Christ. If it were that easy to kill Charles, don't you think I would have done it by now?" He walked into the room, gazing at his reflection in the medicine cabinet before approaching the toilet and taking a seat on the lid.

"What happened to talking to me from the doorway?" Lenore exclaimed, drawing the shower curtain up to her waist.

Richard shrugged. "I can't see you from over there, and I want to hear your ideas. Besides," he smiled, "it isn't like I haven't seen you with your shirt off on before."

"Hey, I have an idea." There was a loud splashing as Lenore rested her feet against the spigot.

"What's that?"

"How about you never bring that up to me again?"

Richard giggled. "You had me all excited for a minute there. I thought your idea was going to have something to do with killing Charles."

"I don't have any ideas on that. I guess you can't suck him dry while Paul isn't looking?"

"Paul would absolutely know if I did that."

"Well, I don't know then. Can't you poison him or something?"

"So I thought about that, actually, but Paul would smell poison. You always smell like Xanax, for instance. It's like your calling card. If I poisoned Charles he'd start sweating the odor of whatever I gave him." Richard looked up at the ceiling and smiled. "Hey, roomie? How many Xanax would it take to kill someone? You can overdose on that shit, right?"

"Yeah, but I thought you said Paul would be able to smell it."

"But if *you* were in the room, it would mask the odor. Paul

157

wouldn't necessarily know it was coming from Charles, especially if we got rid of the body right away. I mean, it's not like he's going to order an autopsy or anything."

Lenore shook her head. "No can do, Rich. That would mean I'd have to hang out the entire time, *and* give up half of my pills."

"Aw, come on. Take one for the team."

"Since when are we a *team*?"

"Don't you want to see Charles dead?"

"More than I want to see you dead?"

"Whoa, killer. Pace yourself."

"Fine. Sure I want to see him dead. But that doesn't mean I want to watch a bunch of people die while we pretend to turn him. Paul told me what happens at these things." She made a face. "No thanks."

Richard brought his hands together. "But that's perfect, actually. Don't you see how that's perfect?"

"Not really. No. What's perfect?"

He rose to his feet, placing one hand on each temple like a fortune teller receiving an important message from the spirit world. "It's all coming together. We'll set Charles up in the living room where he can hang out on the couch. Then I'm going to insist that you stay in there to monitor him. That'll definitely sound believable because he's going to get fucking sick. You agree to stay on the condition that you don't have to watch anyone die. I'll generously offer to slaughter the victims in the laundry room so that you don't have to see anything, and bring cups of blood for Charles instead. A couple days in, I make him a very special cup of blood, and he keels over dead."

"Rich, no offense, but it's going to sound like bullshit if you generously offer to do *anything*. Think of another reason the victims stay in the laundry room."

Richard brought a single finger to his lips, thinking. "My rug. I don't want to get my rug dirty."

"That sounds a lot more like you." Lenore ran all of the steps through her mind, looking for holes. "If Charles is drinking blood, hasn't he already been turned? Isn't it too late to kill him at that point?"

"Nah, there's a halfway phase. That's the one that most people don't survive. If we give him a Xanax cocktail at that point, it's sure to do the trick."

"But isn't the blood going to taste funny? Won't he know there's a problem right away?"

Richard chuckled at this, as if the question were absurd. "Lenore, Lenore, Lenore. You have no idea how delicious blood is, especially when you're hungry. He won't have any idea. Goddammit, I'm a fucking genius. This is going to work. Can you feel it?"

"Yes, you're a ninja assassin, Rich. Congratulations."

"Thank you."

Lenore let out of a deep breath. "There should be fifty-seven pills in the bottle on my nightstand. Take thirty five of them, but *leave the rest for me*. And you're on the hook for getting me more when this is over."

"Thanks, roomie," Richard said, getting up. "Don't forget to scrub behind your ears."

Chapter Nine:
The Elegant Solution

Sunday, 11:00 p.m.

Charles slept on the sofa as Paul and Richard laid a tarp over the living room floor.

"What's that for?" Lenore asked, stopping by on her way to the kitchen.

Richard began to secure the lining with duct tape. "Gotta protect the rug," he said. "Can't be too careful."

"I thought no one was dying in here," she said, narrowing her eyes at the room. Upon further inspection, the sofa on which Charles lay appeared to be covered in saran wrap.

"It could still get messy. Charles might throw up, spill blood, shit himself. God only knows what Captain Useless over there might capable of. I'm not taking any chances." Richard threw the roll of tape to Paul, who proceeded to secure the other side. "How many victims were you planning on for this? And where were you going to put them?"

Paul shrugged. "Six? If we tie them up we can store all of them in your laundry room. I was planning on getting some folding chairs or something from the utility closet."

"Folding chairs?" Lenore wrung her hands uncomfortably, looking like she had just swallowed a toad. "You mean you're going to keep people tied up in there for days? Waiting to die?"

Paul nodded, not meeting her eyes. "Buck up, kiddo. This was your idea."

"No. No, that was *not* my idea," she grimaced. "You can't store people alive like that. I thought you'd just get them as needed. I thought you'd make it quick. I can't imagine anything worse than being tied up in that room back there, waiting."

Richard rolled his eyes disdainfully. "What *difference* does it make? They'll be dead soon enough anyway. Why don't you go back to worrying about popping pills and eating toaster pastries, and leave the important details to the grownups in the room?"

Terrible thoughts sprung into her mind. "But how are you going to feed them?" How would they use the bathroom? Would they be able to hear Richard murder them one by one, knowing that there was no way to escape, no way to stop it?

"*Godammit*, Lenore. This isn't a fucking hospice. They don't need to *eat*. I'll see to it that they stay alive until they serve their purpose and that's the end of it."

Paul frowned up at her, having fastened his end. "I told you this was messy business, kiddo. Just stay out of the laundry room. Rich is right—let us worry about it."

Richard eyed Paul skeptically. "So how are you going to get all those people? We're in this mess because you two dumbasses couldn't manage to find me *one* supplement. How are you going to get *six*? Are you just going to snatch people off the street?"

Paul nodded. "Yeah, that was the idea. There's a shelter not too far from here. I don't think it should be too hard to find victims. Just gotta grab 'em when they're alone."

"That's still sounds a bit risky to me."

"It isn't like we can't cover it up."

"Yeah, but I hate asking for favors."

"I'll be careful."

This was not the first time Lenore had heard the two men talk about covering their tracks, but the conversations were always too cryptic for her to decipher exactly how it was done. It sounded like they had a contact somewhere that would help them out if they became accidentally linked to a murder, and she wondered how far up the chain their connections went.

"Hey," Richard whispered to Paul, looking unnervingly cheerful. "You know who we should get? Let's get the litigious Mrs. Grayson down here. Let's take care of that lawsuit once and for all."

Paul shook his head. "Jesus fucking Christ, you're unbelievable. I thought you didn't want to call in a favor on this one."

"That woman is a grade-A cunt. I can't imagine I'm the only person who wants to see her dead."

"She's seventy years old, Rich. How many enemies could she possibly have?"

"Exactly. Who's going to miss her? I've got the key to her apartment. I'll snatch her up later tonight. We *are* doing this all tonight, right? It's going to be a pain in the ass so I'd like to get it over with as soon as possible."

"Yeah, that's fine. It shouldn't take me over a couple of hours to get five people down here. I think you're being a moron pulling that tenant, though. You're going to end up spending more money getting yourself pulled out of that investigation than you were ever going to spend on that piddly lawsuit."

"Oh, but it'll be so worth it. She dies last. I'm taking those back payments out of her ass."

Paul shrugged. "Whatever you say."

Lenore continued on her way to the kitchen, and when she got there she decided to pull all of the food from the pantry and store it under the bar in the living room instead. Anything to avoid passing by the laundry room on future trips. Anything to avoid thinking about the people inside of it, strapped to folding chairs, waiting for Richard to put them out of their misery.

Monday, 3:25 a.m.

Lenore did not look up from painting her toenails as she heard two more people being dragged through the hallway.

Monday, 5:10 a.m.

"*Hey, roomie. Get over here. Pronto.*"

Lenore paused her video game and followed Richard's voice into the foyer. He stood at the entrance, restraining an elderly woman who Lenore could only assume was the litigious Mrs. Grayson. Richard held the woman's head and torso, allowing her arms and legs to flail wildly about in an effort to wrestle free. Red welts lined Richard's face and forearms.

"Meet the bitch who was suing us," he said, ignoring the screams of his captive.

Lenore nodded, confused.

"Now, I thought there was no way this bitch could piss me off more than she already has, but it looks like I underestimated her."

Lenore nodded, still confused.

The old lady screamed, causing Richard to jostle her around like a cat shaking a mouse in its teeth. "Shut the fuck up, will you?" he said to her. "I'm having an important conversation with my roommate over here. Lenore, do you see the watch this bitch is wearing?"

Lenore nodded, no longer confused. The watch looked like it was made of silver, and explained the welts on Richard's face. Good for Mrs. Grayson. She had put up a fight after all.

"Now what I need to you do," Richard continued, "is get the fucking thing off her wrist. I'd ask Paul to help me, but he's off getting lucky contestant number five. And I'd ask Charles to do it, but—no, never mind on that. I wouldn't trust Charles with anything this complicated. You've got to help me out here."

But Lenore did not want to help him out. She did not want to remove Mrs. Grayson's only line of defense against the evil that would torture and eventually kill her. Over the past few months, Lenore often struggled with what she owed Richard's victims, even when she knew there was nothing she could do to save them. Looking at Richard's latest kill, she thought she finally had her answer; she owed them their ability to put up a fight. She owed Mrs. Grayson her silver watch.

Lenore's lips trembled as she backed away from the pair. "No, Rich. I'm not going to help you."

Richard lurched forward, his victim in tow. "What's this? *You never say no to me. Understand? When I tell you to do something, you just fucking do it.*"

Lenore recoiled, meeting Mrs. Grayson's eyes for the first time since stepping into the room. They looked like fear. "Not this time, Rich," she said, shaking her head. "I won't help you. Please don't make me help you."

"Oh, I think I get it," Richard grinned, swaying with the body struggling in his arms. "I've presented you with a moral dilemma. Gosh, I'm so sorry. Well, let me put it to you another way. Either you take that thing off her wrist, or I'm heading in to the kitchen with her so I can *cut her fucking arm off.*" He smirked as Mrs. Grayson screamed at his latest suggestion. "How's that for a moral dilemma, Lenore? What will our pill popping heroine do? The suspense is killing me."

Our pill popping heroine stared at the ground, defeated. Richard would absolutely make good on his threat to cut Mrs. Grayson's arm off. And what's more, he'd probably celebrate the accomplishment by nailing the geriatric appendage to Lenore's door like triumphant Beowulf at the mead hall. "Okay, I'll do it, Rich. Just—just hold her still. I'll get it off."

Lenore approached the pair with caution, fearing the restrained party might kick her in the stomach if she got too close. Mrs. Grayson had stopped fighting, however, and looked at Lenore with a bewildered, terrified expression on her face. Lenore wondered if cows looked the same way when being led to slaughter, never understanding the reason behind their murder.

"Fucking hurry up!" Richard prompted. "Christ. Just grab the damn thing."

Lenore began unhinging the clasp from the wriggling arm beneath her. God, this was horrible business. But what choice did she have? "I'm sorry," she whispered as the watch came free. "Oh God. I'm so sorry."

Richard repositioned his grasp on the woman, saying, "Don't tell that bitch you're sorry. She was suing us! She brought this on herself. Besides, you did her a favor just now." He smiled wickedly. "She should thank you. Would you like me to make her thank you? I'll bet we could get her to thank you."

Lenore stepped back, ignoring him, clutching the item in her palm. "What do you want me to do with the watch, Rich? Paul said you don't like your donors to keep silver around."

"I could give a shit. What are you going to do to me with it? Tell me the time? I'll cut your arm off, too, if I have to." Richard grasped Mrs. Grayson tightly and began walking her forward. "Keep it for all I care, but get out of my way." He shuffled past her saying, "Say no to me again and I'll strap you to a folding chair with the rest of the hors d'oeuvres."

Lenore walked back to her bedroom with the watch in hand. She placed it on the dresser, sliding some nail files out of the way to make room. Sitting on her bed, she stared at it the way that a mathematician might ponder a complex equation on a chalkboard. How might she use the metal to her advantage?

An old conversation sprung into her mind. *Silver's about as dangerous to us as poison ivy.*

Lenore knew of only one way to die from poison ivy. Smoke from the burning plant could trigger a deadly allergic reaction in the lungs. Other than that, it was a nuisance, but harmless. There was certainly no way to get Richard to inhale a wristwatch.

Muffled screaming in the hallway interrupted her train of thought.

"*Hey, roomie. Paul's back with the final victim. We're about to begin.*"

Elena Hearty

Monday, 7:30 a.m.

Lenore entered the parlor holding a crossword anthology, two packets of toaster pastries, and her 18 remaining pills (down from the 22 Richard had left her). Although still relatively immobile, Charles appeared to have recovered substantially over the past twenty-four hours and looked up at Lenore as she entered the room. Saying nothing, she passed him on her way to the wet bar, where Paul stood behind the counter.

He wrinkled his forehead as she dropped her belongings onto the granite surface. "Hey, Rich. Why does she have to hang out for this? Don't you think she'd be more comfortable staying in her room?"

Richard, hovering by the pool table as usual, grabbed a cue from the rack and took a shot at the eight ball. "She's hanging out because if you two retards want to turn Charles then you're going to watch him the whole time and not make a mess. Lenore's going to guard my furniture like her life depends on it because—at the risk of stating the obvious—it does. She can sleep on the floor."

Paul made a face. "I don't want to hurt her if I get hungry, though. I'm not sure this is such a hot idea." He grabbed a glass from behind the bar and set it on the counter. Lenore wondered if he was going to make her a drink.

Eight ball, corner pocket. "You worry too much."

"*I* worry too much?" Paul gestured to the meticulously placed tarp on the floor.

"What's the worst thing that could happen?" Richard asked, brandishing the pool cue like a weapon. "You kill her and find me someone new? Big fucking deal. Now get on with this stupid fiasco before I come to my senses."

"Well, where's the knife?" Paul asked, searching around the bar helplessly. "Where are those bags I brought in from the hardware store?"

"I've told you three times now I put them in the laundry room with all of the other supplies." He placed the cue back on the rack. "Hang on

166

for a second. I'll grab the knife."

With Richard out of the room, Paul leaned forward, saying. "Thanks for helping out, kiddo. Sorry you got dragged into this. Check out what I got for you." Paul reached under the bar and produced a plastic bag filled with club soda, sour mix, maraschino cherries, and several different types of liquors. "When Rich told me he was making you stick around, I figured the least I could do was make you drinks the whole time. I practically bought out the entire store."

Lenore nodded, barely hearing Paul's words, still processing his earlier concern about what might happen when he grew hungry. How much danger had Richard knowingly signed her on for? Best not to think about it. Best to concentrate on other things.

"Is that for me, then?" she asked, motioning to the glass on the counter.

Paul chuckled. "Nope. For once, someone's going to be pouring blood into a glass around here and it isn't going to be you."

Richard returned with a stainless steel pocket knife and handed it to Paul. "All right let's get going here," he said, standing in front of the bar with his arms crossed.

Paul nodded and turned the knife over in his hands a few times before slitting the back of his wrist. Keeping the knife lodged inside the wound, he began siphoning blood into the glass. "This is absolutely the worst part," he said, twisting the blade. "You have to keep the cut open. If you don't—Jesus Christ, this hurts—if you don't, then the blood starts clotting and it heals too quickly. Jesus. I fucking hate this."

Lenore watched the container fill, thinking that Paul's blood didn't look any different from her own. And why would it? Every drop was stolen from an ordinary human being, just like her.

"I think that's enough to start," Richard declared when blood pooled about two inches from the rim. "Give that to him and if he keeps it down you can give him more in a few hours."

Pulling the knife from his arm, Paul concurred. "Yeah, this is plenty to start. I'll have him sip it." He cocked his head toward Lenore, bringing her into their conversation. "This is how you turn someone, kiddo. First we're going to give this to Charles to drink." He gestured toward the cup. "He has to drink it slowly or he'll throw it back up. If that doesn't happen—like Rich just said—I'll give him another glass in a few hours. We'll do this all day. Once he gets my blood into his system, he's going to get really sick, and he'll be thirsty. After that, we'll give him half my blood, half someone else's, and we'll do that for about a day or two. We gradually start tapering off my blood and use the victim's blood more and more. When Charles isn't thirsty anymore, he's been fully turned. Make sense?"

Lenore knitted her brow. "When does he get teeth?" she asked.

Richard snorted. "Those don't come in for a few weeks. This isn't a fucking movie. Real life works slow. His cells are mutating and shit."

Paul snickered, lifting the glass from the counter. "Yeah, Lenore. What a stupid question. Don't you know anything about science? Charles's cells will be 'mutating and shit.' Rich, I think you should have that published in a medical journal or something." He walked over to Charles, who had been silent the entire time, and knelt beside the sofa. "Drink up, buddy," Paul said, bringing the container to Charles's lips.

Charles lifted his head and took a few sips before placing it back down again. The process continued until the vessel was empty.

Monday 12:00 p.m.

Paul garnished his latest creation with a cherry. "This," he said, "is a Sloe Gin Fizz. Let me know what you think."

Lenore took a sip and nodded her head in approval. "I like it. But what's sloe gin? It taste's fruity."

"There's actually something called a sloe berry. I've never seen one, but I know that's what they use to make it."

"Did they have sloe gin back in the twenties?"

He grinned, resting his elbows on the counter. "Oh yeah, sloe gin's been around forever. I didn't just bartend in the twenties, though. I've done it on and off ever since. Helps me keep in touch. I like to stay current."

"I guess it's a good night job."

"Oh, it's ideal. And—I'm telling you—hotel bars are perfect, because you get people who are alone and in from out of town—"

A low moaning came from the sofa. Charles had become a lot more vocal ever since Richard had gone to bed nearly an hour ago. "Shit, man. I feel like I'm burning up or something."

Paul looked at his watch. "Well, you kept down the first drink. I'm going to give you some more. Do you feel okay? Do you feel like you can handle it? You have to be honest with me if you think you're getting nauseous."

"Nah, I can handle it. I'm good."

Paul lifted the knife and brought it to his wrist.

Monday, 5:45 p.m.

"Paul? Hey, Paul? I need some water or something. Paul?"

Lenore looked up from her margarita to see Paul crossing the room to check on his friend. Charles had finished his third ration of blood nearly an hour ago, and his health appeared to be in rapid decline.

Paul placed his hand on Charles's forehead and called out to Lenore. "Hey, can you do me a favor and bring him a glass of water? Get him a little something to eat, too, please."

"I thought you were going to start feeding him blood," she said, stumbling out of her stool. How many drinks had she had at this point? She looked at the myriad empty glasses atop the counter and thought that even if they weren't spinning around, she couldn't possibly count that high.

Paul shook his head. "It's too soon for that. Maybe tomorrow. I don't want to push this too quickly. He's running a temperature."

Lenore smiled inwardly. Good. Perhaps nature would take its

course. Perhaps she and Richard wouldn't have to kill Charles after all. It seemed like a waste of perfectly good Xanax.

She clumsily filled a cup in the sink and fished a package of toaster pastries from underneath the counter. Fighting to maintain balance, she ambled toward where Paul stood by the sofa. "Here," she said, nearly tripping as she placed the items in his arms.

Paul held the water to his friend's mouth. Charles took several sips, but had trouble swallowing. Large drips spilled from his chin and onto the tarp below.

Lenore watched from behind the coffee table, thinking that Charles looked dreadful, even considering the poor condition he was in before they started. Dark bags had formed beneath his eyes, and his cheeks were flushed with fever.

His eyes met hers as he writhed uncomfortably on the sofa. "This is bullshit," he said. "You don't belong here. I'm gonna eat you." He closed his eyes and murmured something under his breath. "Gonna eat you. Gonna eat you first."

Paul shook his head and put the water on the floor beside him. "He's delirious, Lenore. Don't pay him any attention. He doesn't know what he's saying."

Charles jolted his head upwards like a rattlesnake. "Don't be tellin' her that. I know what I'm saying. She don't belong here. I'm gonna replace her with Deirdre."

Paul smiled, humoring him. "Sounds good, Charlie. We'll replace her with Deirdre first thing." He looked over at Lenore. "See? He's completely out of it."

"Gonna eat her. Gonna gobble her up like a snapping turtle."

"Yep, that sounds great, Charlie," Paul said, pulling a toaster pastry from its package. "Here, try to eat this."

Charles started sobbing for no apparent reason and pushed the food away. *"Don't make me put the eyeball in my mouth!"*

Richard walked into the room, chuckling. "Now, where have I heard Charles say that before? Oh, yeah. Back in the laundry room.

170

Those were good times we had the other night, weren't they? Who knew we had the same taste in women?" He pointed to Paul and Lenore with a bemused expression on his face. "Did either of you guys catch that? I said *taste* in women?"

Paul rolled his eyes. "Very punny, Rich."

"Thanks. You should hear my material when I'm wide awake." He glanced at Charles appraisingly. "Isn't there some way to shut him up? I can hear him yapping all the way in my bedroom."

"What do you want me to do, Rich? Put a muzzle on him? He's got a fever. He's hallucinating. He doesn't even know where he is right now."

"Now that you mention it, it wouldn't break my heart if you shoved something in his mouth for a few hours while I went back to bed." Richard started looking around the room, presumably for items that might suit that purpose.

Paul shook his head. "I'm not going to do that. He might choke. Besides, he needs to eat something. Lenore and I need to keep his energy up tonight."

Lenore, who had reached the limits of drunken stoicism, did not care to hear Charles rant about eating her for the remainder of the evening. "Isn't there something we could give him for the fever, then?" she asked. "Can't we give him some aspirin or something? Won't that shut him up for a while?"

Paul and Richard exchanged a knowing eyeful.

"That won't work," Paul said. "The fever's part of it. Or at least I *think* the fever's part of it. The last time we tried to give someone something for the fever, they died a couple hours later. I don't want to try it again."

She wrinkled her nose. "How many times have you done this?"

"Eleven, I think? Eleven times?" Paul said, looking to Richard for confirmation.

"No, twelve. Remember the experiment?"

"Oh yeah. Yeah you're right. Twelve."

"Has it ever worked?" she asked.

"Once," Paul replied. "Our third try worked. We didn't give her anything for the fever, and we kept her fed the whole time. I'm sure we can get it to work again."

Tuesday, 12:00 a.m.

Lenore awoke to a light tapping on her chest and looked up to see Paul standing over her, poking her with a pool cue. She shut her eyes tightly and rolled over on the floor. "Stop bugging me. Let me sleep. I'm still drunk. I want to sleep it off."

Tap. Tap. Tap.

"Oh God. Don't you sleep? Aren't you tired? I thought we both agreed to get some rest."

He poked her again, harder. "Wake up and hang out with me, Miss Toaster Pastry. I can't sleep."

Lenore started rising. "Can't you get Rich hang out with you?"

"I'm working on payroll. Hang out with Paul until I'm through. And keep it down."

Paul shot her a smug grin and helped her to her feet. "I'm afraid you have no choice. I made you another drink, though."

"The last thing I need is another drink."

"This one will wake you up. And it should bring back a few memories. It's what I made you on your first night here."

Lenore walked over to the bar, where she found an Irish coffee waiting for her on the counter. She downed it quickly, enjoying the warm rush of caffeine and alcohol into system. How long had Paul let her sleep? Perhaps four hours at most.

He waited by the pool table, staring at her intently. "Come play a game with me," he said, grabbing another cue from the rack.

"No thanks. I've never been good at pool and I don't really know

172

how to play. Why don't you help me with a crossword? Or—I have an idea—we should bring my television in here. It's going to be a long week and—"

"Leave the television where it is. I'm not rearranging my house for this shit."

"I'll *teach* you how to play," Paul said, waving her over and handing her the stick. "There's nothing to it." He reached into the ball-return and pulled the seven. "Let's work on bank shots."

Yawning, Lenore drunkenly nodded her head as Paul positioned the balls on the table.

"Now what you want to do," he said, "is hit the cue ball and cause the seven to bounce off the cushion and into the corner pocket. Do you think you can do that?"

"I'm probably too drunk to do that, but here goes." Lenore took an unsuccessful shot, causing the balls to disperse chaotically around the table.

"Terrible," Paul chided. "That was horrible."

"I told you I'm too drunk for this. You know it's bad when you *wake up* drunk. I shouldn't have let you talk me into that Long Island."

"Nonsense. I think you're funny when you've had a few. And I don't think that's your problem at all. I think your problem is that you aren't properly motivated. Let's make this interesting. Let's raise the stakes."

"Great," she giggled. "I'll bet you a million dollars that I can land the seven in this pocket over here." She ran her fingers over one of the openings on the side of the table.

"No good. You don't have a million dollars."

"You'll have to take it in installments." She smiled. "You're going to live forever, right? I figure I'll give you five dollars a week and we'll eventually get there."

Paul chuckled, shaking his head. "That's some very creative bookkeeping, but I think I'll pass. I don't want a million dollars. How 'bout we do this instead? How 'bout I kill you if you don't make that shot?"

They stared at each other for a moment and both burst out laughing.

"Deal," she said, taking aim. The ball fell into the hole. "Holy shit! Did you see that? Did you see it? I'm fucking awesome."

Paul gave her a high five. "See? You just never had a reason to be good at pool before."

"Imagine the time I've wasted."

He reached underneath the table and placed another ball on the surface. "I think you're getting the hang of it. Let's try one more time, double or nothing."

Lenore nodded and once again took aim. The ball landed to the side of the pocket. "Oh that sucks," she said, watching it roll to a stop. "I think I know the problem, though. This is the five ball. Where's the seven? I was a lot better at the seven."

"Who said you got another shot at this?" Paul asked, snickering, moving toward her.

Lenore retreated playfully, feeling the Irish coffee coursing through her veins. "That doesn't count. I'm citing faulty equipment. The entire wager's been compromised."

"A bet's a bet, Lenore. And you lost. It's time to pay up." Paul grew fangs.

"Pay up?" She stepped backward as Paul grabbed her by the wrist.

"Yeah," he said, pulling her toward him, "and I'm afraid I don't accept installments." He brought her wrist to his mouth.

And pretended to bite into it.

They both howled with laughter as he let her go. Lenore wobbled unsteadily, and Paul caught her, placing his arm around her shoulders.

"Okay, Toaster Pastry," he grinned. "Next time it's for real. Next time—"

"There won't be a next time," Richard said, standing in the

174

doorway. "What exactly is going on here?"

"We're just hanging out, Rich. Charles is still sleeping and—"

"You are *not* just hanging out. Let go of her right now."

Paul broke away from Lenore, who, in her intoxicated state, leaned against the pool table instead. He glared at his friend. "Jesus, Rich. What's the problem?"

"When's the last time you ate? How many glasses have you given Charles at this point?"

"He's had four. I haven't eaten yet, but I was just about to."

"No shit, you're about to." Richard gestured to Lenore.

Paul's jaw fell open. "No. It wasn't anything like that. I wasn't going to *touch* her, Rich. I swear. I wouldn't do that. She's my buddy."

"I didn't say you were going to do it on purpose, but you need to go eat. This is how accidents happen."

"I wasn't going to touch her, honest."

"And I'm *keeping* you honest. Get out of here. Your dinner's waiting in the laundry room. Sorry it isn't all young and cute and pliable like my roommate over here."

Paul headed out of the room, raising his arms in irritation. "You've got the wrong idea, Rich."

"I'm sure I do," Richard said, calling after him.

He turned his attention to Lenore, crossing his arms paternally. "So maybe you were too drunk to notice—or care—but Paul had fangs just now. What have I told you about fangs? We only grow them when we're getting ready to *bite into something, stupid.* You need to be more careful. Paul gets very touchy-feely with his victims, and don't let him trick you into believing it's all in fun. He'll joke around about eating you before he actually does it. I know you guys are pals, but he isn't your pal when he's starving like this. Understand?"

Lenore clutched her wrist where Paul had grabbed it, sobered and embarrassed at her naiveté. "Yeah, I understand."

"So that's good. That's good for both your sakes. Paul doesn't *want*

175

to hurt you. He's been really concerned about that, as a matter of fact, and he's been making you all those drinks to keep your heart rate down."

Lenore nodded, astounded that Paul's lighthearted diversion was really a security measure designed to keep her alive.

"But you need to take some responsibility here as well," Richard continued. "Don't play around with him like that. Not when he's low on blood. It isn't safe. I mean, you don't stick your head in a tiger's mouth even when you think—"

"You can save the analogy, Rich. I know what you guys are."

"Never forget it," he said, walking back into the hall.

Paul reemerged an hour later, the front of his shirt soaked with blood. He stopped by the sofa to check on Charles before taking a seat next to Lenore at the bar. "I was just messing around earlier. You know that, right? You know I wasn't going to hurt you, right?"

"I know," Lenore lied. "I believe you."

"It would really bother me if you didn't. I promised you wouldn't die for this, and I'm going to follow through." He looked down at his hands. "But all the same, Rich is right. Stay away from me when I'm hungry."

"You were going to kill me, weren't you?"

He shrugged, not meeting her eyes. "I don't know what I would have done, to be honest."

"*Told you.*"

Tuesday, 4:00 a.m.

"Water. I need some water, Paul."

"Hey, Lenore? Would you bring Charles some water?"

Lenore filled a glass in the sink and walked it over to them.

Charles took a sip and then spit it out. "That don't taste right," he said. "Bitch is trying to poison me."

176

Lenore smiled. How little did he know.

Paul shook his head. "There's nothing wrong what she gave you, Charlie boy. You just can't drink it anymore. You're ready for blood. I'll tell Rich to go get you some."

Tuesday, 4:45 a.m.

Richard garnished his latest creation with a cherry.

"Why are you decorating that cup, Rich?" Paul asked from the sofa. "Just bring it over. Charles is thirsty over here."

"Because I want you to know exactly how stupid this looks." He added two more cherries to the rim as if each one served as a delicate counterbalance. "Christ. I even *feel* stupid doing this. Lenore, on a scale from one to ten, ten being balls-to-the-wall-retarded, how stupid does this look?"

Lenore did not lift her eyes from the puzzle before her. "Rich, remember the last time you asked me to pick a number between one and ten? Remember how I don't like to play that game?"

Richard carried the glass with him to the sofa, saying, "You're no fun, Lenore. I should have given the job to Stacy." When he reached the couch, he handed the beverage to Paul. "So we're doing half and half today? You're going to bleed yourself the next time he needs to be fed?"

Paul nodded wearily. "Yeah. What's bothering me, though, is that the fever isn't going down. I'm not sure he should have any more of my blood until it does. I might keep him on regular blood for the first half of the day and see how he does with it. What do you think?"

"I think it's up to you. He's kept everything down so far, though, and that's the important thing." Richard winked at Lenore as he said this. She raised her eyebrows inquisitively in return, silently questioning whether or not the bedizened cup contained their secret sauce. Richard shook his head; it didn't.

Wednesday, 3:25 a.m.

Lenore polished off her screwdriver. "Okay, your turn," she said to Paul. "Have you got one?"

"Yeah, I've got one. Go."

"Animal, vegetable, or mineral?"

"Animal."

"Is it a person?"

"Yes. One."

She narrowed her eyes at him and smiled. "Is that person in the apartment?"

"Yes," he laughed. "Two."

"Oh, will you guys please shut up?" Richard said, folding his laptop and placing it on the bar. "Christ. It's like stupid in stereo." He eyed the patient on the sofa. "Hey Charles? How are you feeling?"

Charles did not answer. It occurred to Lenore that she had not heard him speak to Richard directly since losing Deirdre. She could not ascertain whether his silence was due to anger, fear, hatred, or possibly some combination of the three.

"I asked how you were feeling, douche bag," Richard pressed, walking toward him. "Are you ready for more blood?"

Paul followed behind. "Don't push it Rich. He just had some an hour ago."

"I'm not pushing it. I'm just fucking *asking him a question*. What's wrong with that?"

Charles's forehead glistened with sweat. "Yeah. I'll take some."

"See?" Richard said, vindicated. "He says he'll take some. I'll go get it for him." He caught Lenore's gaze from across the room and nodded to her.

She took a deep breath and nodded back. It was show time.

Richard left for the laundry room and came back holding large glassful of blood, which he handed to Charles directly. Both Lenore and Richard watched with keen interest as he consumed its contents.

When Charles was finished, he looked up at Richard and said, "Thanks, man."

Richard smiled back at him. "Don't mention it."

Fifteen minutes later, Charles was asleep, and Richard hovered over him, gleefully tussling the other man's hair. "Aw, look at him, Lenore. He's so cute when he's sleeping."

She stood next to Richard with her arms folded, anxiously awaiting Charles's final breath. "Adorable."

"I wonder what he's dreaming about."

"Probably killing me. That's all he's talked about today."

"You've got to admire his focus."

"Leave him alone, guys," Paul said from the bar. "Stop touching his head like that, Rich. Jesus. Just let him sleep. Give him some space."

Charles moaned and twisted at the sound of Paul's voice. "Ugh. Oh, man. Shit. Paul? I ain't feeling so good. Y'all are all fuzzy."

Richard scowled at him. "Was that even English?"

Charles angled his head toward the floor, gagging. "Shit, man. Paul? Paul. Shit, Paul. I think I'm gonna throw up."

Lenore and Richard looked at each other, horrified.

"Oh, no you don't," Richard said, suddenly alarmed. "You need to keep this down. I swear to God I will fucking kill you if you throw up in my living room. Just close your eyes and go back to sleep."

Charles began heaving.

"*Goddamn*, Charles. Don't you fucking throw up on me. Don't you do it. Got to swallow that shit back down. Do you hear me?"

Red liquid projected from Charles's mouth and landed on the tarp below.

Richard, in a state of panic, placed his hand over Charles's mouth, but was unable to stop the deluge. Sensing that his initial approach was doomed to failure, Richard then tried to scoop vomit from the floor and shove it back down the other man's throat, causing Charles to gag uncontrollably.

Lenore watched Richard's last ditch efforts with a sense of detached disappointment. How could someone who took lives on a regular basis possibly be this bad at murder? And why had they not accounted for this scenario? What was the backup plan? She fingered the ten remaining Xanax in her pocket, realizing that even if she were willing to sacrifice the rest of her pills, they would not be enough to accomplish the task.

The string of profanity that erupted from Richard's mouth was unhindered by either logic or restraint. Charles was a dog, his mother was a cunt, his father was some sort of cunt as well, and the whole family evidently took it up the ass. Unfortunately, Charles had fallen back asleep, missing out on some truly imaginative details regarding his grandparents and incestuous second cousins.

"And they called their act, The Aristocrats!" Paul said, walking over with a roll of paper towels.

He wadded several sheets together and started mopping up the mess, but paused a moment later, eying the liquid on the tarp with skepticism. "Hey Rich, what's going on here? What are those white specs?"

Lenore and Richard watched in stunned silence as Paul grabbed one of the larger bits between his thumb and forefinger and placed it on his tongue. He gawked at the two of them. "This is Xanax! Did you guys crush up a bunch of Xanax and put it in Charlie's drink? You did, didn't you?"

Richard shrugged indifferently. "Let's not make a huge deal out of this."

"You don't want me to make a huge deal out of this?"

"He's fine, isn't he? I mean, it's not like it worked or anything."

Paul shook his head in amazement. "You two are unbelievable."

Lenore opened her mouth to speak.

But Paul cut her off. "Don't even look at me right now. I *know* you had something to do with this. My promise is off. If we run out of bodies, you're fair game. You'd better be out of this room the next time I'm hungry."

"Now hang on just a minute," Richard said. "You can't call dibs on her like that."

"Can't I? You just tried to kill Charles, so she's no longer off limits. If *anything* happens to Charlie at this point—if he doesn't make it for *any* reason—she goes to me." He looked directly into Lenore's eyes. "And I'm killing her."

She winced at his words, but then bit her lower lip and nodded. "I'm not sorry, Paul. I'd do it again." She turned to leave. "I'm going back to my room, Rich. I don't think you need me anymore."

"Well, I hope you like it there," Paul called behind her. "Because that's where you're going to spend the rest of your life."

Thursday, 11:00 p.m.

Lenore was staring at the watch on her dresser when she heard a knock at the door. Her heart raced. Perhaps Charles had died and Paul had come to collect his compensation. It was impossible to tell for sure. Once inside her bedroom, the events in the parlor amounted to nothing more than indecipherable noises in the hallway. Either way, it looked like she was about to get an update.

"Come on in."

The door swung open and Richard stepped in the room. "How are you doing in here?"

"I'm decent. How's Charles?"

"He hasn't thrown up again since you left. I don't get it. Out of all the drinks we gave him...it's uncanny." Richard took a deep breath. "It looks like he's in the clear at this point. Just my luck, huh? That's good news for you, though, considering I was going to have to hand you over to Paul if he died. I thought you might like to know."

"Thanks, Rich."

He nodded, furrowing his brow. "How many Xanax do you have

left, by the way?"

"Six." She lifted six fingers. "I've taken a few."

"You're going to start having seizures again. That isn't enough to taper, is it?"

"No. I guess I just didn't think I'd live long enough for it to matter."

Richard pursed his lips and pulled a bottle of pills from his pocket. "I'm probably going to regret doing this, but here," he said, throwing the container onto the bed. "Paul brought these with him on Sunday. He must have forgotten to give them to you, because I found them at the bottom of one of the bags from the hardware store. You'd better start tapering, though. Either that, or you'll need to find yourself a new drug dealer."

"I know."

They both turned to the sound of yelling in the hallway.

"I'm still hungry, man," Charles said, his voice getting closer.

"You couldn't be *that* hungry," Paul replied. "You finished off the final victim only two hours ago. When I eat that much, I'm good for days. It's all in your head."

Charles appeared behind Richard in the doorway, and Lenore was immediately aware of the transformation that had taken place. She watched his long limbs sway with unnatural fluidity as he stared at her, licking his lips. "You said if we ran out of bodies she was fair game."

Lenore clutched her blanket, paralyzed with fear. There was nowhere to run inside the tiny bedroom. There was no protection from the greedy monster lurking at the door.

Paul stepped in front of his friend. "Charlie, let's get out of here. Forget about Lenore. She's going to spend the rest of her life rotting in this little room until Rich finally decides to eat her. What could you possibly do to her that's worse than that?"

"Bitch tried to kill me, man."

Lenore swallowed. So he knew. He knew about the poison. Perhaps

Paul had told him, or perhaps Charles had not been sleeping as soundly as she'd thought. Did it make a difference? Horrible consequences filled her mind.

"I know," Paul said. "And she'll suffer for it, believe me. I'm not helping her anymore."

Richard sneered at Paul. "I don't fucking believe this. Who do you think you are, anyway? You think Lenore's going to suffer without your help? I think that's unlikely. I think she's got more balls than you and your pussy friend put together, and she's going to be just fine without you. *You're* the one who's going to suffer. You should have traded her for Charles when you had the chance, because now you're fucked. Now you're stuck with that mascara wearing freak for the rest of your life, and I think it's time you got it out of my apartment."

Paul stood in silence, his eyes shifting anxiously between Charles and Lenore.

Richard clapped his hands, walking toward him. "What are you waiting for? A restraining order? *Get out of my house!*"

Chapter Ten:
The Encore

The universe had grown colder now that Lenore had fallen out of Paul's favor. In the weeks that followed, she found that even the little things she had taken for granted, such as their conversations in the hallway, had faded into the realm of bittersweet memory. Now he would not even look at her as he passed by, and Lenore found herself longing for their friendship, not caring anymore if it had ever been real in the first place.

And it was lonely. It was lonely to listen to Paul talk to Richard from the seclusion of her bedroom. It was lonely to hear him leave, knowing that he would never again take her with him. And when the pantry was bare, it was lonely to think that there was no one in the world who cared enough to buy her groceries.

Lenore stepped into the library. "Hey, Rich?"

Richard did not look up from the computer. "Yeah?"

"I need food," she said, walking over to examine his baseball card collection. "I haven't eaten in two days. Did you get the notes I left you?"

He placed his laptop down and turned to her. "Yeah, I got them. I've just been busy is all. Mrs. Grayson's turned out to be a much bigger pain in the ass than I'd expected. It's like that bitch is still irritating me from beyond the grave. Her son's claiming I threatened her before she went missing. Can you believe that shit?"

"That you threatened a seventy year old woman in public? Absolutely."

Richard smiled. "Oh Lenore, what you must think of me. Why didn't you tell Paul you were out of food when he was here yesterday? You know that going to the store really isn't my thing."

The words that emerged from Lenore's lips were tinged with unexpected emotion. "Because he's still mad at me," she said, tears forming in her eyes. "He isn't going to go to the store for me. He won't even speak to me. He—"

Richard raised his hand in the air for silence. "You think you're the only person on the outs with Paul? You think he's talking to me about anything besides work these days? He'll come around, though. He always does. You two morons will be playing twenty questions together again in no time, I promise."

But Lenore doubted that. Paul had trusted her, and she betrayed him, even after he had gone out of his way to save her life. There would be no reconciliation. There would be no more trips to the grocery store, or outings to the diner, or zombie movies in the penthouse. There would only be Richard. Richard, and the muted television to keep her company. "Rich, you can't let me starve to death while you wait for him to come around."

"That's ridiculous. You aren't going to starve *to death*. It takes something like thirty days to starve *to death*, and you're only on day two. All right? So chill out and eat some Xanax. Why don't you make yourself a cup of coffee or something?"

"We're out of coffee. We don't even have—"

"Oh for Christ's sake just stop talking. I'll go to the store, okay? I'll go. But you might have to wait a few more days. Now get out of here and stop bugging me. I have a lot of shit to print out before I meet with the lawyer at ten. Maybe I'll stop and get you something on the way back."

"Thanks, Rich."

"I told you to stop talking."

Lenore walked back to her room and sat on the bed. She hungrily eyed the canister of Flintstones vitamins on the nightstand, tempted to consume its entire contents for sustenance. What was the worst thing that could happen? According to the warning on the back of the label, the worst thing involved poison control and a trip to the emergency room. She chewed three tablets, thinking that if she were going to overdose on anything, it would be on her beloved Xanax instead; a fitting end to their tragic love affair.

And that idea was quickly entering the realm of possibility. Because Richard wasn't about to get her more food. He would let her starve to death, not out of malice, but sheer carelessness, like a seven year old forgetting to feed a goldfish.

The front door closed in the distance. Perhaps there was still hope. Perhaps Richard would return with food after all.

Did it even matter? Eventually he would grow tired of the biweekly chore. Eventually he would replace her with someone else, someone easier, someone who hadn't alienated Paul.

Suicide, starvation, or death at Richard's hands. The future swelled with morbid possibility.

Lenore shook her head, hating her options. There had to be another card to play. There had to be some other permutation. There had to be a perfect universe. There had to be an escape.

The silver watch winked at her from across the room.

What are you going to do to me with it? Tell me the time?

Silver's about as dangerous to us as poison ivy.

Poison ivy is only deadly when inhaled.

How could she get Richard to inhale a wristwatch? If only Mrs. Grayson had happened to have a bag of powdered silver on her instead. Now that would have been useful.

The silver watch, laying next to several industrial strength nail files, winked at her from across the room.

But would it work? Lenore's pulse quickened as she approached the dresser. Excitedly, she picked up a file and started grinding it against the chain links. The metal would not yield.

She needed more leverage. Items in hand, she entered the bathroom and placed the watch along the edge of the sink. Then, pushing all of her weight against the file, she slid it along the silver timepiece. After several tries, a small pile of dust began to form beneath her effort.

Lenore ran her thumb along the metal shavings. The filings did not appear fine enough to reach Richard's lungs as she had originally hoped, but perhaps they would still wreak sufficient damage if blown in his face. And any weapon was better than no weapon at all. She would be able to render her captor helpless, if only for a short while.

But where would she store the powder? It would need to contained, obviously, and accessible at a moment's notice. Her eyes wandered to an empty Xanax bottle in the medicine cabinet. Perfect.

Lenore kept an eye on the clock as she pulverized Mrs. Grayson's final fuck-you. She allowed herself to work until 11:30, by which time the watch was three quarters diminished and a respectable amount of particulate filled the receptacle. Richard would probably be home any moment.

And that was a problem because silver specs lined Lenore's hands, hair, clothes and the rest of the bathroom. She would have to act fast. Lenore removed all of her garments and stashed them, along with what was left of the wristwatch, inside the sink cabinet for later disposal. Then she mopped the floor with a paper towel before stepping into the shower to rid her own body of the residue.

As Lenore stood underneath the running water, she pictured the front door, and herself running through it. But it was always bolted shut. If she attacked Richard while it was still locked, she risked being trapped in the apartment with a very angry vampire. She would have to time it just right; she would have to strike the moment he walked through the door.

When Lenore exited the shower, she went through her clothes in an effort to find a decent outfit.

Because she was getting out of the apartment that night.

When the front entrance opened again later that evening, Lenore stood at the other side, her hand poised on the crude chemical weapon in her pocket.

But she hesitated when Charles walked over the threshold instead.

She stepped backwards as he locked the door. And now it was too late to use the silver. Now it was too late, period.

"Ah, look whose heart's racing," he said, a cigarette dangling from his mouth. "I'll bet you weren't expecting to see me."

"Y-you're not allowed to smoke in here," she replied, her mind running on autopilot.

Charles smiled. "Oh, that's right." He threw the cigarette to the ground and stomped it out on the marble tiles. Richard would be furious. "Hey, you know what? I just remembered something." Charles grabbed another cigarette from his pocket. "I don't give a shit."

She nodded, watching him exhale a stream of smoke through his nose. This was bad. This was very bad. What other things did Charles no longer give a shit about?

"Why don't you have a seat, sweetheart?" Charles gestured to the shoe bench. "I've been doing an awful lot of thinking about you lately. I've just been itching for a chance for us to be alone together."

Lenore did not move.

So Charles grabbed her by the arm and shoved her into place. "I told you to take a load off, honey." He stood back and looked at her, cocking his head to the side. "Yeah, that's about right. You know what this reminds me of? Oh, wait. Hang on. Something's missing." He came to sit beside her. "Okay, *now* do you know what this reminds me of? Remember the last time we sat next to each other like this?"

She cringed as he ran his hand along her thigh.

"Dinner theater!" he announced at last. "Those were good times, huh? And, man! You were such a good player. Cool, calm and collected, that was you. Paul still talks about it, you know. He says to me, he says, 'Charlie, the reason Lenore's stayed alive so long is she refuses to *act* like food. She don't get scared,' he says. I think he's wrong, though. I'll bet you do get scared."

He brought his cigarette dangerously close to her ear. "I'll bet you're scared right now. Aren't you, honey?"

She turned away from him. "Rich is going to be back any minute. And he's going to be pissed. He's going to rip your—"

"Rich ain't gonna do shit," Charles said, standing. "And he *ain't* gonna be back any minute. He and Paul are off at some 24-hour grocery store buying more toaster pastries for your scrawny ass." He chuckled. "I hope they keep the receipt."

Lenore looked at the ground, strangely happy to hear that Paul was still looking out for her. "What do you want from me, Charles?"

"What do I *want* from you? I just want to talk. I just want to hang out with you like Paul used to do. Why else would I be here?" He lifted his hand to his mouth in mock realization. "Now, Lenore, you don't think I'm still mad because you tried to kill me, do you? I certainly hope not. It would be awful immature of me to hold a grudge like that." He grinned wickedly. "Still, though, come to mention it, it would mean the world to me if you told me you were sorry. I think that would really clear the air between the two of us."

Lenore remained silent. Third grade retorts went through her mind, such as "*I'm sorry you didn't die from that drink we gave you*" and "*go fuck yourself.*"

"That's okay," he said, chuckling softly to himself. "Sometimes it takes a while to realize what you done wrong. As I recall, I didn't apologize to you until Rich had me do some hard thinking in the laundry room. Maybe you need to do some hard thinking as well. Realize the error of your ways."

"Charles, please," she whispered. "You got what you wanted. What could I possibly do to you anymore?"

189

"Aw, now don't sell yourself short like that, honey. I think there's a lot of fun we can still have together." He exhaled contemplatively. "It's too bad you never got to know my ex-girlfriend, Deirdre. I'll bet you two would have gotten on. You wanna know what Rich did to her that night?"

Lenore shook her head. She did not want to know.

Charles smiled. "He started off real easy with her. He sat her down, just like you're sitting down right now. And he asked her to pick a number between one and ten." Lenore squirmed as Charles tapped the ashes from his cigarette onto her knee. "At first, she didn't want to pick a number. That's why I think y'all would've gotten on, see. She wasn't much for games, neither. But eventually, Rich talked her into it. Wanna know how?"

"No," Lenore replied, bracing herself.

"Did you ever wonder what happened to that pack of Marlboro Lights you left in the laundry room that night?"

Lenore shook her head. She had never given it a second thought.

"Rich used 'em up. Yes siree. He took one out." Charles pulled another smoke from his pocket. "Then he lit it up." Charles, still smoking his first cigarette, placed the second in his mouth and ignited it. He muttered with both of them between his lips. "Then he told Deirdre that he was gonna start putting it on her arm."

Trembling, Lenore pulled her arms behind her back. She slid herself as far as she could against the bench and stiffened, as if she might become part of the furniture.

"Now, don't be scared," Charles laughed, readying the fiery stick in his hand. "This couldn't hurt all *that* bad because she still wasn't screaming even after a few go rounds. What I want to know is whether you'll last as long as she did." He knelt on the ground before her. "Now, do you think you could roll up your sleeves for me, sweetheart?"

"Go fuck yourself." Third grade was making a comeback.

"Hah. You sound just like Deirdre just now. Let me see if I can remember what Rich said to her. Oh, yeah. I think he told her that if she didn't roll up her sleeves, he'd put the cigarette out on her face. Does that sound about right to you? That sounds like something that Rich would say, don't it?"

Lenore's hands shook as she gathered her sleeves away from her forearms.

"That's more like it," Charles grinned. "Now, here's where Rich's game got interesting. Like I said earlier, he told Deirdre to think of a number between one and ten. But if she got it wrong, he'd make up the difference on her arm. Does that sound like a fair game to you? He told her it was important she really tried to get the number just right, because when he ran out of room on her arm he was going for her face after all. And when he ran out of room on her face, he was going for her eyes."

Charles's words sent a wave of nausea throughout Lenore's body, and for the first time in two days she was glad she hadn't eaten anything. So this was what it felt like to be one of Richard's less privileged victims. Helpless. Helpless and terrified.

Lenore looked at the front door with longing. Perhaps she was never destined to pass through it again. But perhaps that was no longer the objective. A new, much simpler, objective had emerged. *Hurt Charles. Fight him off. Take that vial of silver and shove it up his ass.*

"Aw, I'll bet that exit's looking pretty good to you about now," Charles said, following her gaze. "It's always been in the way, hasn't it?" He dangled his keys in front of her. "Betcha wish you had these."

Slowly, Lenore moved her hand toward her pocket.

"Yep, Paul ought to be more careful where he leaves these things," Charles said, gloating. "They were just right out in the open, right out on his kitchen counter, where anyone could take them. It's a good thing they didn't fall into the wrong hands."

Ever so slowly, Lenore slipped her hand inside, clutching the bottle of silver in her palm.

And Charles noticed. "What you got in there, cutie pie? You got something for me? Can I see?"

She froze.

"Come on, now. You can show me." He pulled the container from her pocket and turned it over in his hands. "Well, well, well. Xanax! Why am I not surprised? Now what would you want to take this shit for? Am I making you nervous or something?" He frowned at her condescendingly. "Now, Lenore, I think it's time for an intervention. I just wouldn't be able to live with myself for another moment if I thought I was aiding and abetting this little habit of yours." Charles threw the bottle across the room.

Lenore let out a little whine and she watched it roll to a stop by the coat rack. "When Rich comes back he's going to—"

"We've covered this already, cupcake. He's an hour away at some crack-head grocery store. His cheap ass is probably buying your toaster pastries in bulk. And I'll bet he don't even get you name brand. I'll bet he's going with generic." He leaned toward her. "Now are you gonna pick a number for me?"

She clenched her jaw. What would happen if she didn't pick a number? Charles would go for her face. Oh God. He would go for her face. Lenore unconsciously brought her hand to her cheek. "Five."

Charles slapped his knee. "Now, I knew a clever girl like you would go with five. I knew it right off the bat because that's just what Deirdre did. Rich knew she'd pick five, too, so I guess that's why he went with ten."

Lenore whimpered as he grabbed her arm in his hand.

And she screamed as he held the lit cigarette against her wrist.

"Woo hoo! Let it out, girl! I didn't peg you to scream right away. Deirdre, God bless her, she made it to three without even breathing heavy. I don't think she actually started wailing 'til Rich made it up past her elbow." He met her eyes and winked at her. "Four more, now, and then you get another turn."

Charles reignited the butt and brought it back to her skin.

And he smiled when she screamed a second time.

"You know what just occurred to me? It occurred to me you're

192

learning a valuable lesson here. You got any idea what that lesson might be?"

She quivered in his grasp, feeling like a mouse caught by its tail.

"Empathy," he smirked, releasing her. Charles stood up and took a long drag on his cigarette. "Now, all these years, I just thought Rich was sick in the head for torturing people. After all, Paul doesn't really do that. He don't approve of that sorta thing." He blew the puff of smoke at her. "But now I been turned, I kinda see where Rich is coming from. Gets me all juiced up to hear your heart going pitter-pat like this."

Charles came to sit beside Lenore and ran his hand underneath her shirt. He placed his fingers over her heart. "I'll bet no one's ever told you that you were beautiful, have they, sweetheart?"

When Lenore closed her eyes, tears ran down her cheeks.

"Well, let me be the first to tell you, Lenore. You're beautiful to me right now."

Lenore replied through gritted teeth. "Well, you're still ugly as shit."

Charles's lips formed into an "O" as he pulled away from her. "Girl, you got a mouth on you, that's for sure. We should probably fix that. Can't have you talking trash this whole time." Then he sprung back toward her, steadying her head with one hand, and bringing the lit cigarette toward her mouth with the other. "Open up, cutie pie. Let me see that sharp tongue of yours."

Breathing heavily through her nose, Lenore gathered the fluids in her mouth.

And spat them onto the cigarette, extinguishing the tiny fire at the end.

Her tormenter cackled as he pulled another from the pack. "Well, aren't you clever? You know what? I'll bet you're getting pretty bored with this game. You're probably itching for some higher stakes. Am I right? Maybe I'll make up my own game just for you. How 'bout you pick a number, and if you get it wrong, I just go directly for that left eye of yours? How 'bout that?"

Lenore closed her lids tightly, determined not to pick a number, determined not to give Charles the satisfaction. He would be making for her eyes no matter what she said, and she might as well get it over with. Once he was finished, he would definitely kill her. And that was something to look forward to. That was the prize.

The sound of the lighter flickered in the background, and Lenore could hear Charles pull air into the flame.

"You wanna pick a number for me now?"

Silence.

"Aw, that's okay. Deirdre stopped picking numbers after a while too, you know. I guess she thought it didn't make no difference in the end. That's when Rich started making me pick the numbers instead. And I'll be damned if I didn't guess wrong every time."

A terrible heat radiated next to her cheek.

"Now this'll only hurt for a minute," he said, wiping the tears away from her eye with his thumb.

Lenore tensed and held her breath.

And then the front door opened.

"What the fuck is going on here?"

She peered through half shut eyes to see Richard standing in the doorway, holding a takeout bag from Burger King.

And the front door was wide open.

Richard dropped the bag to the ground. "Charles, what the hell are you doing in my house? How did you get in here?"

"Welcome home, Rich," Charles said, spinning around. "I figured I'd keep Lenore some company while you were away. She seemed awful lonesome when I found her. I thought I'd cheer her up. Play a game with her."

Richard glowered at him with his arms crossed. "You disgusting little motherfucker. Are you smoking in here? What are you doing to Lenore?" His face sobered as he spotted the burns on her arm. "Oh, bad move, Charles. I hope you enjoyed your little taste of immortality because I'm going to—"

"What? You're gonna do *what,* exactly? All those years I spent running around for you and Paul—all that shit's coming to a stop. Now I figure you owe me for Deirdre, and I'm taking what's mine."

Lenore shifted in her seat.

"You keep your ass where it is," Charles hissed. "You ain't going nowhere."

"Don't listen to him, Lenore. Go to your room."

Richard and Charles stood head-to-head. They appeared to be sizing each other up.

And the front door was wide open.

Lenore remained where she sat, staring intently at the bottle by the coat rack.

"I told you to get out of here," Richard said, not taking his eyes off Charles.

"You stay where you are," Charles said, not taking his eyes off Richard.

Then Richard shoved Charles. "Oh, that is fucking *it. I've had it!* I'm the only one who tells Lenore what to do. Got that? Now, I never liked you before you were turned, and I sure as shit don't like you any better now. You get the hell out of here or you'll be joining that slut girlfriend of yours in my furnace."

But Charles wasn't moving. "All this over that skinny bitch over there? This is bullshit, man. Just *give* her to me. Do you have any idea how many of my girlfriends you've killed over the years? I've given them *all* to you! You've gotten *everyone.* You've made me watch!" There was agony in Charles's voice, and in that moment, Lenore pitied him. "Now you fucking owe me. You owe me Lenore and I'm going to have myself a real good time with her."

Richard spat. "I don't owe you shit, Charles. You would have sold your own mother down the river for those pointy teeth of yours. You can't have Lenore. Get over it and go home."

"How are you gonna make me, Rich? You gonna rip my arms out of their sockets again? You really think you can kick my ass now we're on even ground?"

And when Charles said this, Lenore realized that he hadn't really come down to see her in the first place.

And Richard must have realized the same thing. "Well, look who came to pick a fight. Charles, we will never be on even ground because you are a fucking cockroach. And as far as kicking your ass goes, I think I'll be just fine—I've had a lot of practice—but thank you for your concern." Richard walked over to the coat rack and picked it up like it was a toothpick, causing the Xanax bottle to roll around on the floor below. He raised the pole in the air, smiling. "Now, this might sting a little."

Charles ducked with superhuman agility to avoid Richard's stroke. He pulled a dagger from his pocket.

"Oh, how original," Richard laughed. "Are we taking self defense lessons from Angela now? It's too bad you never got a chance to talk to her before she died because I think she would have told you that silver isn't all it's cracked up to be. At least she would have told you that if I hadn't ripped her tongue out of her mouth."

Lenore rose from where she sat.

Richard took another swing at Charles with the coat rack, and managed to hit him squarely on the jaw. Charles was down for a moment, but soon rebounded, coming at Richard again with the knife in hand. From what Lenore could tell, Charles appeared to be hopelessly outmatched; a six inch blade against a six foot pole. How on earth would he ever manage to strike a blow?

As if to answer this question, Charles slid across the floor on his knees, running the dagger into Richard's shin.

Lenore started moving toward the container on the floor.

Richard cried out in pain. "You're going to regret that, Charles." He shook the wounded leg as if it suffered from a muscle cramp.

196

Charles's jaw had begun to swell, and he produced a lopsided smile. "I've been dreaming of doing that ever since I was seventeen years old."

Lenore bent over to retrieve the bottle.

Richard nodded, taking a deep breath. "You've been hiding behind Paul like a little bitch ever since you were seventeen years old, and it's too bad he isn't here to protect you." He began whirling the rack around like a baton. "Because you are so fucked, my friend. I can think of all sorts of creative ways to drag out your death now that you've been turned. I can't wait to watch your skull cave in. I can't wait to break every bone in your body." Richard took a swing at Charles and missed. "And when your bones heal, I'll break them again." He took another swing at Charles, hitting him in the stomach, causing him to drop his knife to the ground.

Charles dashed to recover the weapon, but Richard cut him off and picked it up instead.

Lenore rose slowly, the bottle clenched tightly in her fist. What was her next move? The door. Perhaps she wouldn't actually have to use her weapon after all. The men on the floor seemed far too distracted to notice her presence.

Or so she thought. Lenore felt someone behind her, and looked down to see Charles's arms wrapped around her waist. Then she looked up to see Richard swinging the coat rack at the two of them.

Charles's voice sounded panicked. "Rich, you hit me with that thing, you're gonna kill your girlfriend over here."

Lenore desperately tried to open the container in her hands, but her sweating, shaking fingers were unable to pop the lid.

Richard raised his weapon, undeterred. "Isn't that just like you to start hiding behind someone else. Well, I think you picked the wrong bodyguard this time because I didn't feel like heading to the grocery store this week anyway."

Lenore closed her eyes and waited for Richard to bring the object down on her, but there was only silence.

Charles laughed triumphantly. "Well, didn't I just know it all along? You *like* her. You ain't gonna kill her."

Richard lowered his weapon. "Oh, I'll kill her all right, but it won't be today, and it sure as hell won't be for the likes of you." He wrinkled his brow, approaching the two of them. "So I don't get what you think is going to happen here. You think I'm just going to let you go now? You think you're getting out of this apartment alive?"

"I think we're gonna call Paul," Charles said, strengthening his grip on Lenore. "We'll straighten all of this out with him in here, and—" He looked down to see Lenore still trying to work the cap on the bottle. "Well, if that don't beat all. Lenore's gonna take some pills! Stop the presses!" He grabbed the container from her hands. "I told you this shit was bad for you."

Richard rolled his eyes. "Give her the fucking bottle back, Charles."

"Nah," he said, single-handedly springing the lid. "That bitch has herself a problem and I think I'd be doing her a favor by pouring all that shit out." He raised the bottle over his head and turned it upside down.

And he winced as a stream of powder fell onto his face. "What the—COUGH. COUGH. What the fuck cough—COUGH. COUGH."

A fine mist hung in the air, giving Richard's foyer the surreal ambiance of a fairy tale land. And the fairy tale monsters cowered and cringed. And the house of gingerbread began to crumble.

And our heroine pushed down on the hands that restrained her, and they gave way. She walked into the sparkling cloud with her eyes closed and her hands out, a rare smile on her face. Over this silver rainbow stretched Lenore's perfect universe, and she could not think of a more appropriate gateway to immortality.

"Silver!" Richard cried, retreating from the haze. He clutched his face and screamed. "Fuck. *Fuck!*"

Charles did not scream, however. He was too busy coughing.

And Lenore did not know what happened next because she bolted out the door.

Chapter Eleven:
Quantum Immortality

Lenore raced through the city streets. The concrete floor felt like ice against her bare heels, numbing her toes and causing her to stumble forward. Muscles that had grown weak during her term of imprisonment strained now to propel her, causing a great burning in her legs that grew worse with each passing stride. How long would she be able to keep this up? Judging from the deep breaths she was already taking to maintain pace, not long.

How far had she gone? Half a mile, perhaps? The unfamiliar metropolis offered no landmarks to track her progress, and Lenore was afraid to look back—even for a moment—to judge the distance she had crossed, for fear that Richard might be gaining ground behind her.

And he almost certainly was. Her scent marked the sidewalk below, betraying her location like a fresh trail of breadcrumbs. That trail needed to come to a stop, and soon. But how? A car. She needed to flag down a car and speed away to a place where her captors would never find her. Hadn't one just passed her a moment ago? Why hadn't she chased it down? Lenore's head pounded as she forced more icy air into her lungs. She wasn't thinking straight.

"Excuse me? Ma'am?"

She turned her head to see a man jogging beside her. He looked like he wanted to help her. Everything was going to be okay.

"Do you need help, miss?" the man asked, glancing Lenore's tattered clothing and burns on her arm. "Why don't you slow down for a minute and I'll help you. What are you running from?"

Lenore stopped and opened her mouth to speak, but then closed it again. Why was she hesitating? Surely it was safe to ask this man for assistance. It wasn't like Richard had sent him or anything.

It wasn't like Richard had sent him or anything.

And this was how all of Lenore's panics began, with a thought that she could not shake.

What if Richard has sent him?

The thought took hold of Lenore. It began to tug at her, threatening to drag her beneath the surface like a hidden undertow. But it didn't make any sense. How could Richard have sent anyone? She had only left minutes ago. He was probably still in the apartment writhing on the ground.

What if he isn't writhing on the ground? Did you take a good look at him on your way out? Maybe the silver didn't hit him at all.

The thought was absurd. Richard was grabbing at his face, wasn't he? Besides, even if he wasn't hurt, how would he have sent someone so quickly?

Maybe he called his lawyer friend.

Lenore stared blankly at the man before her, sizing him up. He looked harmless.

Paul looks harmless. They all look harmless.

She wiped a bead of sweat from her forehead. This was irrational. If she couldn't trust the man in front of her, then how could she trust anyone?

You can't trust anyone. They'll be chasing you for the rest of your life.

The man approached her soothingly. "I've got a cell phone you can use. Do you need me to call you an ambulance?"

Lenore backed away from him. What was his deal, anyway? Why would he want to help her? What did he have to gain?

It's a trap. It's a trick. It's a ruse. Run.

She sprinted away, hearing the man call out behind her, "All right, then. I guess you don't need my help after all."

Lenore kept going, feeling a tinge of regret as his words faded in the distance. What if he was legitimately trying to help her? What if he really would have called her an ambulance? It didn't matter. When Richard caught up, and he would, he would just kill them both. Standing around on the sidewalk, even to make a phone call, was a one way ticket back to the apartment, where Charles was waiting to see dinner theater to its gory conclusion, where Paul was waiting to kiss her on the forehead and whisper his goodbyes, where Richard was waiting to thrust her into the furnace.

No, best to keep moving. A car approached, and Lenore angled toward it, eying the driver appraisingly. Was it safe to flag it down? The driver moved his hand to use the turn signal, and Lenore could not be sure, but she did not like something about the movement. It was too fluid. What if the driver was a vampire? Best not to take any chances. She would just wait for the next vehicle. Wait for something safe. Yes, she needed to find something safe.

A police car. Maybe she would hold out for a police car. That had to be safe, right? Once inside, she would explain her situation and— No. No, that was a terrible idea. How many people had she watched die over the past (Three? Four?) several months without lifting a finger? Surely the police would understand—or would they? What if the cops were in on it?

Lenore's mind swirled with conspiracy and betrayal. No one could be trusted. Everyone was out to get her; ready to slow her down, drag her back and eat her alive.

She shook her head for a moment, confused. Something was different. The scenery. The scenery had stopped changing. Why was that? Because she had stopped running. Because she was bent over, heaving, desperately trying to catch her breath. God damn, it was cold. Her shadow in the light of the street lamp appeared to tremble with every inhalation. It looked small, frigid, tired.

An alleyway fractured the line of row homes behind her. That might be a good place to (wait) hide. That might be a good place to (wait for Richard to come and get her) sit and think and figure things out for a while.

Lenore walked into the darkness and rested her head against the brick wall. For the first time since leaving the apartment, she felt safe. But what would she do now? Where would she go? Who would help her?

And then there was the terrible realization that her life was gone. Gobbled up and forgotten, like the endless parade of visitors to Richard's laundry room. She had no job to get back to. No worried family or friends sat vigil by the phone. No lover waited by the cold side of the bed, clutching the sheets at night and dreaming of her return. The world was only full of strangers and monsters and people in between, and she no longer belonged.

A mouse scurried past Lenore's feet, and Paul emerged from the shadows. He came to sit beside her, and brought his hand around her shoulders, pulling her close. "What's going on with you, kiddo?" he whispered. "Why are you letting me catch you?"

When Lenore turned to meet Paul's eyes, she saw that he was smiling, and the playful creases around his lids looked an awful lot like the way back home. And she wanted to tell him this. She wanted to tell him how glad she was to see him, and that she didn't care if he killed her, just so long as he would pretend to be her friend once again, just for a little while longer. But all that escaped her lips were incomprehensible sobs.

He stroked her hair. "Are you having one of those famous panic attacks you were telling me about?"

She nodded tearfully.

"Well, let's just sit here and wait for it to pass. I'm in no rush to get back. You just about scared the shit out of me, you know. I knew something was wrong when I got up to the penthouse and Charlie was missing along with Rich's keys. I knew right away he'd gone down there to give you a hard time. Jesus." He shook his head like someone stirring from a nightmare. "When I got to Rich's apartment and saw that the door was wide open I thought something horrible had happened to you. I know this is going to sound strange, considering that I came here to take you back and all, but I'm just happy you're okay. I would have hated for things to end before I got to tell you I'm sorry. And I am sorry, Lenore. Jesus Christ, I'm so sorry."

"So you're not still mad?"

"*Mad?* Are you kidding? I'm mad at Rich for not telling me you were out of food. When he came by and said you hadn't eaten in two days, I just about hit the roof. I shouldn't have given you the silent treatment earlier. I had no idea you were too scared to ask me for groceries. You know why I couldn't speak to you, though? It's because I knew I owed you an apology. And I swear, one was coming. I'd even told Rich I was going to get you out of the apartment next week."

Lenore smiled and then started sobbing again. "I'm sorry too."

"Shh. Don't be. Don't ever be sorry for defending yourself. And that's all you were doing. You just happen to be a little too good at it." He stood up and pulled Lenore to her feet. "Here, you've got to be freezing," he said, placing his jacket around her shoulders.

Lenore slipped her arms through the sleeves and winced as the cigarette burns rubbed against the silk lining. After several painful attempts, she opted to let her arms hang free instead.

Paul made a face. "Jesus Christ. Is that what Charles did to you while Rich was away?"

"I sure as hell didn't do it to myself." She cringed as he took her arm in his hands and ran his fingers over the wounds.

"Well, if it makes you feel any better, I've seen Rich do a lot worse to people," he said, letting go. "I've done a lot worse to people myself, to be honest." He reached into his pocket and produced a handful of pills. "I brought you your medicine." Paul held the tablets out to her as if trying to feed crumbs to a seagull.

And she responded with like enthusiasm. "Thanks," she said, happily munching.

He frowned at her feet. "I wish I'd thought to bring you some shoes, though. I can't believe you ran all this way with no shoes on. You should have seen the looks some people were giving you."

"I used to run six miles a day back when I was in high school."

"You know, that is not something I would have guessed about you. But it turns out you're just full of surprises. For example, I didn't think it was possible to kill a vampire with silver, but it looks like you found a way." He grinned. "I suppose some congratulations are in order."

Lenore's jaw dropped. "What? What do you mean?"

"Charles is dead, kiddo. He must have inhaled some of that dust because he died coughing up blood all over Rich's new carpet." Paul started laughing. "Rich is so pissed off, I can't even tell you."

"About the rug?" Lenore chuckled in spite of herself.

"About everything. Did you see Rich's face before you ran out of there?"

She shook her head.

"You burned about half of it off. I don't know if his left eye is ever going to grow back."

Lenore smiled. "I put his eye out?"

Paul nodded. "Yeah. That's karma, right? *Empathy*. Maybe Rich learned a little empathy. Who knows? He's mad as hell, though, that's for sure. Good for you. I'll bet you'd been waiting to do that for a long time. How did you ever manage to get your hands on silver in the first place?"

"It came off Mrs. Grayson. Rich let me keep it."

Paul snorted. "That is fucking priceless. I told him not to mess with that tenant. I can't believe you thought to grind silver up like that. Unbelievable. You're unbelievable is what you are. I'm impressed."

"You're not upset about Charles?"

Paul kicked a stone on the ground and watched it land in a nearby puddle. "No. You know what's funny? When I walked in there and saw him dead on Rich's carpet, I was just happy it wasn't you. Charles has changed a lot in the past twelve years, and I don't think I'll be missing him. In the end, I think I'm relieved."

"So how long were you following me?"

"A ways. I could have caught up with you a few blocks ago, but I thought I'd let you keep going a little while longer. I thought for sure you'd let that guy help you. The guy with the cell phone. Why did you pull away from him like that?"

"I was afraid," she whispered, tensing at the memory.

"Of *what*? You'd *won*. Against all odds you did it. You were out. All you had to do was ask someone—anyone—for help. Why didn't you?"

Lenore's lips trembled. "I don't know what I was afraid of. I thought I'd feel safe when I finally escaped the apartment, but I didn't. I felt scared." Frigid tears rolled down her cheeks.

"But scared of *what*? That's the part where you're losing me."

"I don't know," she said, wringing her hands. "How am I..." She trailed off because a terrible question was forming in her mind.

"What, kiddo?"

"How am I ever supposed to function in the outside world now?"

He shot her a wan smile. "I'm not so sure you were doing such a great job with that before I met you. But I'll tell you something—I don't think the outside world is where you fit in. You fit in with me, though, and there's something to be said for that, I think. Charles always wanted to be like me, but with you that wasn't the case. Shit. I wanted to be more like *you*."

"So what happens now?"

Paul met her eyes. "You know what happens now."

She took a deep breath. "Rich is going to kill me, isn't he?"

For a rare moment, Paul was not smiling. "Yeah, kiddo. Yeah, I think he is."

"You'll stay with me?"

"I'll stay. I'll be there the entire time if you'll let me."

Lenore wiped her tears away and nodded, glancing around the

alleyway. "Could *you* do it? Could you just take me right here and get it over with?"

"I knew you were going to ask me to do that, and the answer's no."

"Why not?"

"*Because I'd enjoy it,* that's why. Jesus Christ. Do you really want me to enjoy you like that? I'd feel like I just fucked my sister or something."

"Then don't feed on me. Snap my neck. Just make it quick."

"No," he whispered, growing quiet. "I don't want to snap your neck, Lenore. And I definitely don't want to kill you in some filthy back alley like this." He looked up at the sky. "You know what I want to do, actually?"

"What?"

"I want to get you something to eat. Let's go to the diner. Are you game? Let's warm you up with some coffee." Paul extended his hand to Lenore, and she took it.

The waitress placed a pot of coffee and two empty cups on the table. She seemed to be making a conscious effort not to stare at the burns on Lenore's arm, but the effort failed miserably. "You okay, hon?" she asked finally.

Lenore nodded. "You should see the other guy."

Paul snickered.

The waitress gave them a quizzical glance before heading back into the kitchen.

Lenore shook seven packets of sugar into her coffee. "If I had asked that man on the street for help earlier, would I have gotten away?"

Paul shook his head. "You wouldn't have gotten away, but you would have made it a hell of a lot harder on us, that's for sure. Rich would have had to start calling in favors left and right. You shouldn't have made it so easy." He leaned forward and slid his cup across the table. "Hey, do you think you could fill me up? Let's toast your victory."

Lenore filled his cup.

And Paul raised it, saying "To the biggest bad-ass I know."

She met his glass with her own and smiled. "To me."

He stared at the blood in the container for a long moment before taking a sip. "Are you feeling better now? Not so panicky anymore?"

"Yeah. I feel a lot better now, thanks." And Lenore did feel better. It was good to see Paul again, and it was good to be back at the diner. But mostly, it was good to have six Xanax in her system. And the terrible reality of where they were heading after dinner seemed like business as usual. Richard was going to kill her. So what else was new?

"It's been a while since we did this," Paul said. "Don't you want to ask me how things are going?"

"No. Not really. I'm slightly preoccupied with my own problems at the moment." She sighed. "For instance, my feet are killing me. I'm pretty sure I ran over some broken glass somewhere." She lifted her left foot onto the table. "Do you see glass in there?"

"What, were you raised in a barn or something?" he asked, grinning. "This is a high class establishment. You can't do that type of thing in here." He studied her foot, rubbing his chin thoughtfully. "I don't see any glass, but it's hard to tell. The bottom's completely black. Let's see the other one." He waved her other foot onto the table. "This one I can see something. Tell me if this hurts." Paul pressed his hand against her heel.

"Yes. YES. Shit. Yes, asshole. You can stop pressing on it now."

He looked up at her and smiled. "Just wanted to make sure. Do you want me to get it out for you?"

"Please."

He squeezed her foot and extracted a small shard of glass. "There. All better."

"Thanks," she said, bringing her feet back underneath the table.

Paul leaned back in his seat. "You could have planned your escape a little better. I would have worn shoes, personally."

"The only shoes I've had to wear this entire time have been my flip flops. I had to kick them off when I started running. They were slowing me down."

"I also would have brought my medicine with me," he added, looking very much amused.

Lenore rolled her eyes. "Well, thank God you caught up with me to tell me everything I was doing wrong. Who knows what might have happened."

"Have you decided what you want to order?" he asked, gesturing to the menu. "Get whatever you want. Actually, you know what? You always talk about getting the pie, but you never do. Why don't you get it this time?"

She shook her head. "Paul, I really don't have much of an appetite right now." This was not true, of course. But—deep down—Lenore knew she would be ordering her last meal, and that thought was almost too depressing to contemplate. Better to die hungry.

"That's fine. Let's just sit here. Plenty of time to get your appetite back." He took another sip from his cup. "Would it help if I told you I'm not going to take you back?"

"You aren't?"

"No. Won't do it." He shook his head decisively.

Lenore took a deep breath, trembling, smiling. "What are you going to tell Rich?"

"Fuck Rich. You escaped fair and square and you never have to see him again. You never have to see that basement again."

Paul's phone began vibrating. "Well, speak of the devil," he said. "Rich wants to know if I've found you. Would you mind if I took a picture? Let's set his mind at ease."

Paul aimed his phone at Lenore, and she posed, shooting her middle finger in the air.

"Awesome," Paul giggled. He took another drink from his cup. "That ought to keep him happy for a while."

Paul's phone vibrated again.

"What does he want now?" Lenore asked.

Paul downed the rest of his drink, staring at the message on the screen with a half smile. "I think if I read this out loud they'd kick me out of the restaurant for indecency." He typed something into the phone and hit send before handing his cup to Lenore. "Would you mind giving me a refill?"

She complied. "What did you tell Rich?"

"That's my little secret," he said, closing his phone. "But I don't think he'll be interrupting our conversation again. Let's not even talk about Rich. Let's talk about what we're going to do when we get out of here. Want to watch a bunch of zombie movies tonight? I'll stop by the store and get some toaster pastries. You can stay at my place for a while. Does that sound good to you? You don't have anywhere to go, do you?"

"No," she whispered, stirring her coffee.

"It's settled then." He took another hefty sip. "Is there anything you want to grab from Rich's place and take up with you to the penthouse? You don't have to go in there. Just make a list and I'll get everything you need, okay?"

She watched Paul finish his second cup and stared at the tube in her arm. "That sounds good, Paul," she said softly. *It sounds too good to be true.*

Her heart began racing. "Tell me more things that we'll do when we get back. You won't lock the door on me, right?"

"No, I wouldn't do that to you. Maybe I'll even set you up with an apartment in the building. Would that work for you? Rich would be furious, but I'll bet he'd get over it. I'd help you with rent for a while until you got back on your feet. We'll get you your old job back, even."

Bullshit.

Lenore nodded, wincing at the same time. "And you'll keep my medicine in steady supply?"

"Definitely." Paul grinned at her from across the table, but his eyes were not smiling. "Hey, would you mind topping me off?"

Her hands shook as the released more fluid into the container. "Not at all."

He raised the cup to his lips. "Thanks, I appreciate it." Paul drank deeply. "Why aren't you touching your coffee?"

"I'm not thirsty." Lenore's eyes dashed toward the exit.

"Calm down," he said, following her gaze. "You're doing great. Try to relax. Just keep talking to me."

She shook her head at him. "This isn't *Lamaze*, Paul. Don't try to talk me through this. And stop trying to feed me some bullshit fantasy about how I'll get my life back."

"Lenore, it's going to be okay," he whispered.

"What *exactly* is your definition of okay? Why couldn't you have snapped my neck in the alley? What are we doing here, Paul? What the fuck is this?"

"Jesus Christ. Keep it down. Sorry. I thought this was better."

"That you plan on draining me right here while I have coffee and dessert? That I get a front row seat at my own execution? Does that sound better to *you*?"

Paul flinched at her words. "What do you want from me? Do you have any idea what Rich is planning to do to you? Do you want me to show you the eight text messages he's sent me since I left his place? They're very detailed." Paul took several sips from his cup. "Look, I don't like this either. Do you have any idea how uncomfortable this is for me? I'm sorry I didn't get it over with in the alleyway. Do you want me to take you back there?"

Lenore was silent.

"Believe me," Paul continued. "If I snap your neck, it's going to hurt. Is this really so bad? Is talking to me really such a bad way to go?"

"What do I have to talk about? Oh, wait. I know. Remember when you tricked me into going to the diner with you and then you murdered me? Remember how pissed off I was?"

"Fine. You know what? Don't worry about talking. I'll do the talking, okay?" He shifted in his seat. "I feel like there's so much I want to say to you right now that I don't even know where to begin. First off, I want you to know something terrible—you asked me something about Angela the other night and I'd already forgotten her name. I'm pretty sure that in a few years I won't think about Charlie anymore either, but I'll still think about you. Once you asked me what made you different and I told you it was because you were my friend, but that couldn't be further from the truth. There's nothing I could offer that would either add or subtract from who you are. And you are without a doubt the toughest, weakest person I've ever met, and I'm going to remember you. I'll remember you for the rest of my life."

Lenore glared at him. "I don't need a eulogy, Paul. I already know how awesome I am."

"Okay, then try this on for size," Paul said, laughing. "You were a *terrible* friend. I can't believe you tried to poison Charlie. I can't believe you double crossed me like that after everything I did for you."

She started to chuckle involuntarily. "You know the other day when you asked me if I would have covered you up if you started bursting into flames?"

"Yeah?"

"I lied. There's no way I would have covered you up."

Paul flung a sugar packet at her. "I could tell you were lying! Why would you lie?"

"Why would I tell the truth? You've been playing with me since you met me."

"I play fair, though."

"Well I don't." She flung a sugar packet at him from underneath the table.

Paul jumped in his seat as it hit him on the knee. "Ouch. I can tell that now. Actually, I think I've known that since dinner theater." He stared at her, his smile fading. "There's nothing fair about this, is there?"

"No," she whispered. "It isn't fair. And you're a terrible friend, too, you know. But you're the only one I've got. You're the only friend I've had in years."

He slid his cup to her. "You deserved better, kiddo. I wish I knew how to be a better friend to you, Lenore."

Her face crumbled as she filled the container. "I'm scared, Paul. I'm really scared. I know begging doesn't work with you guys, but I wish there was something I could say to change your mind."

With this, Paul's entire posture changed, and he rested his head in his hands, probably to support the weight of the enormous grin on his face. "Well, that would be terrible, wouldn't it? If this entire time there had been something you could have said to change my mind? And you had never bothered to find out what it was?"

Her eyes grew wide. "*What?* You piece of shit. Don't you think I've been through enough tonight? How long would you have let that go on?"

Paul chuckled. "Two more cups." He wiggled two fingers in front of her. "Stop clenching your jaw like that. I wasn't anywhere close to draining you."

"You piece of shit. You filthy piece of shit."

But Paul was laughing too hard to listen. "You think you're so slick. You barely even filled my cup that last time. I swear, you left that thing half empty. Like that would have helped you. Like that was the make or break."

Lenore grabbed his cup and spit in it. "There. Is that full enough for you now?" She slid it back over to him. "I hope you choke."

"Oh. Very mature. Do you feel better now?"

"Yes." She felt a lot better, actually.

"Do you remember what you said to me the first time I brought you here?"

"No."

"You told me about Quantum Immortality and how you were trying to find your perfect universe. You said there had to be some scenario where you'd escape your fate. And I remember saying something along the lines of you were being overly optimistic, but now I think you might have been on to something. Let's just assume for a second that you never dragged Charlie into that game. He never would have tried to kill you. I wouldn't have tried to turn him. You never would have gotten your hands on that silver. Charlie wouldn't have come over for revenge. Rich wouldn't have forgotten to lock the door. You see what I'm saying? It's almost like you found your perfect universe after all."

"Almost."

"Of course, this isn't your perfect universe, though." He grinned. "It's mine. But I think there might be a place for you in it. You know, I was awfully hurt that you didn't ask me how things were going earlier. As your only friend, I'd think you'd want to know how I was doing."

Lenore watched her only friend take a sip of the blood-spit mixture. "How's it going, Paul?"

"Terrible. Just terrible. Thanks for asking. Rich was right. I never should have turned Charlie. He turned into such a pain in the ass, I can't even tell you. It made me realize how completely dependent I was on him for food, though."

And then Lenore knew exactly where their conversation was headed. "You poor thing."

"Aren't I? I've been trying to find a replacement. Ask me how that's going."

And she prepared herself for a familiar argument. "How's that going?"

"Miserable. Now, the way I see it, you have a pretty big problem on your hands because Rich wants you dead. You need some protection. I also have a pretty big problem on my hands because I've lost my meal

214

ticket. Maybe we could stop being such terrible friends to each other, and we could start helping each other out instead. What do you say?"

And she was happy to lose.

About the Author

Elena Hearty graduated from the University of Virginia in 2000 with a BS in computer science. After that, she bought a house, got married, and had two children, all while working full time to ensure that your online experience is replete with banner ads and pop-up windows.

You can learn more about Elena and her latest projects at http://elenahearty.com.

Something is trapped in the castle, and it wants to feed!

The Sorrows
© *2011 Jonathan Janz*

The Sorrows, an island off the coast of northern California, and its castle have been uninhabited since a series of gruesome, unexplained murders in 1925. But its owner needs money, so he allows film composers Ben and Eddie and a couple of their female friends to stay a month in Castle Blackwood. Eddie is certain an eerie and reportedly haunted castle is just the setting Ben needs to find musical inspiration for a horror film.

But what they find is more horrific than any movie. For something is waiting for them in the castle. A being, once worshipped, now imprisoned, has been trapped for nearly a century. And he's ready to feed.

Available now in ebook and print from Samhain Publishing.

Enjoy the following excerpt from The Sorrows ...

On the way up the mountain, Ben Shadeland flirted with the idea of killing Eddie Blaze. The problem was, Ben could barely breathe.

"Good lord," Eddie said. "You sound like an obscene phone caller back there."

Ben ignored him. Between ragged breaths, he asked, "We still on your dad's land?"

"Only a small part is residential. Sonoma County owns the rest."

Ben looked around. "So we're not supposed to be here?"

"Not after dark," Eddie answered, and in the moonlight Ben saw him grin.

Great, he thought. Trespassing on government land at one in the morning. Trekking around the wilderness was fine for hardcore fitness freaks, but for out-of-shape guys in their late thirties, this kind of hike was a surefire ticket to the ER. If a heart attack didn't get him, a broken leg would.

As if answering his thoughts Eddie said, "You want me to carry you?"

"Go to hell."

When Ben risked a look ahead, the toe of his boot caught on something. He fell awkwardly, his outstretched palms pierced by thorns. He lay there a moment, riding out the pain but relishing the momentary rest.

"You still alive?"

Rather than answering he rolled over and examined his torn palms. The blood dribbling out of his wounds looked black and oily in the starlight. He rubbed them on the belly of his shirt and pushed to his feet.

When they reached the cave Ben had to kneel for several moments to avoid passing out. This was the price he paid, his only physical activity lifting weights and chasing his three-year old son around the yard.

Of course, that was before the divorce. Now he only played with his son on weekends, and when he did he was haunted by the specter of returning Joshua to his ex-wife. The lump in his throat caught him off guard.

He spat and glanced up at the cave. "So what's the story?"

"It's a good one," Eddie answered.

"It better be."

"Come on," Eddie said and switched on a large black Maglite.

"You had that all along?"

Eddie started toward the cave.

"What, we're going in?"

"Don't you want to retrace Arthur Vaughan's steps?"

He stared at Eddie, whose face was barely visible within the cave. "You're kidding."

"I knew that'd get your attention."

Hell, he thought and cast a glance down the mountain. It wasn't too late to go back. He thought he remembered the way, though he'd been too busy trying not to break his neck to thoroughly memorize the terrain.

"This is perfect," Eddie was saying. "One of the most prolific serial killers in California history?"

"I'm not in the mood for a cannibal story right now."

"The deadline's in two months."

"I know when the deadline is."

"Then stop being a pussy and come on."

With a defeated sigh, he did.

Immediately, the dank smell of stagnant water coated his nostrils.

As he advanced, he couldn't shake the sensation of sliding into some ancient creature's gullet, a voluntary repast for its monstrous appetite. The cave serpentined left and right, and several times branched into different tunnels. Ben was reminded of all the horror movies he'd seen with cave settings.

They never ended well.

At least the tunnel was large enough that he could stand erect. In addition to his fear of heights, sharks, and his ex-wife, he was deathly afraid of tight spaces. He remembered fighting off panic attacks whenever he ended up on the bottom of a football pile.

So why the hell was he going to a place where his claustrophobia could run amuck?

Because they were desperate.

"Arthur's first two victims," Eddie said, "were a couple of teenagers named Shannon Williams and Jill Shelton. They were out here hiking and decided to explore the caves."

It was actually Shannon Shelton and Jill Williams, but Ben let it go. Eddie was a good storyteller as long as one didn't get too hung up on facts.

"Little did they know," Eddie said, "they'd wandered into the den of a beast."

Despite the fact that they'd mined for inspiration in eerie places several times, Ben felt the old thrill. Sometimes the tale inspired him, sometimes it was the setting. Often, the music didn't come until days later, when a specific memory triggered his imagination.

Lately, it didn't come at all.

"Who was murdered first?" Ben asked.

"Don't rush it," Eddie said. "I'm coming to that."

They moved up a curving incline that, to Ben's infinite dismay, narrowed gradually until he had to shuffle forward in a stooped position. When the tunnel opened up, he groaned.

The gap between where Eddie stood and where solid ground

resumed couldn't have been more than five feet, but to Ben the space yawned terrible and forbidding, an impassable expanse.

"This was where she fell," Eddie said, gesturing with the Maglite into the darkness. "Jill made it over, but Shannon ended up down there."

Ben stood next to Eddie and peered into the chasm. The flashlight's glow barely reached the bottom. He estimated the distance was sixty feet or more.

The image came unbidden, but once it settled in his mind, it dug in with the tenacity of a tick. He imagined the poor girl leaping and realizing halfway she wasn't going to make it. The hands scrabbling frantically on the grimy cave floor. The amplified scraping of her body as it slid downward. A fingernail or two snapping off. Then the endless, screaming tumble into the abyss.

He hoped it killed her. Goodness knew being eaten alive by Arthur Vaughan was a far worse fate.

"You ready?" Eddie asked.

"Hell yes," he answered. "Ready to go back."

Without another word, Eddie leaped over the expanse and landed with room to spare.

"Your turn," Eddie said.

"I'm not jumping."

"Scared?"

"I don't have a death wish."

"It's only a few feet."

"And a hundred more to the ground."

"Stop letting fear rule your life."

Classic Eddie. Put him in a bad situation and mock him for reacting sanely. Like last month, the double date that turned out to be a pair of hookers. What's the difference? Eddie had asked.

So Ben sat there listening to one girl's stories about her clients' sexual quirks while Eddie got it on with the other in a hot tub.

"Look," Eddie was saying. "I went first so you'd know it was safe."

Ben turned. "I'm going home."

The cave went black.

SAMHAIN
PUBLISHING

www.samhainpublishing.com

Green for the planet.
Great for your wallet.

It's all about the story...

Romance

HORROR

www.samhainpublishing.com

CPSIA information can be obtained at www.ICGtesting.com
Printed in the USA
BVOW071438230212

283673BV00004B/5/P

9 781609 286712